OUTBACK

Also in this series

Domino Island

Other books by Desmond Bagley

The Golden Keel
High Citadel
Wyatt's Hurricane
Landslide
The Vivero Letter
The Spoilers
Running Blind
The Freedom Trap
The Tightrope Men
The Snow Tiger
The Enemy
Flyaway
Bahama Crisis
Windfall
Night of Error
Juggernaut

Michael Davies

Outback

The Desmond Bagley
Centenary Thriller

HarperCollins*Publishers*

HarperCollins*Publishers*
1 London Bridge Street,
London SE1 9GF

HarperCollins*Publishers*
Macken House,
39/40 Mayor Street Upper
Dublin 1
D01 C9W8
Ireland
www.harpercollins.co.uk

First published by HarperCollins*Publishers* 2023
1

A catalogue record for this book is available from the British Library

ISBN 978-0-00-858135-0 HB
ISBN 978-0-00-858136-7 TPB

Typeset in Meridien by Palimpsest Book Production Ltd,
Falkirk, Stirlingshire

Printed and Bound in the UK using
100% Renewable Electricity at CPI Group (UK) Ltd

AUTHOR'S NOTE

I have something of a complicated relationship with Bill Kemp. I've now lived with him through two adventures, spread across the globe and almost five years, and he's been an entertaining companion. Described by Jeffrey Deaver as 'part James Bond, part Philip Marlowe, and all hero', he certainly gets himself into some interesting scrapes, and it's been a delight to bring a few more of them into the light for your enjoyment.

And yet he doesn't quite belong to me.

Bill Kemp – albeit under a different name – was the creation of Desmond Bagley, one of the world's best-loved thriller writers through the 1960s, 70s and 80s. He initially appeared in *Domino Island*, a novel whose first draft was discovered in the archives 35 years after Bagley's death and which was finally delivered to an excited public by his longstanding publishers HarperCollins in 2019. I had the privilege of editing, redrafting and polishing that early manuscript – we ended up calling it 'curating' – and that was how I came to know and cherish Bill Kemp.

I'd known and cherished Desmond Bagley a lot longer than that. My older brother Patrick reminds me that it was a teacher at school, Paul Wickham, who first intro-duced us to the thrills and spills of Bagley's novels; *Running Blind*, *The Tightrope Men* and *The Enemy* were particular favourites. When the opportunity arose to find ways of celebrating the centenary of Bagley's birth, I immediately knew there was more to Bill Kemp that could be explored. His natural resourcefulness, military background and sheer bloody-mindedness made him an ideal candidate for putting through the wringer in a new, original story that would aim not to mimic Bagley but to pay modest tribute to the master and his legacy: sixteen novels over a period of eighteen years until his early death, aged just 59, in 1983.

The project would never have come to fruition without the support, encouragement and hard work of a number of people. Foremost in that group comes David Brawn, Estates Publisher at HarperCollins, who has nurtured the memory of Desmond Bagley – not least by keeping all his books in print – while juggling other behemoths such as J.R.R. Tolkien, Agatha Christie and Alistair MacLean. David's assiduous care of Bagley's literary legacy is a mark both of his professional excellence and of his love of the work, and I suspect his deceased authors owe him just as much a debt as this living one does. David was kind enough to bestow upon me the wonderful editor Sophia Schoepfer, whose perspicacity and attention to detail have contributed considerably to the finished novel. Along the way, the ever-generous Paul Campbell offered terrific advice while another keeper of the Bagley flame, Nigel Alefounder, has always been on hand with an encouraging word. I urge you to pay a visit to his highly informative website at desmondbagley.blogspot.com, as well as Philip Eastwood's comprehensive biographical one, thebagleybrief.com.

Outside the publishing world, I was lucky enough to enjoy a brief but joyous correspondence with Bagley's widow Joan before her own death in 1999. Fortunately for me, Joan's sister Lecia and her husband Peter have, in the years since, made me feel a very welcome part of the Bagley story and theirs is a friendship I continue to cherish. Their love and inspiration have been major factors in my ongoing Bagley obsession and I hope they will feel I have done the family justice with my tribute.

There is, of course, another person without whom this novel would never have happened. For Desmond Bagley – known to friends and family as Simon, for reasons unclear – his wife Joan provided an intellectual sounding board, a safe space in which to play with his stories, and an invaluable first-read editor. Indeed, she herself prepared two of his manuscripts for posthumous publication. I have been blessed with my own equivalent in the shape of my wife Tricia, who has supported and enabled the book to be written. Thank you for being you.

Oh, and if you're wondering about Bill Kemp's original name, there's a story. Bagley christened him Robert Armin, after a member of the troupe of actors for whom Shakespeare wrote and performed. While I was working on *Domino Island*, my sense was that the name Armin was too similar to the notorious Ugandan dictator Idi Amin and might prompt some unhelpful associations in the mind of the reader, so instead I borrowed the name of another Shakespearean colleague for our hero. Bagley had explicitly given permission for the book to be retitled (he had even invited suggestions), so I didn't feel too uncomfortable about tweaking the protagonist's name as well.

I hope Desmond Bagley fans around the world will afford me as much generosity with *Outback*, my centenary tribute to the great man, as they did with *Domino Island*, my cheeky collaboration with him.

Michael Davies

For Tricia – for real this time

And for my boys –
Matthew, Ethan, Alex and Oliver

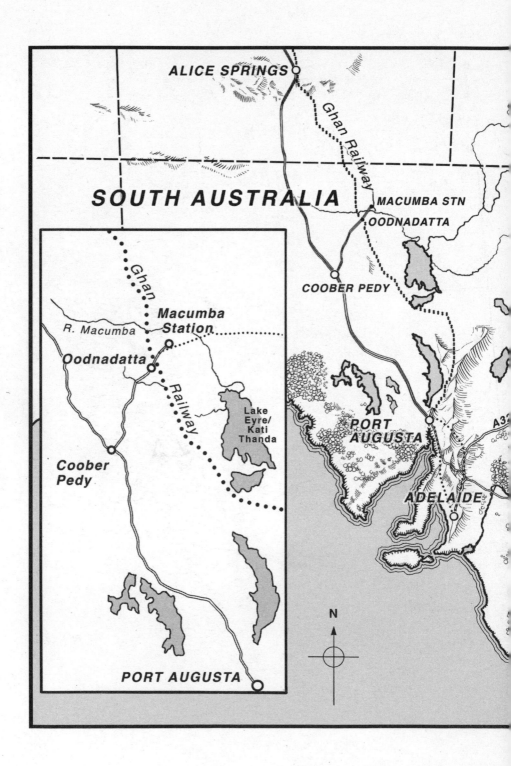

PART ONE: BLUE

I

The first thing that hit me was the coolness of the interior. After the blazing heat of the sand, which weighted down your shoulders like a wet astrakhan, it thumped you with a wall of cold.

The second thing was the utter blackness. Forget adjusting your eyes for a couple of minutes in an unlit room: this was darkness such as I'd never known, even in the depths of the jungle at night. At least there, some creatures emit glimmering hints of their nocturnal activity. Here, contrasted with the searing whiteness of the sun outside, the mine was a void. I stumbled blindly forward for as many paces as the rocks underfoot would allow without serious injury and squatted on my haunches. I was reluctant to look behind me for fear of destroying my retinas with another blast of dizzying light but I could hear Sophie and Adam clattering among the looser stones at the entrance.

'Bloody hell, it's dark,' said Adam simply.

'Watch your footing,' I said. 'It'll take a while for our eyes to adapt so I'd stay put if I were you.'

The clattering stopped and we waited. Even here, a mere ten yards into the mouth of the mine, the daylight from outside was growing thin and opaque while the blackness within yawned like a sleeping giant.

'What can you see?' Sophie's voice reverberated as it fell into the depths of the chamber in front of us.

'Not a damn thing,' I said. 'Can you shine your torch into the shaft?'

She cursed under her breath, the whisper following her question into the dark. 'I left it in the Landy.'

My heart sank. Without the torch, we hadn't got a chance of scoping out the mine as we'd intended. There was nothing for it but to go back to the Land Rover at the bottom of the hill and pick it up. I ransacked my brain to see if there was anything else we might have left behind: if someone was going back to the car, they might as well make it worthwhile.

'I'll go,' said Sophie, pre-empting my offer to play the white knight. As the most qualified member of the team I could have overridden her but along with my seniority came the disadvantages of great age: I had a good fifteen years on her. There was also my natural aversion to extreme temperatures and the mercury was already comfortably – or, more accurately, uncomfortably – above the 100-degree mark in the afternoon sun.

'Bring some more water, will you? There's no telling how long we'll be down here.'

Sophie's boots scuttled back up towards the entrance and I heard her exchange a few words with Adam as she passed him on the way out. I don't know what his excuse was not to exercise a little chivalry and offer to go back to the car instead but moments later he was lowering himself into the steep mouth of the shaft. He was barely three yards behind me when I felt the ground shift beneath my feet. A cascade of loose stones swept down from where Adam was manoeuvring and took away the tentative foothold I'd established. Instinctively, I threw my arms sideways and tried to grab a handful of earth but instead I fell backwards and landed heavily on my rump, the miniature landslide carrying me on uncontrollably.

'Keep still!' I yelled into the darkness, and heard my own voice yelling back.

I couldn't have slid more than a few feet but it was enough to scare me. I'd read about the original miners who plumbed shafts with pickaxes and lowered themselves into timber-lined holes with windlasses in the search for precious metals, and I knew the death toll had been high. I also knew that one of the legacies of those early-century prospectors was a landscape peppered with hidden shafts and tunnels that could entrap the unwary and literally bury them alive. While I was pretty confident Sophie's ancestors were unlikely to have dug a network of underground caverns in this remote corner of the South Australian desert, I'd just as soon not find out the hard way that I was wrong.

I lay still for a full two minutes before daring to twist my head round. Adam was silhouetted against the mouth of the shaft, the edge of his form blurred by the shocking blue of the sky beyond.

'Bill? Are you OK?'

'I'm fine – but don't move. The ground is unstable and I really don't want to go any further in without a torch. Or a rope, come to that.'

'Sophie shouldn't be long. She's got the rope tied round her waist.'

'Looks like we're just going to have to sit it out then.'

I stared up at the ceiling of the tunnel, my eyes now finally beginning to make out some of the crevices and curves of the chiselled and blasted rockface. At a height of more than twelve feet, it felt more like a galleried hall than the entrance to a mine, but the wide opening was designed to prevent collapse. Further in, the shaft was sure to get increasingly narrow and claustrophobic. My mind wandered to the pioneers whose quest for untold wealth had driven them to this wilderness and a life of desolation and danger. I knew from previous encounters with the unimaginably wealthy that riches could do strange things to people. It seemed that the desire for riches could be just as corrosive.

'Seeing any clearer now?'

'Starting to,' said Adam. 'It's still pretty oppressive down here.'

'And we're only a few yards in. Imagine what it must be like half a mile underground.'

'I'm not sure I want to. This is Sophie's adventure, not mine.'

I snorted in the darkness. 'Missing the comforts of the Home Counties?'

'Something like that. I could be sitting in a nice cosy office, wrapped up in a warm sweater, reading personnel files right now.'

My thoughts flitted briefly to the dismal politicking and the prospects of power cuts and a three-day week that I'd left behind in England when I got on the 747 to Sydney. 'You're not telling me you'd prefer the grim, grey British winter to this Australian heatwave, are you?'

'Pros and cons, Bill. Pros and cons. You don't seem overjoyed to be here yourself. I thought someone with your background would be in their element in this kind of environment?'

He was right; most military men would give their right arm to find themselves in my position right now. What with the dramatic location, hint of derring-do and flirtation with danger – albeit in a heavily sanitised, strictly English kind of way – this would be a dream posting for many, perhaps most, of my former colleagues. But I had discovered since leaving uniform that I was not your run-of-the-mill ex-soldier at something of a loss in Civvy Street. For a while I'd found a nice little niche investigating dodgy claims for a global insurance company which had not only taken me all over the world but also introduced me to some extremely interesting people. Some of them I might even be willing to run into again.

'It's the heat I can't stand,' I offered lamely.

'You're better off in here then.'

I could feel my left leg going numb. When I'd slipped and sat heavily down on the loose rock, I'd ended up putting my body weight on my left-hand side and now my buttock was feeling the effects. I tried to stabilise my right foot flat on the floor of the shaft and adjusted my centre of gravity away from the pins and needles. As I lifted myself clear of the shale it moved again and I felt the whole plate of rock on which I was lying shift.

There was a movement above me and a shower of shingle fell round my ears. Adam was trying to shuffle down to grab me but it was the wrong move.

'Stay where you are!'

The movement stopped, and so did the gravel waterfall.

'If this loose stuff becomes any more unstable, we'll both go headfirst down the shaft,' I said. 'And we don't know how much steeper it gets. It could be vertical for all we know.'

'Sorry. I was just trying to help.'

'Thanks for the thought,' I said feelingly, and lapsed into an anxious silence. Where the hell was Sophie? I really needed her with the torch and rope before things got any worse.

Adam was obviously thinking the same thing. 'What's taking her so long?'

I didn't have an answer but a thousand possibilities flooded my thoughts. None of them were appealing, from hostile arachnids to malevolent adversaries, and I pushed them to the back of my mind. This was not a moment to be spooking myself with phantoms: I was in quite enough real danger.

A voice from the mouth of the mine punctured the rising bubble of alarm. 'Everyone OK in there?'

'Just about,' I said. 'But you know that proverbial nick of time people always talk about . . . ?'

A flash of yellowish light played on the shaft ceiling above me and I knew Sophie was trying to point the torch in my direction. 'That any help?'

'Not much. I think the light from outside is still too strong for the torch to be much use.'

'Better get further in then.' She was certainly taking the adventurous spirit bit to heart.

Adam's voice rang out nearer to me. 'Don't start galumphing down here just yet. I've already created one rockfall and we really don't want to see Bill disappearing down a tunnel until we've got him properly secured. Can you send the rope down?'

'Hang on a minute; I'll just unwrap it.'

The yellow beam stopped abruptly and there were sounds of scrabbling near the entrance. It wasn't going to be as simple as throwing me a line: with nothing to fasten it to, it would merely add extra weight to the movable heavy object that was my body lurching around on unstable shingle.

I called behind me. 'Can you find somewhere you can wedge yourself, then keep one end tied round your waist?'

Sophie paused a moment, presumably scouting her environment for something to hold on to. 'There's a big boulder here. If I sit astride it that should keep me steady.'

I'd have given good money right then for a handful of pitons and a climbing hammer but Sophie would have to do. A moment later, the end of the rope went whistling past my head and plummeted into the darkness. Still supine, I reached across to my right and scrabbled around in the stones to find it. I formed a double loop around my wrist and gave a test jerk downwards.

'Hey – what's going on?'

'Just making sure it's strong enough to take my weight.'

'A bit of warning wouldn't go amiss.'

I chuckled. 'Sorry, Sophie. Won't happen again.'

I rolled over on to my belly, trying to hang off the line as little as possible, and began to edge my way back up the tunnel. As I went I clutched new handfuls of rope, more as a comfort than a genuine climbing aid. Each time I dragged on the line I felt the tension stiffen at the top end as Sophie braced herself against her boulder. The light near the entrance blinded me again and I twisted my head away to protect my eyes; in any case, I was back on firmer ground and let the rope go slack.

'What now?' Adam's voice echoed up from the crevice at the side of the shaft where he had tucked himself after the rockfall. I hadn't seen him as I climbed but I must have passed within a few feet of him.

'We'll send the rope back down for you, then regroup and work out how we can actually get into this thing. I suspect we're going to need some more specialist equipment.'

I hauled up the rope, coiling it neatly as I went, then relieved Sophie of her anchoring duties. I positioned myself securely against the rock she'd used, ready to take Adam's weight if necessary, and hurled the untied end of the coil down into the tunnel. It fell a couple of feet from Adam's outstretched arm and he was able to shimmy across and grab it without too much trouble. The ground wasn't as steep there as where I had been lying.

'Wrap it round your waist and then you should be able just to walk back up again,' I said.

Sophie was pacing in the sunlight outside the entrance. 'It's so frustrating. It's taken us all this time to get here – not to mention using up supplies – and now we can't even get into the mine.'

'Sorry,' I said simply. 'When you're this far from civilisation and you encounter dangerous terrain, it's standard procedure to take every precaution available.' Adam was pulling on the rope more than I'd expected and the exertion in the heat was taking a toll on my power of speech.

'I know,' Sophie said. 'I just want to see it for myself.'

I could understand that: if I'd recently discovered that an ancestor of whom I was completely unaware had been a prospector for precious gems in the middle of a wilderness on the other side of the world, I imagine my curiosity would have been piqued too. 'And you will,' I assured her. 'We just need to go back to the farmstead and get ourselves properly kitted out.'

'It feels like another two days wasted.'

The reply I was forming was stifled by a sudden jerk on the rope. The full weight of a man exerted unexpectedly on a line, followed by the impact on your torso as that line reaches its full length, is much greater than most people presume. It ripped the breath out of me and rammed my left thigh heavily against the boulder I was supposed to be using to brace myself. My right foot scrambled for traction but the sandy debris beneath it gave way and I was on the move. I heard Sophie scream as I plunged headlong into the darkness, knowing that Adam was ahead of me ploughing the potentially lethal furrow that I was following. The blinding light was obliterated in a moment by the blackness of the mine's interior and I could only hope that all the sizeable boulders had been heaved aside decades earlier. The thought of coming into head-on contact with one while travelling at this speed was not something I relished; at least Adam seemed to be descending feet-first.

The slope steepened sharply and Adam gave a cry ahead of me as he went over the edge. His shout hardly had time to register before I went over too.

I wasn't sure how long I was unconscious. The luminous hands of my wristwatch were luminous no longer: it had evidently been smashed in the fall, its phosphorescent paint scattered in the dirt. As I started to regain my senses, the first thing I became aware of was Adam softly moaning in the darkness not too far away.

'Adam? Are you all right?'

I never got an answer to my question: from high above me came an alarmed shout from Sophie.

'Bill, is that you?'

'It's me.'

'Oh, thank God. Are you with Adam? I couldn't get either of you to answer me.'

'How long have you been trying?'

'A good five minutes. Is he all right?'

'I don't know yet.'

I began to twist my head around in the hope of making out some dim shape but the blackness down here was even more impenetrable. Looking up, I was vaguely aware of a paler patch high above me but it was impossible to estimate distances with nothing to gauge them by. I decided to resume my attempt to find Adam, who was still making quiet sounds away to my left.

'Adam, can you hear me?'

Nothing discernible came out of the darkness so I tried to sit up – and instantly regretted it. My left hand hurt like hell when I put my weight on it and I could feel warm moisture under my shirt on the left side of my torso. I hoped I'd just twisted my wrist and I wasn't bleeding too heavily but there was no way of finding out. If the pain levels were anything to go by I might have got away with a surface graze. I explored tentatively with my fingers and found a single tear in the material. Beneath the cotton my skin was wet to the touch but my prodding didn't provoke any greater agony so I figured I'd live. That's if I could ever get us out of this hole.

I called back up towards the glimmer of light. 'Sophie, what did you bring from the Landy?'

'Torch, water and all the ropes I could carry.'

'Great.' I offered a silent prayer of thanks for her fore-sight. I didn't fancy yet more delay while she made another return trip to the Land Rover. 'Adam's making some inter-esting noises, which is a good sign: it's the quiet ones you have to watch out for. Mind you, he's not exactly coherent so I'd like to check him out properly.'

'How are you going to do that?'

'I was wondering the same thing myself. The crucial thing is that you stay safe up there: you're our only link to the outside world so it really wouldn't do if you ended up down here with us.'

'Understood. What can I do?'

I thought for a moment. 'Tie the torch to one end of the longest rope you've got and yourself to the other end. Then sling a loop of it round that rock at the entrance and put yourself somewhere you can't slip on the shale – outside the mine altogether if you can. With luck the rope will be long enough to lower the torch down to me.'

'Give me a minute,' she said.

As a way to pass the time as much as anything, I began counting in what I reckoned were one-second intervals. It was a training technique I'd picked up from an idiosyncratic sergeant-major, in which a whole company would sound along with a ticking clock for an hour or more, just to drive the rhythm of the interval into our heads. The idea was that if we ever found ourselves without a timepiece, we could still synchronise a manoeuvre by counting the internal ticks. It was supposed to be more reliable than a pulse, though I'd never actually tried it in the field.

At fifty-eight, Sophie shouted. 'On its way.'

'OK.'

I heard the shingle move but stupidly left my face upturned, hoping to see . . . what? Instead, I got a mouthful of gravel and some loose earth as the torch came over the edge. I coughed and wiped at my face with my good hand then saw that Sophie had smartly switched the torch on before lowering it into the pit. Apart from making it much easier to locate, it also gave me my first sight of my immediate surroundings.

The view was unprepossessing.

Adam was slumped with his back against a wall of the small chamber we were in, hewn roughly into the red soil. I flashed the torchlight around at floor level before pointing it upwards. Three high sides of the chamber led at least twelve feet up towards where we'd fallen from, while the fourth wall had a low opening which led into what must form the rest of the shaft. The gap was probably only two feet square, making it a tight squeeze for anyone, let alone a prospector carrying mining equipment. My first priority was to make sure Adam wasn't badly hurt so I shuffled across to him and shone the torch in his face. There was an immediate instinctive reaction as Adam screwed up his eyes and grimaced: another good sign. I shook a shoulder.

'What?' Adam's voice was slurred and indistinct.

'Can you hear me? It's Bill – Bill Kemp. Do you know where you are?'

I moved the light away from his eyes, pointing the beam down at the chamber floor, and the lids twitched in an attempt to open.

'Adam, can you move? Is anything broken?'

He began to turn his head but grimaced again and stopped. 'What the hell happened?' His voice was clearer now and he managed to force his eyes open, focusing successfully on me.

'I'm going to check you over. Don't move.'

I started with the arm nearest to me but I was hampered by my own wrist, which let me know frequently that it wasn't up to muster. I did the best I could, tucking the torch into my left armpit and using mainly my right hand to pat Adam down gently, searching for any injuries. I didn't intend to cause him further pain but I wanted to know just how badly he was hurt. When I reached his right ankle, I got the answer.

The scream of pain brought a rapid reaction from up above. Sophie sounded terrified. 'Is that Adam? What's happened to him?'

'It's all right, Sophie, I'm just trying to find out. Looks like he's smashed up an ankle pretty badly.'

I was beginning to feel the early pangs of terror myself. If I were to dwell on the reality of our situation for any length of time, I'm pretty sure I'd have felt true panic rising in my throat. What had I been thinking, suggesting we all come into the mine together without somebody staying safe outside? Now, of the three of us, only one was still fully fit and she was hardly in a position to play the rescuer. Adam was a rugby-playing six-footer who outweighed even me, and his incapacitation meant he'd be a literal and metaphorical burden to anyone trying to get him out of this hole. While I was in marginally better shape, my twisted wrist would certainly mean I couldn't keep hold of a rope or anything else designed to haul myself out. There was no way I could carry Adam and even less chance of Sophie pulling either of us to safety. And another troubling thought had crossed my mind: while this derelict mine was self-evidently lacking in the kind of gemstones that had drawn the prospectors all those years ago, I had no such reassurance that it wouldn't contain a host of other, far less appealing, things. I've never been a big fan of creepy-crawlies of any kind, but I knew that Australia was home to a wide variety of extremely unpleasant ones and I had no desire to make the acquaintance of any of them at close quarters.

'Sorry, Bill – I think it's broken.' The expression on

Adam's face in the reflected torchlight told me he was putting a brave face on things. My guess was that he'd probably sustained the odd injury during his sporting activities so if he believed his ankle was broken, then I was prepared to take his word for it. The pained grimace certainly backed up his theory.

'I should say so. Sorry about that.'

'What are you apologising for? It was me who took us over the edge.'

'And it was me who put us in danger in the first place. I should have been much more careful with how we went about exploring this place. I can't believe I was so stupid as to bring us all inside together then leave Sophie as the only one in a safe place. God knows what we're going to do now.'

'Is she all right?'

'I think so. You can ask her yourself.'

As Adam and Sophie traded the concerned exchanges of the beloved in peril, I took another look around. I knelt down in the earth beside the narrow opening and pointed the torch into the void. Bending my head to ground level, I could see a short passageway extending maybe three feet before the shaft widened again into what seemed like a much bigger cavern. I wasn't sure but I thought I could make out some kind of pit prop a few yards ahead. If the mine went any distance into the hillside, it would certainly have needed supports to hold up the roof – though how Sophie's Uncle George could have excavated a seam in such confined conditions was beyond me.

The man himself was as much of an enigma as the mine he'd dug. The fact that Sophie had never even heard of George Deakins less than a month ago made the entire story even more unbelievable; but it was true. And not just the mine: when he'd died a few weeks earlier, Uncle George had left Sophie the whole kit and caboodle – homestead, farm and mining rights, each as worthless as the other. In the middle of the Australian outback, on the fringes of the Simpson Desert, neatly bypassed by the transcontinental rail artery of the Ghan, it was a busted flush. I was willing to bet that no animal had been farmed on the land since the days of the original Afghan cameleers in the 1930s, while any gems that might have lurked in this unpromising corner of the Great Artesian Basin had long since been transported to the jewellery emporia of Amsterdam, Monte Carlo and New York. The relentless red-brown earth, grim and drab in the torchlight, certainly bore no glimmer, of either gemstone or hope.

II

I'd never intended to be stuck underground in the middle of a godforsaken desert. It was all Kenny's fault. *You're at a loose end*, he'd said one day after the excesses of an Aussie Christmas had added a few pounds to my flying weight. *You could help me out.*

I'd known a few larger-than-life characters during my time in uniform but Kenny Hines was easily the largest. A comfortably rotund man with whiskers almost to the sides of his mouth, he had never been troubled by the burden of fashionability. He delighted in his wardrobe of oversized cosy cardigans and capacious slacks and had the air of a man who didn't give a fig what anyone else thought of him or his dress sense. For all that, he was never shoddily attired and always looked trim, even if his clothes hung off him like a shroud. He was a one-off and proud to be so.

The arrival of an Australian in our unit had raised a few eyebrows but it turned out that Kenny's eligibility for our English regiment was derived from his father. Hines Senior had been born not ten miles from my own home town and had served on the Western front in the Great War. There, he'd rubbed shoulders with some of the vast numbers of Anzac troops who came over to support the cause and, when the nonsense was all over and he discovered he'd miraculously survived, he'd been enticed by the thought of escaping the rain-sodden wastes of Europe and followed them back to their homeland. He'd married a local girl and set up shop as an undertaker in Coober Pedy, deep in the interior, employing some of the grimmer skills he'd picked up in the trenches. Kenny had arrived as something of an afterthought, a few years before the next instalment of nonsense.

I was never quite sure why, when he was called up for national service – or 'nasho', as the Aussies affectionately refer to it – he'd wangled things to sign up for a spell in the British Army instead. Maybe he wanted to see something of the world: his family had moved even further into the outback when he was a small child and his experience of life had been limited to the books he was able to lay his hands on. These, however, were many and varied and Kenny was better-read and more knowledgeable on almost any subject than most of the people I'd grown up with in the suburban Midlands.

And I certainly wasn't complaining about Kenny signing up for service on British soil: he was fantastic company, a limitless source of ribald stories and a copious consumer of beer who could drink everyone else in the regiment under the table and back again. He had a knack of getting along equally well with squaddies and officers and he somehow managed to extricate himself from more than one serious scrape with nothing worse than a tut from the CO. It was quite a trick and I wasn't the only person who benefited from it simply by being stood next to him when the igloo was on fire.

We hit it off from the first week of basic training; by week six, we were best friends. I don't know which of us found it more of a wrench when he made the decision to return to Oz but he had his sights set on a career as a lawyer and you didn't get that by playing drinking games in a windswept pub on Salisbury Plain. In the two decades since he'd settled back in Sydney, he'd qualified, served his time as a junior and then struck out on his own, building a quietly successful practice handling everything from divorces to wills. We wrote to each other regularly and occasionally he'd chivvy me about paying him a visit but somehow I never quite made the time. My own globetrotting exploits exposing fraudulent claims against the not-so-noble Lord Hosmer's insurance firm had so far not taken me to the further reaches of the southern hemisphere.

In truth, I'd needed a really good excuse to make the trip; when I found myself jobless but far from penniless after my adventures in the Caribbean, it seemed I had it. Kenny's invitation to stay for a month or so over Christmas came at just the right moment.

Twenty years older, but arguably no wiser, we settled immediately into our old routine. Kenny's wife Dolly was enormously patient with both of us, allowing us to reminisce, drink and stare at the ocean waves without upsetting the equilibrium of the friendship in any way. In fact, she added a new perspective of her own and her talents in the kitchen meant Kenny and I could be self-indulgent layabouts without worrying about where the next meal was coming from. We'd chip in when she allowed it, peeling potatoes or doing the washing up, but there was no doubting who was in charge, and she never let us believe we were taking advantage of her good nature. She was a third-generation Aussie, meaning her family had real history, and she teased Kenny mercilessly about his Johnny-come-lately nationality.

Christmas was as festive a season as I've ever enjoyed, in spite of the strangeness of a midsummer Yuletide. Instead of snow and sub-zero temperatures, I learned to appreciate the constant sunshine and plentiful beaches. Bizarrely, holly, mistletoe and turkey were still very much in evidence but I drew the line at Santa's sleigh being pulled across the night sky by six white 'boomers' – the native Australian kangaroo.

'I'm sorry, Kenny, but Father Christmas has eight reindeer. Everyone knows that.'

'Don't you believe it,' he said, pouring the latest in an already long line of whiskies and passing me the glass. 'You've fallen for the American schmaltz if you accept that.'

'Come off it,' I said. 'I can even name them: Dasher, Dancer, Prancer—'

Kenny cut me off. 'It's a conspiracy by the Yanks. I know you Brits think Dickens invented Christmas but it was that bloody poem that really started off all the guff about Saint Nick and his sack of toys. They've been moulding it in their own image ever since.'

For once, Dolly interrupted our cheerful bickering. 'Does it really matter where it came from? The fact is, it's a bloody good holiday.'

I had to concur. I was indeed having a bloody good holiday.

The best thing about Sydney – or Port Jackson, to give it Captain Cook's original name – was the harbour. Kenny and Dolly lived on the north shore of the famous bay and their home had spectacular views. Since arriving I had spent most evenings sitting on their balcony staring out at a vista I could barely believe was real. Off to the left, the Pacific Ocean was laid out to the distant horizon, with the craggy inlets of the harbour mouth creating a natural barrier to its more elemental qualities: flooding from high tides was a surprisingly rare event. On the slopes opposite stood the city's Central Business District, with its putative skyscrapers and ever-present cranes. Just to the right was the steel maw of the Sydney Harbour Bridge, majestic and monumental, and, at its further base, the extraordinary engineering achievement of the Sydney Opera House.

'We've watched that go up brick by brick,' Kenny told
me on my second evening in the country. He'd clearly
clocked my open-jawed amazement at the gleaming white
structure, bathed in the glow of a Sydney sunset.

'Doesn't look much like brick to me,' I said.

'It's a figure of speech. Concrete and tile, mostly, if you
really want to know. Fifteen years in the making and worth
every penny of the hundred million dollars it cost to build.'

I let out a breath. 'Pretty impressive tribute to Australian
creativity, though.'

'Designed by a Dane, engineered by Brits and clad by
Swedes – but yes, it's impressive.'

I stared again at the billowing shells overlooking the blue
carpet of water. 'Hardly Australian at all, in fact.'

Kenny laughed and handed me another beer.

The new year had dawned – incongruously, in shorts and
shirt sleeves – and I was starting to turn my mind to the
long return flight in a few days' time when Kenny brought
something interesting home from work.

I'd spent the day strolling the paths of the harbour's
northern inlets, whiling away happy hours envying the
sailboats; the grandeur of the backdrop and the size of some
of the yachts made my little tub on the Dart look decidedly
toylike. When I got back to the house, Kenny was already
home.

'Something here that might interest you,' he said before
I even had a chance to offer a greeting. 'Might be an insurance claim in it.'

'You know I don't do that any more.'

'Yeah, right, mate. One whiff of a decent scam and you'll
be off and running.'

I gave him a look that was meant to convey dissent but
we both knew he was right. I was too nosey – and, if I'm
honest, too good at my job – to stay away from it for long.

All it would take would be the right case to hook me straight back into the whole messy business. I didn't even need the fees at the moment: a nice, juicy mystery would do it for me.

'So you think it's a scam?' I asked non-committally.

'Not a scam,' said Kenny. 'But there is something intriguing about it.'

By the time he'd finished outlining the story, my interest had been well and truly aroused. Any remaining objections were half-hearted, at best.

'I haven't got time to go galavanting after fortune-hunters.'

'Why not? You haven't got a job to go back to; you're at a loose end. Why not help me out with a bit of nosing around?'

Dolly emerged from the kitchen, a tray of raw shrimp in her hand. Her diminutive height and slight figure belied her personality, which was large enough to match Kenny's, and her bright blue eyes seemed constantly on the lookout for something interesting to investigate.

'Who's nosing around?' she said.

'Bill is, if I get my way.'

'Oh, bonzer. You'll be staying a bit longer then?'

Kenny had warned me about the opacity of much Australian slang, and Dolly – as a 'true blue' Aussie with proper history – was certainly putting my linguistic skills to the test.

'Bonzer?'

'Yeah, mate. Ripper. I'm stoked.'

Dolly proffered the tray. I took one of the shrimp and dipped it in the bowl of thousand island dressing in the centre. 'I take it that's a good thing?'

She laughed and adopted what she fondly imagined to be a prim English accent. 'Quite so, young sir. We would deem it highly acceptable if you were able to extend your sojourn at our pleasure.'

I looked at Kenny, who raised his eyebrows expectantly. 'Can't argue with that, mate.'

I didn't even want to. The hospitality of this infectious pair was more than enough to tip the scales in favour of exchanging my London-bound plane ticket for an open-ended return. A few more weeks of this, I thought, and I'd be ready to go native. And there was the added incentive of some amateur detective work for Kenny and his client. I never could resist a challenging puzzle.

Maybe if I'd known what this particular puzzle had in store, I might have offered a little more resistance.

The client turned out to be two clients, Sophie and Adam Church. Like me, they had flown to Australia as visitors from the old country, only with more compelling reasons than simply a nice holiday: they were on a mission.

Kenny arranged a meeting between the four of us at his office. It was the first time he'd taken me there – for him, as for most Australians, the Christmas break was sacrosanct – and I was fascinated to see just what kind of empire he'd built for himself in the years since he'd set up his own practice.

The building itself was in an unassuming part of town known as Surry Hills, just south of the booming Central Business District, where older, smaller blocks were becoming increasingly engulfed by a towering skyline. While concrete and glass rose elegantly a few streets away, Kenny's three-storey sandstone pile looked solid and squat by comparison.

'Not much to look at,' he conceded as we approached the front door. 'But you don't really want anything too flashy. Gives the clients ideas above their station. Much better to manage their expectations early, I say.'

I suspected Kenny's skills would mean that most of his clients actually had their expectations comfortably exceeded but I took his point. In any case, the interior was far more welcoming. Warm lighting and thick carpet took us down

an entrance corridor to an open office at the rear of the
building, where two well-dressed receptionists were already
tapping away at electric typewriters, even at this early hour.
One was dark-haired and wore glasses and had a look of
Nana Mouskouri with her short bobbed cut. The other was
a striking redhead in a floaty green blouse, giving off a
distinct whiff of Janis Joplin with her beads and outsize
necklaces.

At the arrival of the boss, they both paused and looked
up.

'Morning, ladies.'

The receptionists nodded a greeting simultaneously, like
a pair of those Olympic synchronised swimmers whose poise
and delivery are meticulously matched, with the slightly
unnerving effect of looking almost mechanical. But their
smiles were human enough and, when they saw me, they
broke ranks.

'Bill, this is Carly and Ruth, without whom this office
would not function. Picked them up a few years back and
it's safe to say they're now indispensable.' The smiles on
the pair broadened. 'Just don't go getting any ideas about
a pay rise.'

Without pausing to watch the women's reaction, Kenny
swept away to a staircase in the corner and beckoned me
to follow. I waved a hasty hello towards Carly and Ruth
– not knowing which was which – and duly obeyed.

The first floor of Kenny's office was truly his domain. A
single room covered the entire storey and, apart from a
huge window at either end, it was head-to-foot in book-
shelves. As well as the obligatory legal tomes, arranged in
colour-coded ranks, there was an eclectic array of other
volumes, from hardback fiction to massive reference books.
I spotted a full set of Encyclopaedia Britannica, along with
a blue-bound edition of Dickens's complete works and
countless atlases, dictionaries and thesauri that signalled

Kenny Hines was something of a renaissance man. There had been books at his home, of course, but this was where the real library treasure trove was housed.

'You're a dark horse,' I said. 'I always knew you were well read, but this is something else.'

Kenny smiled. 'The accumulated detritus of a wandering soul.'

I walked over the thick carpet to an extravagantly bound set of James Bond novels. 'I'd hardly call it detritus.'

'You've got to allow a man his hobbies.'

I ran my fingers over the spines of a rather battered three-volume copy of *Rob Roy*. 'First edition?'

'Naturally.'

'Must have cost a fortune.'

'Less than it's worth, more than I told Dolly. I'm not usually in favour of secrets between spouses, but in that instance . . .'

The rest of Kenny's office was equally well appointed and comfortably luxurious. It rather made a mockery of his protestations outside about clients' expectations. His desk alone filled a third of the available space, a giant double-pedestal thing made out of what I guessed to be mahogany and inlaid with gold-trimmed green leather across its vast surface. Beyond it was what I can only describe as a throne – another outsize, opulent piece of furniture befitting the scale of the room – with two less decadent chairs facing it across the desk. At the opposite end of the room, a large smoked-glass meeting table was flanked by six steel-framed chairs, the only visible concessions to modern living. To my eyes, they seemed out of place in this emporium of antiquated clubbiness.

'What's upstairs?' I asked, pointing at the ceiling towards the top floor of the building.

'Storage, mainly, and I've got a strongroom up there for the confidential stuff.'

He'd created a real empire for himself and I was glad for him.

Kenny took up a position on his throne and gestured at the chairs facing him. I selected one and sat down. 'We've got a few minutes before they arrive,' he said. 'I'll be introducing you as my associate, so don't let on that you're here on holiday.'

I looked down at my casual clothes. 'I'm hardly dressed for the office.'

'Don't worry about that. They'll probably think it's normal for an Aussie businessman.'

I doubted that, even allowing for the informality I was growing to love about this country, but I didn't argue. These were Kenny's clients and this was his meeting: I was just along for the ride.

There was a tap at the door and the Janis Joplin receptionist came in with a tray containing cups, saucers and a large pot of coffee. 'Thanks, love,' Kenny said, and immediately started arranging them on the desk. He set out two empty cups in front of the guest chairs, then filled two from the pot and laid them in front of him. 'Do you want to bring another chair over, Carly?'

She collected one of the steel monstrosities from the meeting table and set it down beside Kenny's throne.

'It's probably best if you sit here.'

I got up and moved round to the other side of the desk, next to Kenny, and Carly picked up the empty tray. 'I'll let you know when they've arrived,' she said, and left.

'How does it look from this side?' Kenny asked.

I surveyed the room afresh and noticed for the first time the view beyond the far window. Opposite Kenny's office building was a pretty little park lined with eucalyptus trees. Through the branches that were festooned with pink and red, the cranes and towers of the business district climbed high over Sydney. Above them, the sun had already painted the sky a striking blue.

'Not too flashy,' I said, and grinned.

We were halfway through our second cup of coffee when the telephone on Kenny's desk rang shrilly. He took his time about picking up the receiver – some kind of power game, I wondered? – and almost barked into the mouthpiece. 'Yep?' A voice that could have been either Carly or Ruth burbled at the other end and he added, 'Send them up.'

He stood up and went over to the door. I watched his expression change into full avuncular Kenny as he saw his clients coming up the stairs, and he stretched out a welcoming hand. 'Ah, so this is the famous Sophie Church in the flesh.'

I heard Sophie's voice before I saw her. 'Mr Hines, it's a pleasure to meet you.'

'Pleasure's all mine,' said Kenny, backing into the room to allow space for Sophie and her husband Adam to enter. 'And you can call me Kenny.'

I'm not sure exactly what I'd expected but it certainly wasn't this. Sophie and Adam were probably in their mid- to late-twenties but seemed much younger. Maybe it was the Australian climate exaggerating their relative youth. Sophie had fair hair – a little too mousy to be truly blonde – and wore a tan-coloured pinafore dress above knee-length boots. Adam, tall and broad in an ill-fitting lightweight jacket, looked like an overgrown schoolboy dragged to his father's office to learn how the business worked. The mop of black hair and the National Health spectacles perched on the bridge of his nose simply added to the effect, as did the battered old briefcase he clutched to his chest. From what Kenny had told me about them, I'd imagined a first impression more professional – slick,

even. Adam was, after all, an accountant, and Sophie ran
her own catering firm. But then, I reminded myself, they
were on vacation too, and my own appearance was hardly
professionalism personified.

Sophie smiled at me from across the room and walked
over, her hand outstretched in greeting. I took it and introduced myself, shaking Adam's hand next.

'Bill's here to help me out,' said Kenny. 'He's got vast
expertise in this kind of area and you never know, he might
turn out to be useful.'

I let the good-humoured dig slide and we all took our
seats.

Kenny looked squarely at Sophie across the green leather
swathes. 'Now then, have you brought the paperwork?'

It took most of the morning to comb through the documents
Sophie had brought from England. For the most part, they
were a mess; many of them were little more than scraps
of scrawled handwriting, while even the more official-looking
typed sheets had been in the wars. Stains and rips revealed
that Uncle George had not been a great one for tidiness,
let alone order, in his documentation.

'I didn't even know I had an uncle until you contacted
me,' Sophie said, selecting a much less worn sheet from
the pile. I could see it was a closely-typed page topped with
a classy navy blue letterhead announcing Kenny's law practice. 'I still don't know how you found me.'

'Long story,' Kenny said. 'Your uncle and I went back a
long way. We grew up in the same town in the outback.
He was always running into trouble in one form or another
so I suppose we were a good match.'

'What about my mother?'

'Victoria – George's sister. Don't tell the missus but I had
a bit of a crush on her when I was a kid. She was a good
deal older than George and me and she was quite a looker.

He didn't talk about her much after she ran off to the other side of the world so I never found out what had happened to her.'

I could barely stand the suspense. 'And what had happened to her?'

Kenny smiled. 'Hold your horses, mate. All in good time.' He turned to a filing cabinet behind his right shoulder and pulled open a drawer, from which he lifted out what looked like a scrolled-up architect's chart, brown and dog-eared with age. He flattened it out on the desk and held the edges down with his forearms. The sheet was covered in dense, technical drawings that I couldn't decipher at first glance and I wondered where Kenny was going with all this.

'What is it?' Sophie asked.

'Oh, this? Some old blueprint for a warehouse or something,' Kenny said. 'But that's not what's interesting.' With a theatrical flourish, he whipped the chart into the air, turned it over and slapped it face down on the desk. 'This is what's interesting.'

Three of us peered at the reverse of the chart, mystified but intrigued. Shaky, pale pencil lines that spidered across the sheet revealed the simple but unmistakable form of a family tree.

Sophie said, 'I thought you'd sent me all George's papers when you wrote to me in England?'

Kenny began taking cups off their saucers and using them to hold down the corners of the scroll. 'There were some things I didn't want to entrust to the mail services of our respective countries. This, for example, is the only copy in existence of George's family tree, as far as I know. I intended to get it copied out and sent to you but when you wrote and told me you were coming over here, I thought I might as well wait and give it to you now.'

'Why? Is it precious?'

'Not in itself. But the information it contains is – to you, at least. It proves that you inherit everything George Deakins owned.'

'Your letter said I might inherit something but you gave no indication as to what,' Sophie said after a pause.

'To be honest, I didn't know myself when I wrote to you. I couldn't be sure that there weren't going to be other claimants crawling out of the woodwork and I didn't know the extent of George's estate. Well, you've seen the will – it's a little bit . . . shall we say, vague?'

Sophie fished among the scraps of paper in front of her and pulled out a handwritten sheet. 'I thought that. All it says is, "I want everything to stay in the family line." Is that even valid as a will?

'He wrote "Last will and testament" at the top and signed his name at the bottom. In the absence of anything to supersede it, that's George's will.'

I was still none the wiser about Sophie's mother Victoria, marked on the scroll with an 'm.' beside her name. Kenny hadn't answered my question about her and when I raised it again it was Sophie who filled me in.

'She died three years ago.'

'I'm sorry,' I said.

'Me too,' she replied. 'There's an awful lot I'm finding out about my Australian ancestry that I'd have loved to ask her about.'

'How did she end up in England?'

Kenny interjected. 'I can tell you that. It's taken some digging but I've uncovered the bald history, as far as it goes. When she left the outback at the age of eighteen she went to Melbourne. There she met an Englishman who was working as a medic helping tackle the polio epidemic – Edward Carrington.'

'My father,' said Sophie.

'Your father. They were married within the year and then he was called up to fight when the Second World War broke out. They sailed back to the other side of the world and it looks like Victoria subsequently forgot she ever had any connections with Australia.'

'I never knew my father,' said Sophie sadly. 'He was killed in the Battle of the Bulge a few months before I was born. I suppose that makes me an orphan now.'

'And the sole heir to the Deakins estate,' said Kenny.

Adam spoke, his voice quiet and tentative. 'What is the extent of the estate?'

'I haven't checked everything's watertight yet, so don't hold me to this, but I've been in touch with some of my old contacts out there and they've filled me in with some details. It seems your Uncle George was the proud owner of an opal mine.'

Kenny knew how to construct a dramatic moment, I had to give him that. Sophie and Adam turned and stared at each other, open-mouthed, taking in what he had just told them.

'And you didn't know about it?' I asked Kenny.

He shook his head. 'I hadn't been in regular contact with George for years, not since coming to Europe for my nasho. He could have set up a five-star hotel for passing nomads for all I knew. He'd sent me the will a few years back, along with a scribbled drawing of the farm – I guess he thought a bigshot city lawyer could be trusted more than someone in the middle of nowhere – but we hadn't seen each other for more than a decade. When I heard on the grapevine that he'd died, I got an old mate to go out to his homestead and pick up whatever papers he could find that looked important. That's where this lot came from.' He gestured at the pile laid out on the desk then pointed across the office. Under the window stood a large packing crate overflowing with papers, which I hadn't noticed before. 'And there's more.'

Sophie picked up the family tree and stared hard at it. 'So this is how you found me?'

'May I see?' I asked her. She put the scroll down again and slid it across the desk towards me, spinning it as she did so. I leaned over it and peered at the faded pencil marks. There didn't seem to be much to old Uncle George's genealogical research but there was apparently enough. The lineage went back two or three generations on his father's side, just one on his mother's. At the level of George and his sister Victoria, it branched out a little, showing her marriage to Edward Carrington and a line leading downwards to the bottom of the scroll. There, in splendid isolation, stood the name Sophie, her date of birth inscribed beneath.

'Must have taken some tracking down, if this was all you had to go on,' I observed.

Kenny snorted. 'You've no idea, mate. It's taken weeks of letters, newspaper adverts – I even had a private eye working on it in London for a while.' He looked accusingly at Sophie. 'You could have done me the favour of at least not changing your name when you got married.'

She smiled back at him. 'Sorry about that.'

I asked, 'So how did you find her in the end?'

'Stroke of good old-fashioned luck, really. The bloke I hired happened to be at a party where Sophie was doing the catering, somebody mentioned her in passing – using her maiden name – and he couldn't believe he'd stumbled across her by complete fluke.'

'It was a bit of a shock for me too,' Sophie said. 'A party guest rather the worse for wear lurching up to me and asking if I was who he thought I was. I almost didn't admit it – you never know with strangers at a party, do you?'

'Good job you did,' I said. 'Otherwise we might not all be here now and you might not be the new owner of an opal mine.'

She turned her attention back to Kenny. 'This opal mine – can you tell me more about it?'

Kenny shrugged. 'Not much. Like I said, I didn't even know about it until a few weeks ago. But in that part of South Australia there was a bit of a gold rush after the First World War – well, not gold, obviously, but the opal equivalent. A lot of the people living there are the children and grandchildren of those prospectors.'

'Is that how George ended up there?'

'Ah, now that story's even more interesting. But I'll tell you what: why don't we continue this convo over dinner at my place tonight? Dolly can rustle up something on the barbie and I can fill you in on the family history – at least, the bit of it that I'm aware of. If I know your Uncle George, I suspect he might still have a few secrets left to be discovered.'

III

Dolly's barbecuing prowess was as impressive as her hosting skills. The longstanding stereotype of Australians throwing hunks of raw meat on 'the barbie' for guests to enjoy with a few beers proved, delightfully, to be rooted in fact: they say that a stereotype has to come from somewhere, and in this instance I wasn't about to challenge it.

Along with the beer, the conversation flowed easily. Sophie and Adam proved extremely good company, and Kenny and Dolly must have thought so too because before the evening was out they'd insisted that the couple stay with them for the rest of their vacation.

'Bill's already bunked down here,' Kenny said. 'And if he's going to be true to his word and help me out, then it'll make things easier if we're all in one place.'

'We couldn't impose on your hospitality,' Sophie said.

Dolly was quick to intervene. 'Nonsense. You can impose all you like. It'll be good to have some youngsters around.'

'Thanks very much,' I said, and she laughed.

The evening also revealed what else Kenny knew of Uncle George's backstory. According to Kenny, the family narrative went back way beyond the first opal prospectors. An Irish ancestor had been one of the huge influx of

European immigrants to join an earlier gold rush in the
state of Victoria in the 1850s. As the city of Melbourne
grew to become the second largest in the British Empire,
its rapidly swelling numbers prompted adventurous types
to try their luck further and further afield, and the immi-
grant Deakins was among the first to search for gemstones
in the interior of South Australia. He had settled down with
a woman from an aboriginal tribe, fathered a son and
between them eked out a living on the fringes of the
Simpson Desert. By 1920, when the town of Coober Pedy
was christened, George's father was simply the latest in a
line of Deakins men to have devoted their lives to the hunt
for untold riches.

'I remember old man Deakins,' Kenny told us. 'Miserable
bastard. I think he'd been out in the sun too long. Mind
you, George could be pretty crabby when he set his mind
to it.' He looked at Sophie, who was sipping a long, cold
drink in a deck chair opposite him. 'Sorry, Soph, but you
come from a line of grumpy old men.'

Adam stepped in chivalrously. 'I believe the family trait
has died out in this generation.'

Sophie shot him a sweet smile, which he returned.

'Anyway,' Kenny went on, 'it looks like George finally
succeeded where his ancestors had failed and managed to
find himself some opals. Good on him.'

'Is there much money in opals?' I asked.

'Depends. Every stone is different, they come in a whole
bunch of colours, and some are pretty much worthless. But
there's a reason why Coober Pedy is the beating heart of
the Australian opal business. All your Christmases will have
come at once if you hit a seam of precious stones – and
there are plenty of the little buggers just sitting in the
ground around there, waiting to be dug up.'

'So why isn't everyone heading for Coober Pedy?'

'You wouldn't ask that if you knew anything about

mining for gems in the desert. I grew up out there until I escaped to the big city when I was seventeen and I can tell you it's no easy life. Opal mining is pretty bloody dangerous. You've got cramped tunnels with no ready supply of oxygen, the chance of cave-ins at any moment, and if there's a sudden storm you can drown quicker than a platypus in a billabong. And that's without mentioning the heat. This time of year, you're looking at forty degrees, easy.'

Sophie looked perplexed and I knew why.

'What's that in old money, Kenny?'

'Oh, sorry, mate – I forgot you blokes use Fahrenheit. Forty degrees centigrade translates to over a hundred of yours. It has been known to reach a hundred and twenty.'

Even allowing for Kenny's propensity for hyperbole, that sounded pretty damn hot to me. I mentally deleted prospecting from my list of potential job options. I was glad that Uncle George was Sophie's benefactor, not mine.

Sophie and Adam checked out of their hotel the following day and moved in to Kenny and Dolly's place. They relished the balcony views just as much as I had and the next few evenings were spent in companionable admiration of the big blue bay and the remarkable scenery this extraordinary city had to offer.

Kenny had a few loose ends to tie up with other cases before he could turn his full attention to Uncle George's will but none of us was in a particular hurry. While Kenny kept busy during the daytime, Dolly served as an excellent tour guide for the three of us and we made a raucous quintet at night, partying into the small hours. Sophie and Adam lapped up my stories of Kenny's youthful antics, while Dolly threw in a few of her own. As for Kenny himself, he tried in vain to protest his innocence but the sparkle in his eyes gave the game away.

On the third evening after the youngsters moved in, Kenny asked me to return to the office with him.

'It's about time we got cracking on Sophie's inheritance, don't you think?' he said.

'I suppose so. But what more can we find out?'

'Oh, I don't know – what sort of house George had, how big the mine is, whether there's any other land involved. That kind of thing.'

'And you want me to do some digging?'

'That's your job, isn't it?'

'Was,' I corrected him.

'All right, was. But you still know how to do it, don't you?'

I had to concede I did, so the next morning I donned the smartest clothes I'd brought with me and joined Kenny in his car.

'This has to be one of the most beautiful journeys to work anywhere in the world,' I said as we headed south onto the Sydney Harbour Bridge for the second time in a week. With the cobalt harbour way below us on both sides and the giant steel framework encasing us as we passed through the concrete gateposts, it was a drive like no other I'd experienced. I sat in awed silence for the full minute that it took us to cross to the far pylons then realised I was holding my breath. I blew it out and shook my head in disbelief.

'Not bad, is it?' he said.

'I can see why you opened your office on the other side of the harbour. That's a hell of a commute.'

We swung into a small car park behind Kenny's office building and I looked up at the sky as we walked to the door. 'Is it always sunny in Sydney?'

'I think you've been spoiled on this trip. There's actually more rain here than you get in London; you just don't notice it in the same way.'

Inside his office, Kenny had made preparations. The smoked-glass meeting table had been set up in one corner, nearest the window overlooking the park, and there were already a number of reference books stacked high. A legal pad and a container of pens and pencils awaited me and he'd even arranged a dedicated telephone.

'We can't have you complaining about the working environment, can we?' he said.

'No complaints here.'

I wasn't about to complain about the volume of research material either. It seemed that Uncle George was disorganised and reclusive and, from the size of the packing crate by my desk, had decided early on to keep just about every piece of paper he ever encountered. Much of it, inevitably, was what most people would regard as junk but I'd learned enough from my old job to know that junk could yield revealing information with surprising frequency. I'd once found a scrap of paper with a scribbled note on it among the effects of a dead man which turned out to change the terms of his will in such a way as to cut out his wife entirely: it didn't make me popular with the widow but it certainly stood up in court. What a man leaves behind can often say more about him than an hour's conversation in life ever could.

Kenny and I agreed that he would plough on with the legal niceties to render Sophie the official owner of her family's opal mine while I would conduct a thorough search through everything else that Kenny had had sent over from the farmstead. He assured me there would be plenty more on site but, for now, this crate contained anything from Uncle George's place that Kenny's local contact had deemed potentially interesting.

'How did you get it here?' I asked as I shuffled my chair round the table for easy access to the crate.

'There's still a few people left from my time out there. I

called a guy I know in Oodnadatta, the nearest town to George's farm.'

'So it's not that remote, then? From the way you've been talking about it, I thought it was miles from civilisation.'

'It is. Oodnadatta is about three hours' drive north of Coober Pedy and George's farm is another forty miles or so out into the desert from there. Hard to imagine anything much more remote.'

'I stand corrected. Who's the guy you called?'

'Smith Penney? Oh, just someone George and I both knew from way back. He was a bit of a larrikin when we were young but he knows his way about out there. He drove out to the farm, packed that crate and shipped it over by plane.'

I peered into the depths of the crate, mentally totting up the hours it was going to take me to wade through its contents. 'And what are you hoping we'll find in here?'

'Hoping? I don't suppose I'm hoping for anything in particular. It's just a case of making sure we know what Sophie can expect from her inheritance. Mind you, where George Deakins is concerned, I don't think there's anything that would surprise me too much. My advice? Keep an open mind and get those investigative antennae of yours twitching. I'd hate for us to miss anything exciting.'

As things turned out, it was Sophie who inadvertently raised the excitement levels. We were on the balcony once more, sipping our drinks and watching the white sails of a flotilla of yachts flit around the harbour; the Opera House writ small.

'Kenny, you still haven't told me exactly what happened to Uncle George.'

Kenny made as if to get up for a refill but Adam reached out a hand and placed it on his arm. 'Why the secrecy, Kenny?'

I glanced at Kenny's face for a reaction. He merely smiled his broadest smile and removed his arm from Adam's grasp with a deft movement. 'No secrecy, mate. I was just trying to spare your wife all the details.'

'What details?' Sophie asked. 'You can tell me: I'm a big girl.'

Kenny sighed and sat back down in the armchair he'd just vacated. 'All right, if you really want to know . . . George Deakins shot himself.'

Sophie let out a little gasp.

Kenny lifted both hands in a placatory gesture. 'I know, I know – I should have told you before.'

Dolly was unimpressed. 'Should have broken the news more gently, that's for sure.' She leaned across and patted Sophie's shoulder. 'I apologise for my husband. Never been great at empathy.'

Sophie shook her head slowly. 'That's OK, Dolly. It was more the surprise than anything. I mean, I didn't even know Uncle George existed until a few weeks ago so I can't really justify a huge emotional outburst.'

'Although he was your only living relative,' said Adam pointedly.

I pressed for more information. 'What else can you tell us about his death, Kenny – allowing for Sophie's feelings?'

'Don't go easy on my account,' she said. 'I'm as interested as the rest of you.'

Kenny shrugged. 'There's not much more I can tell you. From what Smith Penney said, nobody had seen him around Oodnadatta for several weeks.'

'Oodnadatta?' said Sophie.

'The nearest town to Uncle George's farmstead,' I told her.

'That's not too unusual for those parts,' Kenny went on. 'People make the journey into town only when they have to – the round trip is a full day's expedition – and the farmers tend to stock up for long periods if they can. The telegraph keeps folks in touch but that only works if you happen to live on the route of the line so the more remote stations might be out of contact for a couple of months at a time.'

I was interested to know more about that. 'Surely the telegraph has been out of use for years?'

'You'd think, wouldn't you? But the line's still there so they still use it. Of course, the official service has long since gone over to telephony but as a local means of staying in touch, the old wires still work pretty well.'

'I'm amazed they even built a telegraph line across the country,' I said.

'Two thousand miles of it. Thirty thousand-plus poles in the sand. One of the great feats of Australian engineering. And if it hadn't been for that, the rail line might have gone somewhere else entirely. The blokes who built the telegraph just used the route mapped out by the original transcontinental explorers in the 1860s and the train wallahs followed suit.'

'That's the Ghan train?'

Kenny nodded.

'Why is it called that?'

'The official explanation is that it was named after the Afghan cameleers who used to drive the route. There is another theory, though. When the first sleeping car arrived in Oodnadatta from the south, the joke was that it only had one passenger – an Afghan.'

Sophie roused herself from the slough of meditation into which she had fallen while Kenny and I wittered on. 'So nobody thought it odd that Uncle George hadn't been seen for a while?'

'Sorry, Sophie,' I said. 'I didn't mean to derail the narrative.'

She threw me an indulgent smile and turned expectantly to Kenny.

'About three weeks, they reckon,' he said. 'Someone finally tried to reach him on the shortwave radio and when there was no response they finally sent a ute to investigate.'

'A ute? What's that?'

'Ah, sorry. It's short for utility vehicle. Henry Ford nicknamed them kangaroo chasers back in the day – you'd probably call it a pick-up truck in England.'

Sophie nodded thoughtfully. 'And what did they find when they got there?'

Kenny dropped his gaze and his voice was more sombre. 'Place was deserted. George's truck was parked outside so they knew he couldn't have gone far. They found him about fifty yards from the house behind a coolibah tree. Single gunshot to the temple.'

We all sat in respectful silence, waiting for Sophie to speak next. The vibrant blue of the bay, with the setting sun glinting off the waves, seemed altogether too frivolous for the topic of conversation and the awkwardness hung heavy in the air.

Finally she wanted to know more. 'Any idea why he might have done that?'

'None at all. That wasn't the George Deakins I knew as a young man, that's for sure. But then I hadn't seen him for a very long time and the outback can do strange things to a bloke, especially one living on his own and literally digging out a living from the ground. It's a hell of an existence, being an opal miner.'

'I can't imagine,' said Sophie. 'Poor Uncle George.'

She and Adam turned in not long afterwards, even though it was still early. Dolly fussed over them for a while, making sure they'd got bedding and refreshments to see them through the night, and Kenny took advantage of our being left alone.

'Young love. Remember that?'

I laughed hollowly. 'Feels like a long time ago.' I thought

of my first wife and the early days of our courtship, when we flouted the rules to find ways of celebrating our growing feelings that would have made a brigadier blush. Like Sophie and Adam, we hadn't been together long before we married and we were still in the halcyon days of blissfulness when the plane that was bringing her to me in Germany came down in a ball of flames, and the dream was done. I'd been through a second marriage and out the other side since then, but the less said about that, the better.

Kenny broke into my reverie. 'What about the girl who came to stay with you in Devon after that business in the Caribbean? You never told me what happened to her.'

I felt a flush of guilt. Leotta Tomsson had barely entered my head in the weeks I'd been in Australia. In my defence, I don't suppose I'd been in her head much either, given that she'd made things very clear when she first arrived at Heathrow: anything that might blossom between us over the course of that summer would only ever be a fling. I agreed happily. To be frank, I hadn't expected anything of the sort anyway and had only extended my invitation to her to come and stay as a way of decompressing from the traumatic events on Campanilla, passing some sociable time with a beautiful and companionable woman who'd been through precisely the same experience. Over the next few months, our relationship had indeed developed into a romantic one but there was always the looming date of the start of her medical degree on the horizon and when term began she packed her bags and we parted, amicably if with a touch of sadness. I hadn't enjoyed the domestic company of anyone for a very long time, let alone someone so delightful, and I suspected I was going to miss her. That suspicion lasted about as long as it took for the hot Australian sun and the Hines hospitality to work their ministrative magic.

'It was nice while it lasted,' I said simply.

Kenny swirled the remains of the drink in his glass. 'Not "The One", I take it?'

'Too many complications, too many painful memories. But I have to admit she did me some good. She even got me to give up smoking.'

'Bloody hell, mate, I didn't think there was a Sheila walking the face of God's earth who could make Bill Kemp do anything he didn't want to do.'

'Must have wanted to, then, mustn't I?'

We lapsed into a silence broken only by the sounds of the city and the bay. It was a curious mixture of noise: the usual background hum of traffic punctuated every so often by the air horn of a waterborne vessel or a shout drifting up from a slipway out of sight beneath us. It was quite a change from an evening overlooking the Dart.

'You know, Sophie reminds me of Leotta in many ways.'

Kenny shot me a look. 'Tell me more.'

'Oh, I don't know. There's something about her freshness – it's not naiveté exactly but something not far from it. It's almost as if you could toss any problem her way and she'd just take it on the chin and get on with sorting it out. Maybe it's the confidence of youth—'

'And yet she still seems pretty grounded.'

I had to agree. Alongside Sophie's upbeat optimism were the clear signs of someone who knew how the world worked and was preparing to exploit it to her own advantage – not in a manipulative way but with an inner strength that would serve her well, whatever life threw at her.

'Adam's a lucky man,' I said.

I reflected on the young newlyweds who'd brought their intriguing mystery to Kenny's door: where Sophie was confident and outgoing, Adam seemed reserved. Sophie was chatty and familiar; Adam verged on the monosyllabic. While it's one thing to date someone who's your polar opposite in almost every respect, it's quite another to want to marry them. Then again, my second wife and I turned out to have little enough in common.

'Do you know how they met?'

'Bit of a whirlwind romance, as far as I can make out,' said Kenny. 'When I first wrote to her in the spring – that's our spring, not yours – I don't think he was even on the scene.'

'There's no accounting for passion,' I said, and drained my glass. 'Look at Dolly – she fell in love with you.'

IV

The first threat came in a letter, hand-delivered to Kenny's office two days later. That part of it at least was a relief: whoever sent it didn't seem to know where he lived. Kenny and I were back at the old routine, me trawling through dog-eared papers, him riffling the textbooks for case law to make Sophie's inheritance watertight. It was Ruth, the dark-haired receptionist, who brought the letter upstairs.

'This has just been dropped off by a courier. Thought you might want it now, rather than wait for your morning coffee.'

Kenny didn't look up. 'Have a gander, will you, mate?'

'Really? Could be confidential.'

He lifted his head from the tome he was studying. 'How long have we known each other? If I can't trust you with anything in these four walls, we might as well give up now.'

I overcame my misgivings and opened the plain envelope. Inside was a single folded sheet of notepaper with no identifying markings, just three lines of handwritten scrawl: *The Carrington girl must abandon her claim on the Deakins mine. It doesn't belong to her. If she won't, she'll be made to pay.*

I flipped it over but there was nothing on the back. I looked again at the envelope, but it too was blank.

'Kenny.'

He grunted.

'You need to see this.'

I walked over to his desk and dropped the sheet under his nose. His expression remained inscrutable as he read it. Then he reached out to the phone and picked up the handset.

'Ruth, who delivered this?'

I could hear her voice on the other end of the line but couldn't make out what she was saying. Kenny listened for a minute then hung up without saying anything more.

'So?' I asked.

'No help at all. Motorcycle courier still wearing his helmet with a blacked-out visor pulled down. Ruth says she's never seen him before. He just tossed the letter on the counter and left.'

It made no sense to me. Kenny had found it difficult enough tracking Sophie down in London, so who else could know about her inheritance? The only conclusion I could reach was that it had to be someone from the mining community out there in the desert. But that threw up other questions: how did they know that Sophie even existed? And, more worryingly, how did they know that Kenny was the lawyer acting on her behalf in the case? Maybe Uncle George had told someone about his long-lost niece back in the old country and how the mine and everything would go to her when he popped off. But the note was clear: *It doesn't belong to her.* Clearly, somebody else reckoned they had a stronger claim to the site – and its potentially valuable contents. If that was the case, though, why not contest the estate openly, through the courts? Why all the cloak-and-dagger business of a mystery motorcycle courier and an anonymous note? And why, above all, offer such a ridiculously melodramatic threat?

'Best not mention this to Sophie,' said Kenny, and returned to his books.

For the rest of the morning, I struggled to concentrate on the task in hand. The bizarre letter lay on the table in front of me, taunting me with its unanswered questions and diverting me from sorting George Deakins's documents. I toyed with the idea of digging out all the discarded papers from the bin where I'd already thrown them and starting all over again, just in case I'd missed something that might shed light on the whole business. I went over them in my mind and came to the conclusion that no, I was actually good enough at my job not to have passed over some vital piece of evidence. If there was anything to be discovered, I had yet to stumble across it.

At lunchtime, I found I needed fresh air. Kenny declined my offer to bring him a sandwich back so I let myself out of the front door and crossed the road to the little park opposite the office. A hot sun was beating down but the leaves of the trees provided quite good coverage so I strolled for a while and soaked the warm day into my bones. I knew the signs of something gnawing at my brain well enough: I'd had plenty of years truffling out niggling half-thoughts about insurance claims I'd investigated for Western and Continental. So far in Sophie's case there hadn't been much to keep me interested. It was a pretty straightforward probate specimen and I knew Kenny didn't really need my help. I suspected he'd only asked me to give me something to do and maybe to keep me hanging around in Australia a bit longer. I'd gone along with it because I was enjoying the company of an old friend and his delightful wife and the truth was that the longer I stayed Down Under, the more I liked it. Sophie and Adam hadn't exactly been an intrusion on my holiday but the focus had definitely shifted from my cosy little trio with the Hineses and I had been starting to feel rather antsy. Admittedly, I had no job, or much of a life, to return to in Devon but whatever the circumstances, it was still home.

And now this. A naked threat – albeit a vague one of indeterminate meaning. With no clue to its origin, I knew Kenny's strategy would be to ignore it. He'd made that much clear with the attention he chose to give it on its arrival. I guessed he would carry on as before until something concrete happened that forced him to change tack – an official alternative claim, for instance, or maybe a court order. To my mind, though, the letter could not simply be swept under the carpet: the underlying ultimatum carried more than a hint of menace and it wasn't down to Kenny and me to make the decision about how to proceed.

'I think Sophie deserves to know about the letter,' I said when I got back to the office. 'After all, it is her case.'

We chucked it back and forth for a while, debating the pros and cons of telling her, and Kenny finally conceded with good grace. What swung it was my argument that, if the boot were on the other foot, he wouldn't want to imagine that his lawyer was keeping anything from him.

Kenny broke the news to Sophie and Adam over one of Dolly's delicious dinners that evening. He needn't have worried about her sensitivity to unknown menaces: if anything, it galvanised her.

'Who the hell thinks they can push me around like this?' she demanded, waving the letter in an angry fist. 'Hiding behind anonymity, threatening God knows what – it's the act of a coward. If somebody feels they have a greater right to that mine, then let them come and tell me to my face.'

'I don't think there's much danger of that,' said Kenny. 'If they had a genuine claim, they'd have brought it in front of a court by now.'

Dolly passed a bowl of vegetables to Sophie and looked down the table to where her husband sat facing her. 'Do you think we should report it to the police?'

Kenny shook his head. 'No point, love. They wouldn't

be interested. Not in an anonymous note as vague as that. I think somebody's just chancing their arm, hoping Sophie might get scared off and leave the whole thing well alone. And if she did, there's a chance they might come out of it pretty well. It's a bit like the Wild West in some places out there and possession, as they say, is nine-tenths of the law. With no one to challenge them, they might just waltz onto George's land and take it for themselves.'

'What about the other townsfolk in Oodnadatta?' I asked. 'They'd have something to say about it, surely?'

'They might . . . if they knew,' said Kenny. 'I don't think you blokes have quite grasped what we're dealing with here. There's a lot of miles between the town and the Deakins farmstead and even more to the mine. The terrain is bloody hostile, too. Nobody in their right minds would go out there unless they had to so if someone had their heart set on grabbing George's property, they could probably do it without people in Oodnadatta being any the wiser.'

There was an edge to Sophie's voice when she spoke. 'Well it's not George's property any more. It's mine. And no faceless bully is going to intimidate me out of it.'

I believed her.

The next day Sophie announced her intention to go to the Deakins farmstead.

The opposition to the plan was unanimous. I tried a paternalistic tone, telling her the outback was no place for an English rose, and quite rightly she gave me short shrift for it. Kenny launched into a long lecture about the perils of the desert, including some gruesome details about the effects on the body's systems of a bite from one of the many venomous spiders and other creepy-crawlies that inhabited the Australian wilderness. Dolly clucked like a mother hen concerned for her chicks. Adam, meanwhile, flatly refused to entertain the notion or even to discuss it. More of his innate reserve, I supposed. How the two of them were ever going to survive marriage I couldn't imagine.

'Show me this place I've been hearing so much about on a map,' Sophie demanded.

Kenny, like me, had always had a fondness for topography. He went immediately to a shelf in his study where a long line of Australian Government maps were ranged and pulled a few down.

'The problem, Sophie my girl, is that you'll struggle to find it on any of these maps. The scale is so enormous and the land so poorly surveyed that the information you're after just doesn't exist.'

He unfolded one of the sheets and spread it out on the dining table.

'What scale is this one?' I asked.

'One to one million.'

I let out a soft whistle.

Adam said, 'What does that mean?'

'It means,' I said, boggling at the idea, 'six inches on that map represent nearly a hundred miles on the ground.'

Kenny leafed open an atlas and dropped it on top of the map. It showed the whole of Australia laid out across a double-page spread. He jabbed a finger at it. 'Here's Coober Pedy. Now, on this one, Oodnadatta doesn't look too far, does it?'

Sophie shook her head.

'Best part of two hundred K,' said Kenny, and snapped the book shut. He leaned over the map underneath it and pointed again. 'If you look at it on here, you get a better idea. Roughly four hours in a ute over that terrain. And you're not even there when you get there.'

'What do you mean?'

'Oodnadatta just happens to be the nearest town. Macumba Station is another forty K beyond that and George's place is an hour on from Macumba. It just keeps getting more and more remote.'

Sophie frowned. 'So where exactly is Uncle George's farmstead?'

'Somewhere about there.' Kenny dropped a finger onto the map and started to swirl it around in a large circle. 'Hard to be more precise as they haven't printed the map that'll show it yet. The government's cartographers have been surveying the interior of Australia since 1961 and they've still only covered a fraction of it. Your best guide is Mount Sarah – here – and Lake Eyre to the south-east. Macumba Station is about a third of the way from Mount Sarah in the direction of Lake Eyre. George's place is somewhere north-east of that.'

Sophie picked out a topographical feature on the map. 'This looks like a river.'

'After a fashion,' said Kenny. 'Depends on the weather and the season. Sometimes there's water, sometimes there isn't. There are a few billabongs along the route that generally stay wet most of the year but you can't guarantee it.'

'What about the transcontinental train?' I said.

'The Ghan? Runs through Oodnadatta – for now.'

'Why "for now"?'

'Plans are under way to re-route it via Coober Pedy. That river can flood just as easily as it dries up and when it does it has a nasty habit of washing the line away. Solution? Shift the whole thing a hundred miles to the west.'

Inwardly I marvelled at Kenny's facility to switch between the Australian metric measurements and our old-fashioned English imperials. I knew it came from his time spent in the northern hemisphere but it never failed to impress me.

He went on, 'In five years' time, that old narrow-gauge line will have gone and there'll be a new standard-gauge connecting Adelaide to Darwin. That's great for the rail users but it will leave Oodnadatta rather cut off from civilisation – if there was ever any civilisation to begin with.'

I looked again at the map. 'Good God. You weren't kidding when you called it remote, were you?'

'Finally getting the picture? And that's why it's madness to talk about going out there.' He turned to Sophie. 'Your best bet is to put the whole place up for sale with the land agent in Oodnadatta and hope there's somebody crazy enough to put in a bid.'

For a while, it looked as if Sophie might just have been persuaded. Kenny and I spent the next couple of days continuing our increasingly tedious search through the paper trails, finding little to support her inheritance claim except one document from a company based in Sydney, addressed to George, which made some oblique reference to a title deed. Without any evidence that it related to the mine, we set it to one side as intriguing but unhelpful. Slightly more useful – potentially, at least – was George's hand-drawn plan of the Deakins farmstead, showing the relative positions of the house itself, a well nearby, and a track that was marked with an arrow and the words 'To the mine' off to the north-east. Comically, a little way to the west of the house, a small circle was labelled 'TREE' in capital letters. The sketch was hardly Ordnance Survey quality and looked like it been dashed off in a hurry but it conjured up something of the site's sprawling nature.

The tedium was relieved two evenings later when Adam returned from a solo shopping trip with a black eye.

'Oh my God,' said Sophie, rushing to coddle him and lead him gingerly to the settee in the living room. 'What on earth happened to you?'

Adam willingly gave in to her attentions and dropped into the chair, one hand over the bruised eye. 'I can't believe it. I was beaten up.'

Dolly darted into the kitchen and I guessed she was going in search of medical supplies.

Sophie peered anxiously at the purpling mark on Adam's face. 'Beaten up? Who by?'

'I don't know. There were two of them. They came up from behind me when I was walking down the street and grabbed an arm each. They bundled me into an alleyway and forced me up against the wall.'

Dolly returned from the kitchen with a small tray containing a dampened flannel, a glass of water and some tablets that I took to be painkillers. She sat beside Adam on the other side from Sophie and passed her the flannel, which she dabbed against his eye.

In between flinching at her touches, Adam continued his story. 'One had an arm across my throat and the other said they wanted me to deliver a message. Then the first one just lamped me and they ran off.'

'Could you describe them?' asked Kenny.

'Not really. They both had sunglasses and sports caps so I couldn't really see their faces. It all happened so fast – I wasn't really taking it in.'

He looked as though he was on the verge of tears and Sophie wrapped her arms round him and pulled him close.

'I don't understand,' she said. 'What message?'

I pointed at the bruise that was swelling under Adam's left eye. 'I think that's quite a message, don't you?'

'Don't tell me we shouldn't report this,' said Dolly, looking sharply at Kenny. I suspected her Australian pride was offended by the thought that a guest in her home should have been assaulted by two of her compatriots.

'I'll get onto it,' I said and went to the telephone in the hall.

The two police officers who knocked on the door an hour later were perfectly pleasant but without any detailed description of the attackers there was little they could do. Kenny brought out the threatening letter and the officers studied it with mild interest but, as they delicately pointed out, it didn't offer much in the way of clues. One of them recorded the assault on Adam in his notebook and advised us that they would pass all the information on to a senior officer. If there was anything else they needed they would get back in touch. They were in the house for barely fifteen minutes.

The second letter arrived the following morning. It was just as mysterious, came in a similar blank envelope, and carried a message even blunter than the last.

Drop the Deakins claim. You have been warned.

The only difference with this letter was that it was delivered to Kenny's house. Someone had been doing their homework.

Once again Kenny made to shrug it off. 'It's probably someone in Oodnadatta trying their luck.'

I wasn't buying that. 'It's a hell of a lot of trouble for someone in Oodnadatta to go to. Getting two threatening letters hand-delivered by a courier in Sydney? Arranging for two thugs to beat up Adam? Not to mention the fact that whoever it is has now managed to track down your home address.'

'That's not difficult. Anyone with a copy of the lawyers' register and the Sydney phone directory could do that,' said Kenny. He looked unconvinced nonetheless.

A phone call to the police added this latest development to their growing dossier but if we hoped their response was going to be anything other than perfunctory, we were disappointed. They were sorry but there was still nothing they could do.

On the balcony that evening Sophie announced she'd made a decision.

'I don't like all this mystery motorcyclist stuff, especially now they've come to your house,' she told Kenny. 'And the attack on Adam is the last straw. Much though it pains me to give in to bullying, I'm going to take your advice and sell up. Can you help me do that?'

Kenny nodded. 'Of course – but are you sure that's what you want?'

'What I want seems to be immaterial. Ditto Uncle George. It's what these bullies want that's the most important thing right now. I'm not willing to put you and Dolly in danger, especially after all the hospitality you've shown us.'

She reached out a hand to Adam, in the chair next to hers, and squeezed it.

'You couldn't have been kinder to a pair of wandering strangers and we're very grateful.'

Kenny laughed. 'You haven't seen the bill for my professional services yet.'

Adam looked relieved and leaned towards his wife. 'You're sure? You just want to let it go?'

The reluctance was plain to see on Sophie's face but she nodded. 'All this unpleasantness isn't what we came to Australia for and I'd rather not have our trip tainted any more than it has been already. Let's just rid ourselves of the whole Deakins headache once and for all.' She turned back to Kenny with a decisive look. 'Put the lot on the market.'

A niggling thought struck me. 'Listen, if there's someone out there who's desperate for Sophie to drop her claim to the mine, how are they going to feel about her putting it up for sale?'

'Good point,' said Kenny. 'But there's no arguing with the law. If George's will leaves it to Sophie then it belongs to Sophie, no matter what these clowns say. If they want it so badly they can always buy it from her on the open market.'

Sophie frowned. 'Have you definitely proved that it belongs to me?'

'As good as. Nothing has come to light to suggest anything different and Bill here has been pretty thorough with his searching.'

Too damned thorough, I thought bitterly, recalling the days I'd put in at Kenny's office poring over scraps of rubbish. Still, that was the job – even if I wasn't actually getting paid for it on this occasion.

'Might be worth making the sale as public as possible if you want to make sure the bullies are off Sophie's back once and for all,' I said.

'Another good point. You're full of bright ideas this evening, aren't you? I'll tell you what: I'll get in touch with the land agent in Oodnadatta and ask him to make an initial valuation. The word'll get round in no time that it's going up for sale. That should do the trick.'

'And what about here in Sydney?'

'What about it?'

'Well, we're making the assumption that whoever wants Sophie out of the picture is based in Oodnadatta but what if they're not? Shouldn't we put a public notice in the *Morning Herald* just to be doubly sure the news gets out?'

Kenny stroked his chin thoughtfully. 'Mmm. Not a bad idea either. And I might drop a line to that company whose letter we found in George's papers talking about a title deed, see if they can shed any light on whether there are any other interested parties. They had a Sydney address, didn't they?'

'That's if they're even still in business.'

Kenny slapped his hand down on the table next to him. 'Will you stop making these good points, please, Bill? It's getting very disconcerting.'

On the basis that there was nothing left to find, and even if we found it Sophie would still be selling the mine and farmstead, Kenny and I abandoned work on the probate case. He resumed his normal duties representing the good and not-so-good of north Sydney while I turned my thoughts to the long trip back to Blighty. I was fast running out of excuses to stay and three weeks into the year I began packing my suitcase.

The day was a warm and sunny one – not blisteringly hot but pleasant enough for short-sleeved shirts – and Sophie decided over breakfast that she would explore the local neighbourhood in more depth rather than take the now familiar trip into the city centre. I wondered if the assault on Adam had spooked her and she was nervous about venturing too far but I said nothing. Adam declined to accompany her, saying he would prefer a spot of sunbathing at the famous Bondi Beach, which he knew would bore Sophie rigid. With admonitions ringing in his ears to take particular care, he set off soon after breakfast while Sophie and Dolly cleared up the breakfast things. Kenny had left for the office a good half-hour before the rest of us were even awake.

'Do you know what? I think I'll come with you,' Dolly said to Sophie as the three of us put away the last of the crockery. 'What about you, Bill?'

I demurred. 'I'd better get on with my packing. But you two have fun.' I was emptying the second drawer of the sideboard in my room when I heard the impact.

It wasn't the crunching sound of metal against metal that you get when two cars collide but the sickening thud of a high-speed vehicle making contact with something much softer. In two steps I was at the window, looking out over the street behind the house. As I got there, I saw a large black saloon car picking up speed as it headed away up the street and I wondered what it had hit. The answer lay in the middle of the road, right outside the driveway.

Dolly was supine, her limbs twisted into an ugly contortion. Even from this distance, I could make out her eyes gazing unseeingly up at the sky.

On the far side of the road, Sophie was sitting with her back against a parked car, staring in disbelief at the horror

before her. It must have taken me less than thirty seconds
to reach her but already there was a small crowd gathering.
Some had clearly heard the collision from houses nearby
and dashed out to see what had happened. Others were
the drivers of cars which had arrived on the scene and
stopped to help.

'Stand back,' I shouted as I ran from the driveway. Two
or three people stepped away from Dolly as I approached
and I knelt down beside her, the bile rising in my throat
at the sight of her blank eyes. I reached out for her right
arm, twisted awkwardly towards her shoulder, and felt for
a pulse. I tried several different positions on her wrist,
hoping that it might be my own incompetence that was
preventing me from finding one, but in my heart I knew
she was already gone. A trickle of blood from the corner
of her mouth confirmed the nightmare.

I switched my attention to Sophie, still propped up a few
feet away in the street. She looked terrible – hair strewn
across her face, tears streaming down her cheeks – but at
first appraisal she didn't seem to have been injured.

'Are you OK?' I asked stupidly.

She collapsed in a torrent of sobs, burying her head in
both hands. I moved over to her and tried to cradle her as
best I could but her position and the ferocity of her crying
made it almost impossible to get an arm around her. I
wanted desperately to know what had happened and
whether she'd seen the car that had taken off at such speed
but now wasn't the right time. She'd need a lot of care
from her husband to get over this.

The next few hours were some of the hardest I'd ever
faced. Seeing combat colleagues killed or injured is not the
same as a violent civilian death and I had to draw on all
my reserves of compassion and fortitude. After the emergency services, who appeared with remarkable alacrity and
immediately took charge of the situation, my first call was

to Kenny's office. A kindly policewoman had offered to get one of the boys in blue to go there and break the news but I figured it would be better coming from me, even if it was on the end of a telephone.

It was bloody but necessary. Kenny refused to believe me at first but he soon realised that this went far beyond the realms of a tasteless practical joke and I could hear the tremor in his voice as the truth sank in. I suggested that he get a taxi home rather than attempt to drive and I was pleased when he agreed. There was no sense in putting even more danger out onto the Sydney streets. He was home in twenty minutes, by which time Dolly's body had already been taken away and the street cordoned off for forensic examination. I saw him staggering down from the top of the hill, where the cab dropped him off at the police tape, and went to meet him.

'What the hell happened, Bill?'

I didn't think that mentioning my immediate suspicions would be helpful at that point so I played things with a straight bat. 'We're not really sure, other than that it was a hit-and-run. Dolly and Sophie were crossing the street when a car careered down here and ploughed into them. Sophie says Dolly was on the side nearest to it and took the full force. Sophie was thrown clear and ended up over there.'

I pointed at the parked car where I'd found Sophie, diverting Kenny's attention from the chalk marks in the middle of the road. Several police officers were milling about doing their thing and one was waiting for us at the entrance to the drive.

'Mr Hines?'

I nodded on Kenny's behalf.

The officer was young – probably no more than twenty-five – and I wondered why he'd been given the job of looking after the victim's widowed husband. It quickly became apparent that he was good at this job.

He took off his sunglasses and laid a comforting hand on Kenny's arm. 'I'm so sorry, Mr Hines. We'll be doing everything we can to support you.'

There was a fire of fury in Kenny's eyes. 'Just find the bastard who did this,' he said. 'And bring him to me.'

Kenny was taken inside and he and Sophie were well looked after by two policewomen, who parked them side by side on the settee in the living room and, over the course of the next couple of hours, gently teased the few facts of the story out of Sophie. I made myself useful supplying endless cups of tea for them and the officers outside and I watched with morbid fascination as the forensics johnnies plied their grim trade. At one point around lunchtime I was called back inside the house to give a statement but there was little I could tell them that added anything substantial to the narrative. I was soon back in the kitchen, rustling up some basic sandwiches.

The menial task in that environment was enough to bring reality crashing into my brain. The kitchen had been Dolly's domain and now here I was, buttering slices of bread to cater for the people who were dealing with the aftermath of her brutal death. It was all I could do to stay on my feet and I don't mind admitting that the tears flowed freely.

V

The funeral was scheduled for a week later.

Kenny took on the task of making all the arrangements himself. I guessed he was trying to keep busy to take his mind off things so I left him to it, offering refreshments periodically. I'd deferred my departure indefinitely and he'd talk when he was ready. In the meantime, if I forced the issue I knew I'd be making myself a nuisance.

With little else to occupy her, Sophie was slowly driving herself mad, replaying the incident in her mind and asking herself what she could have done to prevent it. She told me as much on the third day after the tragedy and I tried to console her by telling her there was nothing anybody could have done. I could see she didn't believe me.

Adam's efforts to comfort his wife, meanwhile, seemed minimal, even with some pretty hefty prompting from me. I was glad that she seemed to have an inner strength to fall back on, while he spent much of his time alone in their bedroom, reading books. Grief is a strange thing and takes people in different ways but I did think he could have stepped up to his supporting role more effectively.

The night before the funeral there was a knock on the door of my room. We'd all turned in early in preparation for the difficult day ahead but I didn't imagine any of us would be getting much sleep.

'Come in.'

I'd anticipated Kenny, perhaps brandishing a bottle of whisky. What I didn't expect was Sophie Church tentatively poking her head round the door. Her long hair hung around her neck and shoulders and I realised I'd only ever seen it pinned up before.

I swung my legs off the bed and stood up, not knowing the correct etiquette for a late-night visit from an attractive woman whose husband was in the next room.

'How are you coping?'

She shrugged. 'I'm not looking forward to tomorrow.'

'Don't feel bad about it: I don't think anyone is.'

She sat on the edge of the bed and her head dropped. I pulled over a chair from the desk that stood near the window and sat opposite her. Ignoring the protocol, I reached across and gathered her clasped hands in mine. When she looked up, her eyes were moist.

'I don't understand what's going on, Bill.'

'What do you mean?'

She paused before speaking again. 'Why is Dolly dead?'

I sighed. In the days since the tragedy, none of us had openly broached the possibility of a link between Dolly's death and the two threatening messages but it had hung in the house like an unspoken confession. Even now I couldn't bring myself to air it.

'Come on, Sophie, we've been over this. Hit-and-run drivers may be the scum of the earth but you can find them all over the world. Dolly was just unlucky.'

Sophie gave a slight shake of her head. 'I don't think so.'

I let go of her hands and leaned back in my chair. I studied her face, trying to decide whether this line of discussion would be helpful or not, while she stared back at me with a curious look – was it defiance?

'What are you thinking, Sophie?'

Her words were steady and calm but there was an under-lying steeliness to her voice. 'I think that accident was meant for me.'

She stopped as if to let the implications of that sank in. If she was right – and she was merely verbalising the thought that had been troubling me for the past week – then the 'accident' had been no accident at all. I hadn't seen the impact itself, only heard the sickening thud, so I couldn't pass comment on how it had unfolded but if Sophie believed it had been deliberate I wasn't about to contradict her. I did want to know why she thought that way.

'What makes you say that?'

'Think about it, Bill. There have already been two warning letters from an anonymous source, both threatening consequences if I don't drop the claim on the mine. The first one specifically said I would be made to pay, and Adam's black eye was the result. Then we made a big show of not giving in to the intimidation – we even put a notice in the newspaper announcing it – and the next thing that happens is a hit-and-run right outside Kenny and Dolly's door.'

It was exactly the same thought process I had been through myself. The chain of logic did look a little relentless. But I was too long in the tooth to jump to any conclusions just yet.

'Sophie, what do you remember about the accident itself?'

She dropped her head again and the hair fell around her face, obscuring her eyes.

'I'm sorry to make you relive it but this could be really important. Talk me through exactly what happened.'

She seemed to draw on that inner resolve once more and lifted her head to look at me.

'We were going out for a walk and Dolly was on my left

as we stepped out of the drive. We'd checked the street for traffic before we crossed the road and then, out of nowhere, this big black car came bombing down the hill. I've been racking my brains to try and remember if I saw what I think I saw or if I just imagined it.'

'And what do you think you saw?'

She paused. 'I think I saw it swerve into the middle of the street, directly at us.'

I couldn't imagine the torture Sophie must have put herself through the last week. If, like me, she had reached the conclusion that Dolly's death was connected to the threatening letters and her claim on the mine then she'd be feeling bloody about the whole business.

'Have you spoken to Adam about this?'

She shook her head. 'I don't think he really knows what to say to me or how to help. Now he's fast asleep but I can't stop going over and over it in my mind and I just had to talk to someone about it before tomorrow.'

I leaned forwards and took hold of her hands again.

Her voice was small. 'It's my fault Dolly's dead, isn't it, Bill?'

'You can't think like that, Sophie. No, it damn well isn't your fault; it's the fault of whoever was driving that car. And if you let them make you think that way then they've won. Let's say you're right and you were the intended victim, then there's only one way to fight back: we have to find the driver of that car. And if it turns out to be the same person who wrote those letters, then the payback for Dolly's death will be a lifetime behind bars.'

I kept an eye on Sophie all through the funeral. I stood beside Kenny, putting an arm round his shoulders as the coffin was carried out of the little crematorium's chapel, but my attention was on her. She was a different person from the night before, when she'd left my room an hour after arriving, her eyes still wet with tears and her spirit all but broken. This morning, in the thin Sydney drizzle, she looked invincible: her hair was piled up at the back of her head, held in place by a stylish black hat with a wide brim, and the sombre suit and coat she wore made her all the more imposing. She cut a figure of determination, strength and potency and I wondered what had happened during the night to make her so. I suspected it wasn't Adam's influence. Beside her, he seemed small and listless, the remnants of the bruising around his eye giving him a curiously livid complexion.

I didn't get a chance to talk to her at the wake; I was too busy shepherding Kenny from guest to guest, accepting condolences and nodding sympathetically. The north shore hotel where it was being held overlooked the Pacific and after a couple of hours of platitudes and shrimp sandwiches I guided him outside. The rain had stopped and the sun was glinting in the puddles that had gathered on the terrace.

'You've done enough, Kenny,' I said, sitting down beside him on a patio settee sheltered from the elements by a large parasol. 'Dolly would have been proud.'

He made a dismissive sound and stared out at the ocean. 'If Dolly had been here she'd have had something to say about the catering.'

In spite of the occasion I laughed. 'Yes, I imagine she would.'

'But she's not here, is she?' There was bitterness in Kenny's voice. 'And the police are no nearer to finding the bastard who was driving that car. So I haven't really done her proud, have I, Bill? I haven't brought her killer to justice or made anyone pay for her death. No one's been punished except for me and that poor girl in there.'

He waved a hand in the general direction of the hotel. 'Sophie?'

'Yeah, Sophie. I wish I'd never got involved in any of

this. George Deakins was a long time in the past and I should have just left him there.'

'You're too good a lawyer for that,' I said. 'George needed a kind of justice, too, making sure his estate stayed in the family, and you were the man he chose to deliver it. I don't think you're about to give up on that now.'

Kenny gazed unblinkingly out to sea. 'You're right,' he said eventually. 'But it's going to be the last job I do. I've decided I'm shutting up shop.'

'What will you do?'

He shrugged. 'Haven't thought. There'll be a payout on the life insurance – I've already been in touch with them about that – so I won't have any money worries. I might just chuck it all in and come to England. How do you fancy a house guest of your own?'

'You know you're welcome any time, Kenny. It's not a huge cottage and the views aren't quite as expansive as this but I think we'd rub along pretty well. All you have to do is say the word.'

'Let me get Sophie's case out of the way and I may well take you up on that. What about you? What are your plans?'

It was my turn to shrug. 'You don't need me kicking around any more so I'll probably get on a plane one of these days.'

'What about Sophie?'

'What about her?' I hadn't had a chance to tell Kenny about my conversation with Sophie and the theory behind the hit-and-run. It seemed cruel to mention it now, even though there was a strong argument for going back to the police and seeing if they could establish a link with the mystery motorcyclist and his anonymous threats. There was something highly disturbing about the sequence of events which I couldn't shake off.

'The two of you seem to have formed quite an attachment. Is there anything you want to tell me?'

I laughed again. 'Don't be ridiculous. I'm old enough to be her . . .' – I stopped, unwilling to complete the sentence – '. . . big brother. And besides, she's got a husband to look after her. She doesn't need me any more than you do.'

'I wasn't talking about what she needs.'

The sly old bastard. I knew better than to let this conversation run on any further so I stood up. 'I'm getting a drink. Do you want one?'

Whatever plans I might have made for a return to England, Sophie blew them apart the next morning. The four of us – Kenny, Sophie, Adam and I – were deliberately taking things slow, recovering from the emotion of the funeral and taking the day to contemplate life after Dolly. That was going to be harder for some than others, of course.

We were sitting on the balcony with a pot of coffee, watching the sun arc across the city, when Sophie made her announcement.

'I know what you said about the pointlessness of visiting the mine but I've decided I want to go.'

I felt a lurching in the pit of my belly. I'd been expecting something like this since the newly resolute Sophie had appeared at the funeral so it hardly came as a surprise. Having made the connection with the warning notes, she was clearly looking at it with a new perspective.

Kenny tried to object. 'Now listen, Sophie, it's just not safe—'

I interrupted him. 'Kenny, I think Sophie might have a point. You've been very clear about Oodnadatta – the Wild West, I think you called it – but the fact of the matter is that Uncle George's mine is now Sophie's to do with as she pleases. If I were in her shoes, I'd want to take a look at what I'd inherited.'

Sophie threw me a grateful smile. 'Thanks, Bill.'

'Besides,' I went on. 'There's something else.'

All eyes turned to me so I launched into the speech I'd been mentally rehearsing for this precise eventuality. I'd only needed Sophie's decision to allow me to deliver it.

'What happened to Dolly was unforgivable. Sophie is of the view – and I must say I'm inclined to agree with her – that it was no accident.'

The two men in my audience both began to speak at once. I waved them down and ploughed on.

'Someone has been trying to get Sophie to abandon her claim to the mine. That much we know to be true. Whoever it is has also made it clear that they would go to some lengths to make that happen. *She'll be made to pay*, they said. Now we don't know if that was an idle threat but subsequent events would suggest otherwise.' I nodded towards Adam, whose black eye had faded to a grey shadow. 'It could be that Dolly died in a cowardly hit-and-run accident but for my money the timing is too coincidental and there's a suggestion that the car swerved deliberately in order to make impact.'

Again Kenny tried to intervene at this news but I overruled him.

'The fact that Sophie managed to escape injury was, I believe, a matter of pure luck – appalling luck for Dolly. And if that's right, then it means the potential threat hasn't gone away. In fact, our little notice in the *Morning Herald* may have provoked rather than pacified our mysterious bully. I'm not saying it was the wrong thing to do, or that anyone is to blame for what happened next, but I'm increasingly convinced that Sophie is in real danger.'

Kenny finally managed to get a word in. 'Even if what you're telling us is true, how does it help Sophie to go trekking around in the outback?'

I looked directly at Sophie as I spoke. 'I don't know about anyone else but I want to see justice done for Dolly. If we can't do that here in Sydney, and the police don't seem to be getting anywhere with that, then I'd like to try flushing out our opponent on neutral territory – and by neutral, obviously I mean potentially lethal. I think there may be two birds to be had with our one stone. Not only can we get Sophie her mine but we might also put the finger on Adam's attackers and Dolly's killer. And a visit to Uncle George's farmstead is just the trap we need. Which leaves only one question: Sophie, how do you fancy being the bait?'

The longer we stuck around in Sydney, the more chance there was that our unseen foe might try to strike again. Without some kind of public announcement to the effect that Sophie had dropped her claim, they would naturally assume she was choosing to ignore their warnings – which increased the risk to her with every passing day. I reasoned that they might hold off for a few days at least, given the attention being afforded to Dolly's death by the boys and girls in blue, but we wouldn't be able to protect Sophie indefinitely. As it was, Kenny kept her pretty much under house arrest, sending out me – or, more usually, Adam – for supplies. Sophie complained about the assiduousness of his care but when I reminded her that he was probably overcompensating for not being there for Dolly, she relented and allowed him to swaddle her both metaphorically and literally, with a blanket or shawl when the temperature dropped in the evenings.

I made myself busy with arrangements for our impending journey. My first idea had been to fly to Adelaide then take the Ghan train direct to Oodnadatta before hiring an off-road vehicle to head out to the Deakins place. It didn't take much thought to rule that one out: if there was someone on Sophie's heels, we'd have been sitting ducks in an overnight train carriage. The alternative of an overland drive from Sydney was a far less attractive proposition but did

at least have the advantage of being unexpected and flex-
ible – providing we managed to avoid a tail from the start.

What would happen when we got to Oodnadatta was
another matter entirely. Kenny was still of the opinion that
it was somebody local to the site who was trying to get
their hands on the Deakins property. I was less convinced,
figuring that executing the kind of deadly stunt they'd
pulled outside Kenny's house needed more coordination
than could be achieved from some remote corner of the
outback. Either way, we were walking into a minefield.
There was no doubt in my mind that there would be
someone hostile at the other end of our trek. I wanted to
be ready.

Besides the practical preparations – hiring a Land Rover,
kitting it out with several weeks' worth of equipment,
packing all the necessary fuel, water, supplies and radio
gear – I had to undertake a crash course in outback survival.
Kenny introduced me to an aboriginal friend of his and
Dolly's, Ruby McKenzie, who gave me the lowdown on
what to expect and how to deal with it. Ruby was a white-
haired, wrinkle-faced septuagenarian who had known
Kenny since his childhood in Oodnadatta and had followed
him out of the red interior a few years after he left. She
brought with her an encyclopaedic knowledge of the bush,
gleaned from untold generations of ancestors who had lived
in harmony with the land, working with it and alongside
it to craft an existence of resilience and fortitude. In those
few educational hours with her, I had my eyes opened to
a seam of practical and ancient wisdom that would have
taken a lifetime to understand fully. I had one afternoon.
I learned fast about which critters can kill you – basically,
all of them – and avoiding a slow, painful death in extreme
temperatures. And the temperatures were going to be
extreme: Oodnadatta, I learned, held the record for the
highest ever documented in Australia and proudly boasted

it was the driest town in the driest state on the driest continent. More than once during my whistlestop education I seriously considered dropping the whole idea but recalling Dolly's contorted body on the street outside the house was enough to refocus my mind.

We were less ready than I'd have liked, given the multitude of eventualities we might face, but I couldn't risk waiting any longer. Kenny made a half-hearted attempt at offering to come with us but I soon quashed that one: we needed him to coordinate operations in Sydney, where he could keep one eye on the police investigation and another on our progress, advising and encouraging from afar. Besides, it was barely a fortnight since Dolly's death and he was in no fit state to go crashing around the outback.

It was a stunning early morning under a brilliant blue sky when Sophie, Adam and I wedged our rucksacks into the last available space in the Land Rover and hit the road.

PART TWO: GOLD

PART TWO: GUIDE

I

I'd planned three full days of driving to get from Sydney
to Coober Pedy. In the event, we did it in two. There was
something unsettling about the prospect, however remote,
of being followed and the sooner we got to George's place,
the quicker we could start getting to the bottom of this
damned murky affair.

A flight and train journey would have been considerably
more agreeable. Land Rovers are built for neither speed nor
comfort and the three of us were squashed into the rickety
interior, hemmed in by survival gear of every kind from
knives and compasses to jerry cans and tarpaulins. Sophie
and Adam had joined me for the last hour or two of Ruby
McKenzie's training session and she'd drummed into us
that our lives could very easily depend on how prepared
we were to face whatever the bush might throw at us. And
that was without taking into consideration an unknown
enemy with their sights on the Deakins mine.

The first thousand miles were the easiest, and the fastest.
We made it to South Australia in thirteen flat-out hours,
taking the new Barrier Highway east and crossing the state
border just past Broken Hill late on the first evening. We
took the driving in shifts, a couple of hours at a time, and

found we made better progress than I'd expected. I didn't want to risk stopping near the road overnight so I pulled off after a few miles of utterly featureless landscape, up a track that seemed to lead nowhere, and drove for another twenty minutes before pitching camp. We emptied the Land Rover and I let Sophie and Adam make a nest in the back while I laid out a tarp in the lee of the car's western flank to protect myself from the morning sun. We threw together a modest supper, which we ate staring up at the Milky Way, and gratefully succumbed to sleep.

Barely seven hours later we were on the road again. None of us had slept particularly soundly and we were all keen to keep moving, a sense of foreboding gnawing at our heels. At Port Augusta we picked up the Stuart Highway, the great north-south continental artery that followed the original route – and took the name – of the Scottish explorer whose early expeditions in the middle years of the nineteenth century uncovered much of the country to European colonisers. I surmised that the metalled road we were now following offered a much quicker traversing of the terrain than Stuart's horses had managed.

It might have been the main road linking the Timor Sea off Darwin to the Great Australian Bight but the route was as desolate as any I'd driven – and that included the enormous prairie highways across Midwestern America. Populated areas had fallen away soon after we left Port Augusta and for mile after mile we ploughed through utterly featureless swathes of red sand adorned with scrubby green plants and bushes. Nothing seemed to stand taller than a few feet while the vast canopy above us acted like a giant incubator, slow-baking us as we crawled, ant-like, across the map.

With precious little to break the tedium, I looked out for anything that would pique my interest. I knew kangaroos could be a danger to traffic, and I'd warned Sophie and

Adam to keep a sharp eye out for them when it was their turn behind the wheel, but the lack of any real ground cover meant even this ubiquitous Australian marsupial was nowhere to be seen. We passed the occasional truck heading south but only once did we encounter any other vehicles going north.

We were nearly three hours out of Port Augusta and it unnerved me. Sophie was driving and I had the navigator's spot in the front seat – although there was no navigating required on this barren stretch. I noticed the black Range Rover first as a tiny speck in the left-hand wing mirror as we eased round a bend in the road. It was probably a mile behind us but within seconds I could see it was gaining fast.

Sophie saw it too and I sensed her unease as she stole quick glances at the rear-view mirror.

'Adam, take a look at that car coming up behind us and tell me what you can see,' I ordered.

'What car?' he said, shifting round as far as he could among the crates and equipment. 'Oh, right. That car.'

'That car.'

'It's moving pretty quick. I can see at least one passenger besides the driver but there could be more – it's hard to tell.'

I turned my attention to the road ahead of us, hoping to see a track where we could pull off. If they were following us we'd have no chance of outrunning them so our best bet would be to stop and take up some kind of defensive position. If it was just another innocent road-user, then pulling over to let them pass would simply be the polite thing to do.

Less than two hundred yards away the road opened out into a makeshift junction as a turning struck off to the right. A green road sign revealed that the township of Woomera lay in that direction. I signalled to Sophie to pull over in the dirt beside the junction as I searched my memory for the name, which was ringing bells. After a moment it came to me: Woomera was the semi-secret home of the Anglo-Australian Joint Project, a Cold War defence system that tested long-range weapons out here in the desert.

As we slowed to a stop, I heaved myself round in my seat to get a better look at the car. The glaring sunlight reflected off its windscreen and I couldn't make out the interior at all but it was showing no sign of letting up speed. If it was pursuing us, then the driver seemed intent on ploughing straight into us; I knew with a sick feeling in my stomach which vehicle would come off worse.

Then, as it bore down with unrelenting menace, the Range Rover suddenly swung to the right, across the junction, and raced off into the distance leaving a trail of dust.

I breathed out heavily. 'Just some Aussie jockeys heading for the rocket range.'

'Translation please,' said Sophie.

I laughed. 'There's an air base a few miles up that road where they test intercontinental missiles. My guess is that the occupants of that car were personnel from the Australian Air Force – jockeys, we used to call them in the Army.'

'I see. Nothing for us to worry about, then?'

'Nothing for us to worry about.'

Five hours later we made it to Coober Pedy. It helped that there were no speed restrictions on this stretch, although the quality of the road surface away from the few sparse settlements dropped dramatically. Even with a foot to the floor and the gearbox hammered to its limits we averaged a meagre fifty miles per hour and I watched the fuel gauge tumble seemingly by the minute. What also appeared to be shifting markedly was the temperature, and I got Adam to cut his speed in the last shift before the town, hoping to give the engine something of a break in the searing heat.

As we neared Coober Pedy occasional signs warned of

the dangers of concealed mineshafts dotting the landscape. I wondered what kind of madness would induce anyone to leave the safety of the road and head out into the sand in such a barren place, especially at this time of year. The extreme conditions would spell almost certain death for anyone but the most experienced local.

Occasional snippets of conversation about the brightness of the sun or the warmth of the wind blowing in from the Landy's open windows were about all we could muster above the relentless noise. I don't know what Sophie and Adam were thinking about but I found it hard to focus on anything but the gruelling miles still ahead of us. We'd decided to approach Oodnadatta from the south-west, partly because the track would be marginally better than the alternative across the vast salt flats of Lake Eyre but also because I still had a lingering fear that there might be someone on our tail and the detour offered the possibility of confusion – albeit a slim one.

Sophie broke what had deepened into a half-hour's silence as we neared the first building on the outskirts of Coober Pedy.

'Can we stay somewhere with a roof tonight, Bill?'

I shared her hankering for anything approaching home comforts but I remained nervous. 'I don't know, Sophie. It doesn't feel particularly safe, even out here. In fact, especially out here.'

'I know you're right but I can't face another night like last night. And I know it's not your fault but you and Adam stink, quite frankly.'

She might have put it more diplomatically but Sophie was right. We all desperately needed a wash.

Having made such good time, I was beginning to consider the possibility of bypassing Coober Pedy altogether and making straight for Oodnadatta that evening. Sophie's plea put paid to that, although I also had doubts about the prospect of a comfortable bed the further we travelled into the wilderness.

I pointed out a motel sign and Adam rolled the Land Rover up to its front door. As we came to a stop, I realised that the entrance was carved into an escarpment of rock – one of the traditional dugout caves that provided accommodation for many of the town's residents. Ruby McKenzie had told us about them back in Sydney: they kept a constant temperature in a way that air conditioning simply couldn't match and they'd been a feature in the vicinity since before the town itself had been formally incorporated in 1915.

'This'll be a novel experience,' I said as we made our way into the motel.

My room was basic but had a certain authentic charm about it. Hewn from the sandstone and siltstone of the Stuart Ranges, it was half-timbered to waist height and featured a bed with a soft mattress and a sink with running water, which the good burghers of the town had thoughtfully plumbed in from a bore hole sunk into the Great Artesian Basin. Never had cold ablutions felt so utterly blissful and I returned to the motel's dining room an hour later much refreshed and far less offensive to the nose.

'Let's not make it a late one tonight, shall we?' I said to Adam and Sophie, who were already perusing a menu. The temptation for copious quantities of cold beer was enormous but I wanted an early start and a clear head.

We ordered and fell into easy talk about the climate. Put three Brits together anywhere in the world and they'll start a conversation about the weather; we were no different. The weather, on the other hand, was. Against all advice, we'd spent two blistering days on the road through the height of the sun's heat and, although we'd made sure to stay well hydrated, our bodies just weren't acclimatised, even after the weeks in Sydney. I felt hollowed out and the young couple in front of me looked as if they'd aged ten years in the past 36 hours.

I changed the subject. 'Right – plans for tomorrow. I'd like to be on the road before seven. That way we can reach Oodnadatta before the heat gets too ridiculous.'

I had no real idea of what to expect in Oodnadatta – still less in the desert beyond – but I was hoping Kenny's old pal Smith Penney might offer some clues. Kenny had given me no address or way of contacting him but, with a population of just a few hundred, the town could not hide him for long. Our first port of call would be the pub.

'I'm guessing we're in for quite a rough ride in the morning. There'll be no such luxuries as a metalled road so we're going to have to make some adjustments.'

Adam looked up from his mutton stew. 'What kind of adjustments?'

'Tyre pressures, for one thing. We'll need to let some air out before we set off. The last thing we need is to hit a rock with an inflated tyre. It's all very well carrying a spare but if we lose one it'll be all over – we'd have to come back to Coober Pedy at least, and possibly even go back to Adelaide. You just can't risk wandering about out here without a spare for any longer than absolutely necessary.'

'Anything else?'

'Speed. We've done well so far but there's no way we can keep up the same kind of average on a dirt track. I reckon we'll be lucky to make forty miles an hour, and quite possibly much less. It's only a hundred and twenty from here to Oodnadatta but that'll still make it an arduous morning. And that's before we even think of going on to Uncle George's place.'

Sophie interrupted. 'Are you planning on doing that tomorrow?'

'I don't know yet. Let's see how the day works out. If there's somewhere reasonable to stay in Oodnadatta then it might be worth sticking around tomorrow night – maybe chat up some locals for background information – and go on the day after. I'm still worried about being followed, though, so it might be best to keep on moving. I'll make that decision tomorrow.'

Adam's voice took on a sullen tone. 'I thought we were all on this expedition together.'

'We are, but don't start playing silly buggers with me. There's got to be one of us who takes the lead and I'm assuming that role as of now, in case you hadn't registered it before. As Kenny's clients, you're my responsibility and you'll damn well do what I tell you or else we might all die out there. Got it?'

As I lay in bed that night, rolling around to find a comfortable position in which to sleep, I wondered if I'd come down a bit hard on the boy. But what I'd told him was true: our lives could depend on what happened over the next few days. And I wasn't about to put mine in the hands of an accountant from Surrey, no matter how sullen he became.

The track was even tougher than I'd feared and it took us the best part of four hours to reach Oodnadatta the next morning. Dropping the pressure in the tyres might have helped avoid any bursts but it made for some brutal handling and we scraped little over thirty miles an hour as I dodged the bigger rocks and hauled the steering wheel back into line with monotonous regularity. I made the decision early to take on this leg entirely myself: I didn't want to put the others in the position of jeopardising the trip by misjudging a pothole or clobbering a kangaroo. As we left the motel, the bronzed Australian boy on reception broke the surprising news that the route to Oodnadatta was called the Kempe Road and – ironic or not – I took it as a sign that my decision to helm this stretch was the right one.

Two hours in, I was not so sure.

'Are you sure you don't want one of us to take over?' asked Adam as I swerved to evade yet another dangerously large boulder in our path. I couldn't tell if there was a hint of sarcasm in his voice.

'You just concentrate on the map-reading,' I said, and Sophie laughed. The road lay dead straight for miles in front of us, with scrubland stretching out on either side to the far horizon and not even the suggestion of a branch track.

'Can you imagine living out here?' she said.

'No – and neither can anyone else from the look of it. Even the early prospectors tended to gather around watering holes so I don't think you'll see much in the way of a remote farmhouse like you might back home.'

'What about the cattle stations?'

'That's about as close as you'll get,' I agreed. 'But even they are their own little communities, apparently. Kenny told me that Uncle George's farmstead was something of an anomaly round these parts. He was a real loner and only travelled as far as Oodnadatta when he had no choice. Macumba Station was about the limit of his sociability.'

'Sounds like a pretty dangerous way of life,' said Adam.

I grunted. 'As George found to his cost. It took them weeks even to find out he'd died.'

Sophie turned her head away and stared out at the wilderness. I suspected I might have overstepped the mark.

'Sorry, Sophie. I didn't mean to—'

She looked back quickly and I could see I hadn't upset her.

'No, it's fine, Bill. I can hardly grieve for someone I never knew, can I? I was just thinking of my mother. She must have known this road, these people, this landscape. I'm wondering how much it shaped her character.'

'One of life's great unanswerables. It's an impossible

question, like whether Beethoven would have written better music if he'd been able to hear. But if you ask me, being brought up somewhere like this would have to have some kind of impact on a person. You could hardly grow up here without being affected by the scale of it, the remoteness, the challenge . . .'

'The weather?' offered Adam, and we all laughed.

As Kenny had warned us, Oodnadatta was something of a one-horse town – except the one horse had evidently died decades ago, leaving the locals with not much to entertain them but the weekly mail run from Coober Pedy and the occasional train passing through. A battered old tin sign hung loose from a pole jammed into the ground declaring that this was the hottest and driest town in the country and we were welcome to it.

The Kempe Road approached from the south-west and I could see the rail line swinging in to meet us from the south. For the last mile or so the track ran parallel to it and, across to our left, a makeshift runway allowed supplies to be flown in as required. That was about as urban as it got. 'Town' was putting it rather generously. Oodnadatta amounted to little more than a ramshackle collection of huts strung out haphazardly along a central road, with a handful of dirt tracks leading off for no more than a hundred yards in any direction. I estimated it would take less than ten minutes to walk from one end of town to the other. The resident population I knew to be no more than two hundred – although Ruby McKenzie had told me that number could swell by half as much again in the laughably-named tourist season, when hardy backpackers and adventurers in search of a dinner-table anecdote would hack out here in the footsteps of John McDouall Stuart to goggle at the locals and snap their souvenir photographs. I'd also learned that at least half the population was aboriginal, made up of Arabana tribespeople for whom Oodnadatta was a stopping point on trade routes that dated back tens of thousands of years. Its name meant 'mulga blossom', after the dominant shrub across much of the Australian interior, although the town wasn't actually settled until the railway came in 1890. It was railway workers who made up most of the rest of the population. I'd expressed surprise that the Ghan hadn't turned it into a bigger centre but discovered that the train passenger who stopped and dismounted in this remote spot was rare to the point of nonexistence. With the recent announcement of plans to move the line further west, the long-term future of Oodnadatta looked decidedly doubtful.

Without any real alternative, we pitched up outside the only available lodgings, a beaten-up, single-storey corrugated shack backing onto the railway which grandly announced itself as the Transcontinental Hotel. I was in dire need of a cold beer and I just hoped the hotel bar would be able to oblige.

The dark interior took some adjustment from the blinding light outside but the noise was the biggest shock. It seemed like the entire town had decided to take its lunch break at the Transcontinental Hotel. The place was packed with people and the chatter resounded off the tin walls with an effect not unlike a swimming pool.

I edged my way through the throng, leaving Sophie and Adam near the door, and tried to catch the attention of the stocky man behind the bar. He seemed reluctant to break off from the jokey conversation he was having at the other end of the counter so I raised my voice above the crowd and shouted.

'Can I get a beer here?'

The impact was startling. In less than half a second, the tumult subsided and the room fell silent. I felt a hundred eyes boring into me as I feebly waved a dollar bill in the direction of the barman.

'I'm just after a drink,' I said plaintively.

The barman strolled to my end of the counter, fixing me with a look I could only interpret as hostile.

'Yeah, mate – you and all these other blokes.' He waved a hand around the room. Despite the heat, I felt a chill in the air.

Then his face cracked into a huge smile.

'No worries, mate. We're only messing with you.' He reached for a glass and a can, which he put on the bar in front of me.

Instantly the hubbub returned, accompanied by some good-natured laughter at my expense. I let out a breath of relief and slapped my money on the counter.

'I'll admit you had me there. I thought you locals might not be too receptive to a bunch of outsiders crashing your pub.'

'Nah, mate,' he said. 'All welcome here – didn't you see the sign?' He stretched out a hand, which I took gratefully. 'The name's Jack. Jack Cadison.'

I introduced myself and waved Sophie and Adam over from the door.

'Two more beers?' asked Jack, and served them up without waiting for an answer.

We sank our first round in record time and ordered more. I didn't need the hydration – water was a much safer bet for that – but the sharpness of the hops at the back of my throat and the cool tingling on my tongue were things that good old dihydrogen monoxide couldn't supply.

'So what brings you out here?' Jack asked halfway through the second beer. 'It's not exactly the season for sightseeing.'

'Personal stuff,' I said. 'A relative of Sophie's used to live around here.'

'Is that right? And who might that have been? Everybody

knows everybody in these parts so we're sure to have known them.'

'George Deakins,' Sophie said.

Jack looked surprised. 'No way! I didn't know George had any relatives. What was he to you?'

'My uncle.'

'Well, bugger me. I thought he was the end of the Deakins line. In fact, I think most people round here did. I'm not sure anyone's even been out to his farm since he was brought in: I don't think anyone expected some kind of heir turning up to claim the old place. Not that there's much to claim, mind you.'

Out of the corner of my eye I noticed Sophie shoot me a look of mild alarm.

'What do you mean?' I asked innocently. If George had been living as a hermit out on the farmstead for the last few years of his life, I guessed he probably hadn't been flush with the earnings from his opal mine.

'Place is a wreck,' said Jack, then caught himself and looked up at Sophie. 'Sorry, mate. I forgot he was your uncle.'

I stepped in to divert any awkwardness. 'How do you know the place is a wreck if no one's been out there for weeks?'

'Oh, it's been like that for years, not weeks. I don't like to speak ill of the dead, and begging his family's pardon and all that, but George Deakins was not a houseproud man. I only went out there a couple of times in all the years I've been here but on both occasions it was little more than a tumbledown shed. He wasn't a big one for furniture, your uncle, and I'm not sure he even owned a broom. Mind you, the way the sand blows in from the Simpson, there's not much point trying to keep on top of it anyway.'

The news was not good, although I don't think Sophie

had ever imagined she'd be the new owner of a sparkling palatial residence with glorious views over South Australia. But there was worse to come.

'Look, I'm sorry, Sophie: I don't know what you were expecting when you decided to hike all the way out here but if you're hoping Uncle George has left you a tidy little opal mine, I'm afraid you're going to have to think again. The house is a wreck and the mine was abandoned years ago. I'm not sure if the family ever got anything meaningful out of it but if they did it must have been decades ago. You're not going to thank George for leaving everything to you.'

We sank two more beers as we mulled over what Jack Cadison had told us. Sophie seemed disappointed that we'd wasted so much time and effort on a dead duck but Adam was surprisingly philosophical about it all.

'It's not the end of the world, is it, Soph? I mean, it's only been a few weeks since you didn't even know you had an Uncle George so you're no worse off than you were then, are you?'

'I suppose you're right,' she said. 'It doesn't change what happened to Dolly, though. There's still a big fat question mark over that. I can't help but believe that the hit-and-run was related to George's mine in some way and I feel a huge weight of responsibility for it.'

I leaned over and put a soothing hand on her knee. 'I've told you before: none of that is your fault. Even if the accident was somehow connected, you didn't ask anybody to run her over. That's entirely down to the driver of the car, whoever they were.'

'I'm entitled to know the truth about what happened, aren't I?'

'Of course you are,' I said. 'If nothing else, maybe that's something we can lay to rest on this trip.'

'And if what that barman says is true, about the mine

being worthless, then why has someone gone to all the trouble of warning us off so dramatically?'

That had been bothering me too. 'I don't know, but it looks to me as if Uncle George's mine might be worth something to somebody. All we have to do is find out who, and how much.'

Sophie looked thoughtful. 'So how do we go about doing that?'

'We find the only person we know in Oodnadatta and start asking questions.'

Adam was confused. 'But we don't know anyone in Oodnadatta.'

'Oh yes, we do. Or, at least, Kenny does. We're going to pay a visit to Smith Penney.'

In a small town like this, word gets round fast when strangers arrive with an interesting backstory and we were still drinking beer when a giant of a man with a shock of blond hair strode into the hotel bar, surveyed the place briefly and singled us out. He was beside our table in three huge paces and spoke directly at me.

'I hear you're sticking your nose into business that isn't yours,' he announced without preamble.

I stood up, hoping to level the playing field, but he had a good four inches on me. I tried putting a decisive note into my voice as an alternative but there was no denying who the alpha male was in this conversation.

'It's not my business and it never really has been. This is Sophie Church – she's employing me to do some research for her.'

The man glanced down at Sophie, who had sat up and was bristling at this gruff intruder. He looked back at me.

'You lot think you can come over here, trample all over the place digging up ancient history – well, I'm here to tell you that you can't. I'll say the same thing I said to the other blokes: clear off out of our town. We don't want you, we don't need you and you're nothing but trouble. Get the message? If you're still here after sundown, I'll be back to make sure you leave. Now get out and go back to where you came from.'

'I don't know who you think we are—' I began. But the giant had already left.

Jack Cadison had seen the whole thing and came over from behind the bar. 'Don't worry about him – that's our local larrikin, Smith Penney.'

Penney had found us first.

'He's a bit of a charmer, isn't he?' I said, sitting down again. 'What did he mean when he said he'd be back to make sure we left?'

Jack shook his head. 'Don't pay any attention. He's all mouth and no trousers. He's a good guy to have around in a ruck but he'd start a fight with his own reflection if there wasn't someone in the bar for him to have a pop at.'

Sophie shifted uneasily in her chair. 'I don't want to cause trouble for anyone.'

'There won't be any trouble,' said Jack. 'I'll see to that. And you don't need to worry about Smith. He had a run-in with some blokes a few days ago and they outnumbered him so he came off worse. His pride was dented so now he's throwing his weight about, trying to prove he's still top dog around here. But he's harmless enough.'

I wasn't so sure: Penney had seemed pretty rough around the edges to me and, back in Sydney, Kenny had described him as the bad boy of the bunch when they were youngsters together. I suspected Smith Penney might be able to cause us quite a bit of harm if he set his mind to it but I let it drop with Jack.

'Is it safe to stay here tonight?' I asked.

'At the hotel? Yeah, sure, mate.' Jack sized up our little group. 'How many rooms do you want?'

'Two,' I said. 'One for me and one for these lovebirds.'

Jack broke into a grin. 'You're in luck. The honeymoon suite is available.'

I didn't sleep well again that night, turning questions over in my mind. Smith Penney was our only connection to the Deakins mine and, for whatever reason, he'd nailed his colours very clearly to the mast. With his blunt message in the hotel bar, he had left us in no doubt that he wanted us out and I wasn't convinced he could be persuaded otherwise, even with the dropping of Kenny's name. There had obviously been a misunderstanding of some sort but I was damned if I knew what it was and I was far from certain that I could straighten it out in a plain-speaking conversation with the man. I feared he might have a go at me on sight, without giving me the opportunity to explain who we were and what we were doing here. He seemed exactly the type to throw a punch and ask questions later – or maybe not ask questions at all. I'd seen plenty like him and learned the hard way that often the best method of defusing a volatile situation is to walk away from it completely.

Kenny and I had been speaking to each other at the same time every evening to check in on our respective progress. Shortwave radio is a fine tool for this kind of long-range communication and we had agreed back in Sydney that regular contact would enable us to follow up on any leads Kenny might dig up – and allow him to chase up anything that we uncovered in the outback. When I spoke to him after my encounter with Smith Penney I had questions. But Kenny got his news in first.

'The office has been burgled.'

'What?' I was aghast. Two threatening letters, the attack on Adam, a fatal hit-and-run and now this: somebody was really keen to put us off this job one way or another.

'There's no chance it was a coincidence, is there, Kenny?'

'Not a ghost of a chance, mate. Eight years I've been in this office and I've never had a problem. We lawyers are under strict obligations to make sure everything's kept under lock and key. You'd be hard-pushed to find a bank with stronger security. I didn't take you to the top floor but I've got a strongroom that's like Fort Knox up there, what with the safes and alarms and whatnot. But as soon as we start digging about in the George Deakins business, suddenly everything goes to hell. No, this wasn't a coincidence. Any run-of-the-mill burglar would at least have stolen something when they ransacked the place. This lot turned it all upside down – but took nothing.'

'Have you reported it to the police?'

'Of course, but what are they going to do? These were professionals so there aren't going to be any fingerprints.'

I was stumped. I warned Kenny to take particular care of himself in the light of this latest development and we said goodnight. It was only after I ended the call that I real-ised I hadn't asked him about Smith Penney. Other concerns – such as Kenny's welfare – had rather taken priority.

There was nothing I could do about that from this distance so instead I thought more about Penney. I tried to figure out if we even needed him. His local knowledge would be invaluable, that was for sure, but he couldn't be the only person in Oodnadatta who could fill us in on Uncle George and his eccentric lifestyle. On the other hand, Kenny had known Penney growing up and had enlisted his help sending over the crate of documents from the farmstead: if a Sydney lawyer was inclined to rely on him, that suggested a level of trustworthiness.

Half an hour later, thanks to one of those middle-of-the-night lurches that the brain is much too willing to indulge in, I was back on the other track. Penney was transparently a wrong 'un, we'd be insane to trust him with anything more serious than a beer, and our best bet was to steer as clear as possible. Nagged by seething doubts, I managed to convince myself that he'd probably undertaken a thorough search of Uncle George's property, farm and mine, and anything of any value was now securely in Penney's possession. It was totally apparent to me that he had robbed Sophie of any meaningful legacy and the lawlessness of this godforsaken wilderness meant she would never come close to claiming her inheritance.

As the hours passed, I was able to drag rational thought back to the surface of my consciousness. I decided to wire a message back to Kenny, asking him to approach Smith Penney from his angle and let Penney know that we were not the enemy. With a bit of luck, Kenny could sort out whatever the misunderstanding was and we could all go back to square one.

Finally, I slept.

The respite was temporary. I was up early to make preparations for the next leg of our journey – we would reach the Deakins property by lunchtime, I hoped – and I went out to start loading the Land Rover. I opened the rear door and hoisted a couple of heavy trunks into the vehicle, then began my usual inspection of the bodywork and wheels for signs of wear or damage from the rugged terrain.

When I reached the bonnet, the spare tyre stared accusingly at me. No attempt had been made to hide the gash that was ripped into its tread.

'What the hell is that?' asked Adam when I showed it to him and Sophie thirty minutes later.

'That, my friend, is Smith Penney being as good as his word. He really doesn't want us around here.'

'You think that was him?'

'I'm damned sure it was. That tyre has been slashed by something much bigger than a Swiss Army knife, I can tell you. It would take a large blade or machete with considerable weight behind it to punch that kind of hole into a tyre that thick. Somebody big and heavy is very keen for us to head back to Sydney and there's only one person we know who fits that bill in these parts.'

Sophie's voice was shaking with fury. 'I think we should tell the police.'

I broke it to her gently that I had already tried that route. As soon as I found the vandalised tyre, I headed across the main street to the office of the solitary law enforcer in Oodnadatta, intending to register a formal complaint. If nothing else, it would lay down a strong signal to Smith Penney that I wasn't about to be pushed around by a casual bully. The door was locked but through the glass panel I could see a uniformed man moving around inside so I hammered on the wooden frame and gestured forcefully to be let in. I should have been alerted by the laid-back stroll with which the officer approached the door.

'What is it, mate?'

'My Land Rover has been attacked by someone with a knife.'

'Is that right?'

'Can you let me in so that I can make a statement?'

'Mate, we don't open for another hour.'

'But I know who it was.'

'Is that right?'

'Yes, that's right. Now do you want my statement or not?'

There was a pause.

'Mate, we don't open for another hour.'

Sophie was almost as outraged as I was but there was nothing to be done. Smith Penney had got the upper hand. I'd already established that there were no spare Land Rover tyres to be had on demand in Oodnadatta, and Penney would likely have known that too. He was condemning us to a slow, careful journey back to Coober Pedy.

It was Adam who stepped up. 'We could just go on anyway.'

Sophie and I stared at each other.

'Look, Smith Penney wants us to go back. Regardless of who he thinks we are, there's obviously something he doesn't want us to know about at George's place and he's willing to indulge in a spot of petty vandalism to achieve it. And don't forget there are people back in Sydney who don't want us to pursue Sophie's claim to the mine.'

I grunted. 'All of those sound like pretty good reasons to head back if you ask me.'

'Or bloody good reasons to carry on,' said Sophie.

I looked hard at her. She had a fieriness within her that belied her years and I sensed Adam's words had stirred something up – maybe the same Deakins family trait that had kept George plugging away at the opal mine in the face of insurmountable odds. I knew the decision ultimately had to be Sophie's.

'What do you want to do?'

She glanced at Adam, who raised an enquiring eyebrow. Then she appeared to make a decision.

'Spare or no spare, I'm not going to be stopped by the likes of Smith Penney. I say we go on.'

II

There was another possibility that had been haunting me. Despite sounding so certain with Adam and Sophie that the damage to the tyre had been carried out by Oodnadatta's resident hooligan, I did have a doubt: it was just possible that the thugs responsible for Dolly's death had somehow managed to track us down.

I tried to put the thought to the back of my mind. After all, if they had located us, there was little to stop them doing the same to us as they had to Dolly. The outback gendarmerie's performance so far hadn't instilled a huge amount of confidence in me and I suspected it would be all too easy literally to get away with murder in this remote place. And yet here we were, all packed up and ready to hit the road again, our only setback a slashed spare tyre. It could have been a lot worse – fatal, in fact – so I was definitely leaning more to the Smith Penney theory than the invisible assassins.

Even so, I wanted to take as few risks as possible. We were already putting ourselves in considerable personal danger simply by continuing the trek to George's farmstead and – call me old-fashioned – I maintain a certain professional pride in keeping my clients alive, at least until they've signed the cheque. Technically, Sophie and Adam were Kenny's clients but I was acting on his behalf so the pride fell to me.

The result was that I decided to switch gear; instead of rushing to get where we wanted to go, I was suddenly going to take the journey inexplicably slowly. We could have traversed the twenty-four miles to Macumba Station – the next logical stopping point – that morning, heading on to George's place the same day. On paper, we'd have been bedded down at the farmstead that night and beginning our hunt for any metaphorical buried treasure the next day. My plan, however irrational it appeared, was to take at least two days over getting to the farm. My thinking was that if it appeared irrational to me, then how would it look to anyone who might be following us? At worst, they might make the assumption we were tourists rather than treasure-hunters and decide to let us be; at worst, we'd look hopelessly lost in a scorching desert and they might be tempted to leave us well alone and let the outback do its killing job for them. It was a tenuous kind of logic, I'll admit, but it was all I had at the moment and any advantage we could secure, however slim, could be important.

There was the added bonus of allowing us to give the Land Rover a much more gentle run through the barren landscape. She'd taken quite a beating since we left Sydney and, although the manufacturers had made a highly successful business out of building vehicles specifically for this kind of terrain, I didn't want to push my luck. At the end of the day, she was still a bag of man-made metal bits cranking against each other under a tin shell: in extremes like these, she hadn't a hope against the elemental forces of Mother Nature if they chose to do their worst.

I hoped the gear-change theory might wrongfoot anyone watching our movements closely. But there was another potential audience I needed to take into account: the casual observer. For them, I had a different ruse. The first thing I had to do was convince Smith Penney and anyone else who might be marginally interested that we were actually heading back to Coober Pedy. I made a big show of getting Sophie and Adam to hang around for a couple of hours in the hotel complaining to anyone who'd listen that this godforsaken place was absolutely the back end of nowhere and they'd had enough. They could take the climate no longer and the tyre was the final straw. Meanwhile, I restocked the Land Rover with fuel and water on the pretence that we needed the supplies to get us back to civilisation. The only person I didn't include in the subterfuge was the mechanic at the town garage: I needed him to order me a new spare for the Land Rover. I just had to hope that he wasn't a big pal of Smith Penney's and wouldn't let on that I was planning to return at some point.

Then I paid another visit to the local constable, for form's sake as much as anything, and succeeded in filing an official complaint about the vandalism to the Land Rover's spare tyre. I offered him the name of my prime suspect but he declined to make a note of it. I also laid it on thick with him about our leaving town in disgust.

Once I was happy that enough people had heard about us retracing our steps to the south-west, I sent my wire to Kenny asking him to try and square things with Smith Penney, and we finally hit the road.

I'd hatched a plan to drive out on the Kempe Road in the direction of Coober Pedy for a mile or so, to where the road parted company with the rail line and veered off to the right. Another half-mile on from there, a minor track joined it from the left, winding across a dry watercourse. If we took it steady and struck lucky, we'd be able to turn off onto the scorched riverbed, totally out of sight from the town, and pass underneath the arches of the iron railway bridge before looping round through a series of shallow valleys to join the Macumba Road a few miles north-east of Oodnadatta. Given that we had no back-up for the tyres, it was a high-risk strategy, but the value of throwing any pursuers off the scent by satisfying the locals that we had scarpered to safety in the south outweighed the possible dangers on the track. If the worst came to the worst and we did lose another tyre, then we'd just have to hike back into town and wait for the next train.

The riverbed was rougher than I'd expected. As well as rocks and boulders of varying sizes, it was also strewn with woody shrubs and cacti, some of whose points would have proved just as lethal to a tyre as Smith Penney's knife.

'Are you sure this is a good idea?' Sophie asked after half an hour of lurching around in the cab with me and Adam as I dodged the obstacles.

'Nowhere near as sure as I was when we left Oodnadatta,' I said without taking my eyes off the ground immediately in front of the Land Rover. 'The sooner we can get back onto the Macumba Road, the better.'

For some reason, I'd imagined the Simpson Desert to be a barren, moonlike landscape covered in red sand and little else. The reality was very different: hilly, golden countryside shimmering in a heat haze and swarming with flies and plant life. The shrubs seemed to be able to draw water from even the most arid of spots and, off the established track, proved more of a hindrance than the rocks.

'There!' Sophie pointed off to the left, where a V-shaped gap in a neighbouring dune revealed the Macumba Road, an extremely missable dirt track that followed the crest of another slope a few hundreds yard ahead. At our current rate, it would take us about an hour to reach it.

'Let's stop and eat,' I said, diverting the car into the lee of a nearby incline. There was no chance of avoiding the midday sun completely but it would give us a little shelter if we hunkered down with our backs to the sand.

Sophie began rustling up some food while I gave the car a routine check. Adam strolled off in the direction of the track up ahead.

'Don't go too far,' I warned him. 'Stay within sight of us and keep covered up as much as you can.'

Adam nodded vaguely and stuffed both hands in his pockets as he walked away.

Ten minutes later, the three of us were sitting lined up like ducks in a shooting gallery, our backs against the car in an attempt to maximise the shade.

'What's the plan, Bill?' Sophie asked, tucking into a rudimentary sandwich of dried beef and mustard.

'Get to the track then take it as slow as we like in the direction of Macumba Station.'

'Do they know we're coming?' asked Adam.

Sophie made an affectionate mocking sound and smacked him on the arm. 'Of course they don't, dumbo. That would defeat the whole object of pretending we were going back to Coober Pedy, wouldn't it?'

'Oh yes,' said Adam, and fell silent.

I took the opportunity to broach my latest idea with them. 'In fact, they're not even going to know we've been.'

'What do you mean?'

'I mean I don't think we should pay a visit to Macumba Station at all. We'd only be giving the game away that we were still hanging about and the fewer people who know that, the better. We've got supplies to last us a week or more so we don't need to call in.'

Sophie popped the last hunk of bread into her mouth and licked her fingers. 'But the track doesn't go anywhere else. How can we avoid it?'

'We do the same as we're doing now: we get to within half a mile of the place then find an off-road trail that will skirt around it without being seen.'

Adam snorted. 'As if this expedition wasn't dangerous enough.'

Sophie turned on him with some ferocity. 'Have you got a better idea, Adam? It seems to me that Bill is the only one using his nous around here. If we're being followed by the same people who got Dolly then this expedition could get a whole lot more dangerous so it makes perfect sense to keep out of sight as much as we can. Have you got something in mind, Bill?'

As it happened, I had. I took out the document that passed for a map in this part of Australia and jabbed a finger at it. The sketchy topography showed that Macumba Station stood in the bend of a river that was itself an offshoot of the Macumba River a little further north. Its location had evidently been selected by early settlers because of its proximity to a waterhole which, with the rivers completely dry at this time of year, would be a lifeline for the ranchers and their stock.

'We can avoid the cattle station if we leave the track somewhere back here,' I said, dragging my finger down and to the left, where the Macumba Road arrived in a dead-straight line from the direction of Oodnadatta. Another branch of the river crossed the route further down but it would mean miles of off-road crawling across literally uncharted territory in searing temperatures before we met the Macumba River and could pick up the track again north of the station.

'That's certain death,' objected Adam, but Sophie again waved him quiet.

'Do you think we can do it?' she asked me.

Now was not the time to be expressing my own doubts so I nodded sagely.

'I wouldn't have suggested if I didn't.'

We stopped for the day about half a mile short of a raised piece of land, on the other side of which I believed Macumba

Station would be visible. The riverbed we were planning to use headed away to our left, dropping into a gentle valley which might offer some protection from the elements and from prying eyes, so we left the track behind and snailed our way for what I hoped would be a safe distance into the bush. I knew we'd been lucky so far that we hadn't seen any sign of life, even though we were nearing the station, and I was hoping that luck would hold out.

The trail of dust we were creating as we drove out into the sand was bigger than I'd have liked so we stopped sooner than planned and made camp. It would be light for hours to come but we were all tired from the efforts of the drive and the heightened enervation of feeling like potential targets. We ate a cold meal – I didn't want to chance the smoke from a fire being seen from Macumba Station – and I tried putting in a call to Kenny but I was more than an hour earlier than our allotted time and he wasn't on the receiving end. I decided to give it a miss that evening and hope that he wouldn't be too alarmed. Besides, I figured, he was probably still in the middle of a major clean-up operation at the office.

The temperature was beginning to drop when Adam excused himself and wandered off on his own for the second time that day.

I looked at Sophie and gestured in Adam's direction. 'Is he all right?'

She pulled a face and shook her head. 'I don't know what's wrong with him. He's probably just jittery about this whole trip – he's blown hot and cold about it ever since we first talked about coming to Australia.'

'Do you want to tell me about it?'

'Nothing much to tell, really. You know we haven't been together very long, don't you?'

I nodded. 'How did you meet?'

'He'd been tasked by his office to arrange the catering

for some event they were hosting and out of the Yellow Pages he picked me. I'm not sure if I believe in destiny but I certainly believe in romance.'

'Love at first sight?'

'Something like that. He swept me off my feet rather.'

'"Who ever lov'd that lov'd not at first sight?",' I quoted.

'No, you've lost me with that one.'

'Something dredged up from my school days. I had an English teacher who was particularly pernickety about that quotation. Everyone thinks it's Shakespeare but actually it's Shakespeare quoting Christopher Marlowe.'

'I'll take your word for it.'

I stared across at the low hill where Adam had gone walkabout. 'Can I be honest? You don't seem the type to me.'

'And what type is that?'

'The type to be swept off her feet. There's a practical streak in you a mile wide and I can't imagine you wouldn't have weighed up the pros and cons of getting married so quickly after meeting someone. How long was it?'

Sophie laughed. 'Exactly two months. And I'm not sure whether to be flattered or offended.'

'Be flattered, please,' I said, smiling back at her. 'All I meant was that some people are ruled by the head and some by the heart. If you'd pressed me to a wager on the subject, I'd have put my money on the head taking precedence with you. I think it's sweet that you proved me wrong. Not that it's any of my business.'

'You're right about that. But if you'd asked me six months ago if I'd be married and hacking about on the other side of the world today, I'm sure I'd have laughed in your face. It's surprised me just as much as anyone.'

I made as if to ask another question but Sophie cut me short.

'And before you say it, I'm fully aware that people regard

us as the odd couple. The loud, excitable girl paired up with the quiet, measured accountant – it doesn't match most people's expectations, does it?'

'Oh, I don't know. They say opposites attract and you two seem to fit that description pretty well.'

'We certainly do,' she said. 'But most people don't see what I see.'

'The hidden Adam behind the accountant façade?'

'There really is one,' she said eagerly, her face coming to life. 'He's kind and generous and funny and he's about the only person who's ever been able to make a friend of my cat . . .' She threw me a glance and grinned. 'But you don't want to hear all that.'

'I'm always happy to hear about other people's contentment. Freud would probably call it transference.'

I stared out into the desert and she lapsed into smiling contemplation. I let her rhapsodise silently for a moment before interrupting. 'So when did the prospect of Australia rear its head?'

Sophie looked thoughtful. 'It was just a few weeks after we met. When I mentioned I was considering coming out here, I thought it would put our romance on hold for a while. In fact, it had the opposite effect. A fortnight later, he proposed in a cute little Italian restaurant in Soho and a month after that we were married.'

'Sounds idyllic.'

'You know what? It was. I've never met anyone like him before and I can't imagine life without him now.'

Sophie's portrait of her husband didn't really square with the Adam I'd met but no one really knows a relationship from the outside. Maybe there was more to Adam than I could fathom. For the sake of my delightful travelling companion I was willing to give him the benefit of the doubt.

'You said he was a bit up and down about the trip?'

She nodded. 'He seemed very keen to begin with.'

I wondered if he might simply have wooed Sophie for the opportunity of getting his hands on her inheritance but I didn't say so and dismissed the thought as deeply uncharitable.

'Then he changed his mind – didn't think it was a good idea to travel halfway round the world on what he called a whim. It got to the point where I almost threatened to come without him, but he relented.'

'I've been on the receiving end of your persuasiveness,' I reminded her. 'I'm not surprised.'

Sophie gave me a look. 'You old charmer.'

'Guilty as charged.'

The night was at its blackest when I woke, stirred by something I couldn't place. Somewhere close by, a noise had roused me.

I glanced at my wristwatch, where the luminous hands informed me that it was three-fifteen in the morning. I looked up at the Land Rover, wondering if a sound from Adam and Sophie had woken me, but all seemed still there. Lifting my head from the rolled-up sweater I was using as a pillow, I screwed up my eyes to make my ears work harder and listened to the night.

I ignored the background hum of insects and tried to focus on anything out of the ordinary – a scuffle in the nearby undergrowth or an unexpected footfall in the sand. I found it hard to imagine that anyone could have found us this far off the Macumba Road but, given the feathers we seemed to have ruffled back in Sydney, I was prepared to believe anything was possible. If someone had discovered us, they were clearly relying on the element of surprise, creeping slowly up on our little encampment to catch us sleeping and unaware. I cursed myself for not setting up a night watch, with the three of us taking it in turns to stay awake and stand guard.

After nearly two minutes of straining, I heard it again. This time there was no mistaking the sound of a growl.

Not long after leaving Coober Pedy we'd crossed over to the northern, unprotected side of Australia's famous dingo fence, which had kept the south-east corner of the continent relatively free from the notorious sheep predators for the best part of a century. Now Ruby's warnings rang again in my ears. Attacks by these desert dogs on humans were, admittedly, few and far between and they mostly targeted infants or small children but incidents involving adults were not unheard of and had been known to prove fatal. I tried to recall what the prevailing advice was if one were to come into close contact with a dingo but all I could do was wonder what had attracted the animal in the first place. We'd lit no fire, been careful to tidy up our leftovers and offered little in the way of tasty morsels for a hungry dingo.

I reached into an inside pocket of my jacket and pulled out a small torch. Estimating the direction from which the growl had come, I pointed and was about to push the 'On' button when I heard another snarl, much closer and from the opposite side of the camp.

I flicked on the torch and executed a swift 360-degree circuit of the immediate vicinity. What I saw alarmed me considerably.

A group of six or seven dingoes stood, heads lowered in anticipation, less than twenty yards from the Land Rover towards the slope Adam had climbed earlier that evening. A lone animal – evidently the pack leader – was scarcely ten feet from me, teeth bared, eyes flashing gold in the reflection of the torch and an unpleasant look on its face. It seemed that I was the tasty morsel.

The danger from those canine incisors was more immediate than any threat a Sydney ne'er-do-well could present right now so I took the only action I could think of. I leaped to my feet and yelled furiously at the dominant dingo, waving my arms frantically. I must have looked like a crazed loon, prancing in the sand, and my idiocy was compounded by the fact that I couldn't properly extricate myself from the sleeping bag that held my legs cocooned in its folds. I tripped and fell face-first into the dirt.

I heard a ferocious bark from the direction of the closest creature, followed by several more from the group further away, and I was suddenly aware of something landing heavily on the sleeping bag. I swung my legs round and lashed out in the limited way that my encumbered limbs allowed, feeling the animal's teeth ripping at the material. In seconds, I realised, the rest of the pack would be on me and I'd be torn to shreds. I threw out the arm that was still holding the torch and connected with something bony and wet – a snarling snout, I guessed. In the moment of respite that followed, the headlamps of the Land Rover lit up the night, and I dived for cover under the tarp.

I sensed, rather than saw, the Landy roar past me, but I clearly heard the stomach-churning thud as it made contact with a dingo.

Moments later, Sophie was dragging me from the sleeping bag and checking me over.

'Bill, are you OK? Did it get you at all?'

I shook off her ministrations and got to my feet. 'I'm fine, Sophie – but only thanks to you. What the hell happened?'

'A pack of dingoes,' she said.

'That much I gathered. Have they gone?'

'I hope so. I think I took out their leader.'

I looked around but couldn't see any sign of the dingo she'd hit with the Landy. 'Maybe it was hurt. That could make it dangerous – we'd better load up and ship out before it decides to come back.'

I climbed into the driving seat and shifted the car into reverse. As I turned to check over my shoulder, I found

myself looking straight at Adam, hunched in the back with
his arms wrapped round his knees and a frightened look
on his face. He'd clearly been no help at all as Sophie drove
to the rescue. Ignoring him, I backed the Landy up to where
my sleeping bag lay in tatters on the ground. When I turned
back to look out of the windscreen, I could see Sophie
staring horrified at the ground where the vehicle had stood
moments before.

There in the red dirt lay the mangled, bloodied corpse
of the dingo.

Dawn broke as we reached the point where our tributary
joined the main Macumba River. The flat plain widened out
before us, greenery lining its bed as plants dug their roots
deep into the earth in the search for moisture. The last stretch
of the journey had been even slower than the rest of our
off-road meanderings, partly because of the terrain but also
because we were picking our way on side lights alone for
fear of revealing our position.

Given that we'd managed to avoid any trouble of the
human variety in the twenty-four hours since leaving
Oodnadatta, I judged we could risk stopping for breakfast
and I was glad we did. The beauty of the sun rising ahead
of us over the mighty Australian desert was breathtaking.
Watching the golden light gradually shorten the shadows
on the slopes and flush a stunning blue into the enormous
sky above our heads was a privilege I took the time to
appreciate, in spite of our situation. I was surprised at how
quickly the temperature climbed, too, and we soon discarded
the fleece-lined jackets that had kept us warm overnight,
replacing them with sunglasses against the dazzling morning
glare.

'Now we're past Macumba we can take our time getting
to the Deakins farm,' I said in answer to a question from
Sophie about the day ahead. 'We could still run into cattle

ranchers from the station so let's keep a low profile and stay in the dips of the dry creeks wherever we can. The longer we can avoid getting back on to the track, the happier I'll be.'

Adam said, 'We're going to have to pick it up at some point, though.'

He was right and for some reason it niggled me. I knew we'd need to find the trail sooner or later – it was the only sure route to Uncle George's place – but to have that fact pointed out by the least accomplished navigator in our group was annoying, nonetheless.

'At some point,' I repeated noncommittally.

We barely made it out of second gear the whole time we stayed off the trail. It didn't bother the engine particularly – we were going so slowly that the revs remained low – but it did make for a boring drive. The only thing that kept me alert was watching the red sand ahead for obstructions. If we lost another wheel out here, we'd be dead for sure.

After two draining hours behind the wheel, we reached the trail on the north-eastern side of Macumba Station. I held back from the track itself, parking up behind a dune and getting out to scope the territory. Keeping low in case of any vehicles or mounted cattle men on the road, I crept up to the top of the ridge and peered gingerly over. My hunch was that the traffic on this desert side of the station would be far less busy than on the Oodnadatta side but I didn't want to take any chances. I looked back down the trail, not really expecting to see much as I hoped we'd left Macumba miles behind us. In fact, less than two miles away, I judged, I could see the buildings of the cattle station and I realised we'd almost completely doubled back on ourselves as we followed the riverbed. From a couple of miles south of Macumba, all we'd achieved was a big round trip fetching us up a couple of miles north of it.

I swore and turned back to the Land Rover. The only

positive from my exploratory trip was that there had indeed been no traffic on the trail but that was about all I could muster up. I felt slightly better when I reminded myself of an old CO, whose mantra had been mercilessly drummed into me: time spent in reconnaissance is seldom wasted.

'Never mind,' said Sophie when I broke the news. 'At least we're still moving in the right direction and there's no sign of anyone following us.'

'Good point,' I said, surprised at how relieved I was about that. If we could make it to George's in good time, then we stood a fair chance of being able to search the place thoroughly for any clues about who might want to get their hands on the opal mine. I also wanted to check out the farmstead as a possible garrison against intruders. That meant having enough supplies to keep us going longer than any opposition, who would struggle to maintain a siege for long in this climate. Provided George had looked after the place reasonably – although I had my doubts about that after what Jack Cadison had told us – I reckoned we should be able to see off any potential attack and stake Sophie's claim once and for all.

There was something else that continued to intrigue me: the mine itself. George had evidently found something underground out in the Simpson Desert and yet he'd never cashed in on it to any great extent – or so it seemed. Of course, he might have been one of those hermit types who hoarded his riches simply to gloat over them. One possibility that crossed my mind was that we might happen upon a stash of uncut opals concealed somewhere on the property. I couldn't work out what the alternative might be. It made little sense for George to have drained his mine dry but then lived out the rest of his life in the middle of nowhere in relative poverty. So where had the money gone? And how could Kenny and I find a way of letting Sophie get her hands on it?

These were questions that were not going to be solved on a dirt track miles from anywhere. Our only hope of finding answers was to press on to the farmstead.

I could never have imagined the madness that awaited us.

III

I caught sight of the farm as the track topped a small rise about half a mile to the south-east. From this distance, it looked pretty much as I'd imagined it: a main building constructed of wood, a couple of smaller outhouses standing separately some distance away – one of them probably what the Australians called a 'dunny', for toilet purposes – and a fenced-off area that would have penned in whatever livestock the farm might have dealt in during its long life. Then the track dipped again and the Deakins property disappeared from view.

As we rounded the final corner a hundred yards short of the farmhouse, I let out an involuntary gasp.

The place was a ruin.

Daylight flooded through the outer walls of the main building, revealing gaping holes in the fabric of the house. Corrugated sheets from the roof lay strewn around the outside while what remained of the outbuildings were little more than frames staked out in the ground, their roofs collapsed and rusted, leaving only the carcasses of shacks. The front door of the house hung limply from one hinge and several windows were smashed.

'What the hell?' said Sophie.

We entered the fenced-off compound. I stopped the Land Rover with a lurch and stared hard at the house.

'What's up, Bill?' Adam asked.

I lifted a hand to silence him and sharpened my ears against the desert wind. The state of the house was not indicative of natural dilapidation: someone had got here before us. And for all I knew, they might still be there.

'Wait here,' I said, opening the door and starting to climb slowly out of the Land Rover. 'I'm going to check it out.'

Sophie reached out a hand and grabbed my arm. 'Are you sure that's wise? Somebody could be lying in wait for us.'

'That's exactly why I'm going to check it out,' I replied and shook my arm free. 'Sophie, you get in the driver's seat. If you see or hear anything remotely untoward, turn this thing around and head back to Macumba Station as fast as you can. Don't stop to find out what's going on – just hit the gas. Got it?'

'I'm not leaving you here,' she said.

'Just do what I tell you, all right? I'm not putting you in any more danger than I have to and if that means you getting back to safety, then that's what you're going to do. No arguments.'

She fixed me with a stare. 'There's no guarantee I'll be any safer back there, though, is there?'

I couldn't argue with that. If someone had been out to the Deakins property, there was a strong likelihood they'd called in at Macumba Station along the way. They might even be staying there. That would mean the station was no safer for Sophie than being out here – and possibly much less safe if she'd left me behind to face an unknown enemy at the farmstead.

'OK, while I skirt round to check out the house from behind the well over there, back up the Landy out of sight behind that last rise and wait until you hear from me.'

'How long are we supposed to wait?' asked Adam.

Sophie punched him on the shoulder and slid across into the driver's seat, looking back at me. 'Go on, then, if you're going.'

As I moved away to the left, crouching low with the sandbank behind me, I heard her jam the Land Rover into reverse and the engine noise lessened as it disappeared behind the dune. I made for a taller tree, which from Ruby's description I guessed to be a coolibah, and took refuge behind its thick, twisted trunk. I shivered as I remembered that George's body had been found near a coolibah tree and wondered if this was the one but I couldn't stop to think any more about that. I was barely fifty yards from the house and, if there was someone inside, there was no chance that they hadn't heard us approaching. I had to hope that they hadn't seen me get out of the Land Rover and make a dash for the tree.

From a shirt pocket I pulled out the hand-drawn sketch I'd found among George's documents back in Kenny's office, checking redundantly that it matched what I saw in front of me. Between me and the main building stood one of the outhouses and a walled-off circle about ten feet across, which I took to be the well. I hazarded that the outhouse would not be the dunny: it was unlikely that anyone would position a waste site so close to the water source.

I waited a full five minutes, watching the windows of the house closely for any hint of movement. I half-expected to see the glint of a rifle barrel in the sun but immediately chided myself for letting my imagination run away with me.

Nothing happened.

I shimmied closer, stopping for cover at the outhouse. I was right – it was not the dunny but a storage shed for some old tools and, bizarrely, a bicycle. I grabbed a claw hammer and hefted it in my hand to feel its weight before tucking it into my belt. Then I crawled on my belly to the well and stuck my head over the wall to get another look at the house.

Still there was no sign of life but I wasn't about to start taking chances now. I glanced back to where the track rounded the little rise, making sure the Land Rover and its occupants were out of sight, and assessed my options. In front of me there was twenty yards of open space leading to the rickety front door. Across the width of the house ran a verandah, perhaps four feet deep, that put the door and windows in shadow with the sun at its current angle. I was pretty sure that if anyone was lurking at any of the openings, or even moving about inside, I'd see their silhouette against the light breaking through from the back wall of the house, where loose timbers had fallen away from the frame.

I watched for another five minutes and saw nothing. Taking out the hammer in case I found I was going to need it, I heaved myself to my feet and scurried across the open space to the left-hand end of the house, where the side wall had no windows or doors. There were plenty of gaps in the woodwork here, too, and my silhouette would be equally visible to anyone inside, so I dived feet first into the sand at the base of the wall and rolled myself tightly against it, where I could see no holes.

The whole time since I'd left the Land Rover, I had spotted no sign of anyone either in or around the property. I judged that our nemesis would almost certainly be armed, which would put us at a serious disadvantage. But it also meant that, in the absence of any shots fired, they were unlikely to be in the immediate vicinity.

I waited another five minutes before testing out my theory.

'Well, that was a bit of a damp squib.'

I shot Adam a dark look but he was right. All the chicanery and shuffling about that I'd done to avoid being seen from the house had been a complete waste of time and effort. There was nobody there.

Which is not to say that there hadn't been somebody there at some point in the not-too-distant past. This was not the normal detritus of a man who'd died a few weeks earlier: this was the wreckage of a thorough ransacking by people who didn't care how they left the place afterwards. Slats had been thumped out of the clapboard walls, floor beams unceremoniously ripped up, and cupboards and boxes torn apart by strong hands. Someone had been looking for something.

Sophie swept some dusty debris from a weather-beaten settee and sat down, resting her elbows on her knees.

'I don't understand, Bill. What on earth is going on?'

I shook my head in sympathy. 'I don't understand either, Sophie. But clearly someone has been searching for something and thought they'd find it among George's things. Maybe they found it and left. Or maybe they didn't find it, which suggests one of two possibilities: either it was among the crate of stuff that got sent to Sydney or . . .'

'Or what?'

I hesitated, not really believing what I was about to say. 'Or it's still here.'

Sophie lapsed into a thoughtful silence.

There was a third possibility which I hadn't mentioned. Kenny had asked Smith Penney to come out to the farmstead after George's death and package up that crate. It was entirely possible that Penney had found whatever it was the searchers had been looking for and removed it from the house. If so, it was back in Oodnadatta and we'd almost certainly never know what it was. That eventuality had its attractions – what we didn't know couldn't harm us and all that – but my curiosity was itching seriously now.

Sophie stood up decisively, jolting me out of my mental

musings. 'Well, we'd better conduct a search of our own, then.'

'Don't hold your breath,' I said, gesturing at the ruins of George Deakins's life. 'This place has been comprehensively demolished. If there was anything here to find, don't you think they'd have found it already?'

'You said it yourself, Bill. Whatever it is could still be here. So let's look.'

'We don't even have a clue what we're looking for. At least with a haystack you know you're trying to find a needle.'

Adam stepped in from the back door, where he'd been staring out at the wilderness beyond the farm.

'I'm with Sophie,' he said. 'We might as well give the place the once-over. We haven't got anything else to do, have we?'

'Apart from go home,' I muttered, more to myself than the others, but Sophie laughed.

'Let's give it a couple of hours, shall we? Shouldn't take us any longer than that to sift through this lot. There isn't much to sift, after all.'

So for the next one hundred and twenty sweaty, uncomfortable minutes, we trawled through the rubbish that littered George's house. The previous search had been thorough, that was certain, and I didn't expect to find anything of use as I turned over wooden boxes, picked up scattered clothes and rummaged through the ransacked cupboards. My expectations were not overturned: there was nothing.

Adam went out to search the two outhouses and peer in vain down the shaft of the well but he found nothing either.

It was Sophie who hit upon the disturbing discovery.

'Bill, Adam – come here, quick!'

Adam was still outside so I got to Sophie in the bedroom first. She was standing over the bed, pointing at the wall a few inches above where a filthy, torn pillow spilled feathers onto the mattress.

'What is it?'

The question was superfluous. From the door, I could see that she was pointing at a spatter of blood on the timber wall.

Adam crashed in behind me and stopped dead. 'What do you think it means?'

I was cautious. 'Could be nothing. Could be some injury George picked up that he never bothered to clean. Could be a hundred different things.'

'Oh, come on, Bill,' said Sophie, wild-eyed and trembling. 'Even living in these conditions, he was hardly likely to leave a bloodstain right above his head while he was in bed. No – you know perfectly well what this means. Uncle George didn't kill himself: somebody shot him. Right here.'

She pushed past us and went back into the main room, where she sat heavily on the settee. I could see her shoulders shaking as she sobbed silently and I nudged Adam to go and comfort her. He took the hint and sat beside her, putting a hand on her knee.

'It's OK, Sophie . . .'

She erupted and railed at him through her tears. 'It's not OK, Adam. This is the second person we know of who's been killed because of this bloody inheritance. Dolly was the first and now Uncle George. Who's next – you? Bill? How many more people are going to die because of me?'

She collapsed into sobs again.

I went over to the settee and sat on the other side of her. 'It's not your fault, Sophie. You didn't do any of this. For God's sake, you don't even know what this is about – how could you be responsible?'

'If I'd listened to those threats and given up my claim to the mine, at least Dolly would still be alive. You can't tell me that's not true because it is.'

'Didn't your mother tell you that you must never give in to bullies?'

She looked at me with fire in her eyes. 'Even if it saves lives?'

I could have argued that point with her all day and all night but now was not the time. Instead I said, 'I know it's early but I'm going to see if I can raise Kenny on the radio.'

I walked outside to where I'd moved the Land Rover and began to set up the transceiver equipment. There were a few things I wanted to ask Kenny, not least what he knew about any enemies George might have made. I wasn't thinking of childhood quarrels or spats over spilled beer – I was looking for information about opal valuations, land disputes, stuff like that. Anything that someone might feel strongly enough to do damage over. I also wanted Kenny to go through the contents of that crate one more time. I knew in my heart I hadn't missed anything important but double-checking was about the only option we had left available to us. And then there was the whole question of Smith Penney and his immediate antagonism towards us. I was hoping Kenny would be able to shed some light on that.

The sun was still blindingly hot and I reached into my shirt pocket for a handkerchief to mop my brow. Instead, I pulled out the tattered map of the farmstead. I put it down on the driver's seat of the Land Rover for safekeeping and was just about to fish again for the handkerchief when I glanced back at the drawing and stopped, open-mouthed.

Uncle George was shouting at me. In capital letters.

'I don't know how I could have been so stupid,' I said as the three of us retrieved whatever tools we could lay our hands on from the outhouse. I'd been hoping there might be an axe – just in case I had to chop the damn thing down – but there was no such luck. We grabbed a couple of hammers, a large bolster and a long-handled crowbar and hurried over to the coolibah tree.

'I saw this thing marked in capitals when I first found the sketch in the crate but I thought it was just some silly joke – pointing out really obvious features of the landscape for comic effect. I can't believe I didn't realise George was leaving a treasure map.'

Sophie had recovered herself rapidly with the news of the clue and seemed as eager as Adam and I to investigate further. She beat both of us to the tree and immediately ran round to the far side, where a split in the trunk was more accessible from ground level.

'It's hollow,' she yelled triumphantly as we arrived on the scene, panting with the heat. She dropped the crowbar and scrambled up into the 'Y' of the split, leaning close to the hollow opening to peer inside.

'Watch out, Sophie!' I shouted, catching her just before her head disappeared into the crevice. 'You don't know what might have made its home in there.'

She recoiled fast and lowered herself from the tree. 'Like what?'

'Oh, I don't know – spiders, scorpions, snakes. The usual deadly crew for this part of Oz.'

She took a step further from the tree and grimaced.

'I wouldn't worry too much,' I went on. 'We're carrying anti-venom and medicine for most things in the Landy. But it might be easier not to get bitten or stung in the first place.'

'How are we going to look?' Adam asked.

'Good question. We can start by shining a light down there.'

I collected the torch from the Land Rover and climbed up into the crook of the branches, where Sophie had crouched moments before. Pointing the beam into the hole, I strained my eyes to look for anything resembling George's secret treasure – whatever it was.

'Hand me that crowbar, would you, Adam?'

He passed me the heavy metal device and I grasped the claw, lowering the lever end into the crack and wafting it around as best I could. I didn't want to go so deep that I had to put my hand inside the trunk, so I hoped the hollow didn't stretch down to ground level.

I was in luck. With two inches of the crowbar still visible outside the cavity, it hit something metallic.

'Bingo,' I shouted. 'We've struck gold.'

It took us twenty minutes to excavate the side of the tree at about the level where I estimated the container to be situated. Even accessing it from the side of the trunk, the same dangers would apply regarding critters wanting to defend their home so we took it slow and steady and when we were about to break through I got Sophie and Adam to stand back while I put on a thick leather glove from our equipment bundle. Using the crowbar, I punched through the innermost layer of the bark and took a swift pace backwards.

A small cascade of crumbling wood fell away from the gap, followed by a few beetle-like creatures that scurried off into the dust. Nothing else moved so I stepped forward and wedged the crook of the crowbar into the tree. I teased the edge of the cranny and pulled away more bark, opening the hole to a height of about six inches. When I backed off this time, the top of a metal cylinder tipped gently out of the darkness and came to rest neatly in the opening.

I reached out with my gloved hand and lifted the cylinder clear of its hiding place.

'Bloody hell,' said Adam simply.

The canister proved as difficult to get into as it had been to find. I started out gingerly, trying to jimmy the lid off with the crowbar before switching to the hammer and bolster but they didn't work either. I guessed there couldn't be anything too fragile inside, given that it had evidently been subjected to the full battery of elemental forces at work in this part of the world, but I also wanted to take care not to damage any paperwork that might be stored in it. I wondered how long it had been out there and concluded that George, if it had in fact been George, had expected it to remain hidden for some considerable time – years, even. I shook it, gently to begin with then more forcefully, to see if I could feel the movement of any loose contents. All I could make out was some shuffling from end to end, which I took to mean it contained only papers of some sort. I jolted it in one direction, attempting to shift everything up to one end, then set to work with a rusty hacksaw I found among the tools in the outhouse. Even though we'd moved into the relative cool of the house, with a breeze blowing through its wreckage, I was sweating like a carthorse by the time I finally made it through the outer casing.

'Let me have a go,' said Adam, taking the hacksaw from my hand and leaning over the canister.

'Take it easy,' I said. 'Make sure there's nothing at this end of the tube that might be damaged by the blade.'

I was happy to let him complete the task and within a few minutes he'd sawn the end completely off the canister. He tipped it upside down, put a hand over the opening and shook.

At first I couldn't make head nor tail of the scroll of documents that fell out. They seemed very old, very dog-eared and very dull. Some were dated, going back decades – nearly a century in one instance – and they were written in the kind of abstruse jargon that is the stock in trade of lawyers all over the world. I flicked through them quickly, looking for anything that stood out as significant, before passing them to Sophie. They belonged to her now, after all.

Adam looked over her shoulder as she perused them.

'What are they, Bill?' she asked eventually.

'Damned if I know. But if they are what's caused all this mayhem, they must be important. I'll ask Kenny when I talk to him – it's almost time for our scheduled call. Meanwhile, we should start thinking about bedding down for the night.'

Sophie looked surprised. 'You mean here? Is that safe?'

'I don't think anyone's coming back in a hurry. I imagine they thought they'd stripped the place bare and have moved on to search somewhere else. And if they did to Uncle George what we suspect they did, then this is going to be the last place they'd return to. No, I think we're probably as safe here as anywhere and at least it has the benefit of a roof.' I looked up at the gaping holes above us and smiled ruefully. 'Well, you know what I mean.'

We agreed that Adam and Sophie should have the house as their overnight lodgings. Understandably, Sophie was not keen to use the bedroom so they decided to lay out camp beds in the living room. I valiantly offered to sleep outside but I was happy to do so: besides wanting to give them some semblance of privacy, I was enjoying the capacious night skies of the outback with their myriad constellations and almost mystical immensity. As long as the creepy-crawlies – and the dingoes – kept to themselves, I'd be perfectly content in the open air.

Kenny sounded distant and crackly when I finally made contact. I knew that shifts in atmospheric conditions could affect the quality of shortwave radio transmissions, creating the phenomenon known as 'skip zones' where reception could fail, but it had become all too apparent that this was frequently worse at night. Through the static and occasional drop-outs, I managed to fill him in on our suspicions about George's death. He immediately wanted to call the police to get the case reopened as a murder inquiry but I talked him down from that one. For one thing, the boys in blue seemed to be making little progress with their investigations into Dolly's hit-and-run – whether deliberately or not it was impossible to say – and for another, I could really do without Kenny stirring up a hornets' nest with our mystery enemy and setting them back on our trail while we were stranded out here. There would be plenty of time to get George's death looked at with fresh eyes when we were safely back in civilisation.

Kenny was reluctant to let it go, especially as he was now in constant touch with the police about his burglary too, but he seemed willing to be diverted when I told him about the papers we'd found stashed secretly away in the tree trunk. He pushed for more information.

'There's not much I can tell you, Kenny. They look pretty dry to me.'

'I thought everything was dry out there in the summer?'

I sighed. 'We don't have the time or the call quality for jokes.'

'Fair point, mate. Give me the gist – what do they look like?'

'Like legal bumf. I've been trying to get my head round the details but it's beyond me, I'm afraid. There is one you might like to check out, though.'

'Fire away.'

I sifted the papers to find the document I wanted. 'It's on letterheaded paper from a company in Sydney called Hamilton and Irvine.'

'Good Australian names,' he said.

'Kenny! What did I just tell you?'

'Sorry, mate. You were saying . . .'

'Well, it's pretty old – more than a hundred years old, in fact – and it's addressed to a Valentine Deakins.'

'I don't recognise the name.'

That answered that question. 'It makes reference to an exchange of title. What does that mean?'

'I'm not a property specialist but every house has a title deed and sometimes the deeds to one place get swapped for another, usually in lieu of some kind of payment that's owed. The exchange of title is the document that records it. Does that bit of paper have details of the properties involved?'

I scanned it but could only find reference to a 'Deakins Farm' – presumably George's place. It was starting to look as if the property he'd purportedly left to Sophie might not have been his to bequeath at all.

'What do you think it was exchanged for?' I asked.

'No idea. Give me the address of the legal firm and I'll do some digging at this end. Could take a couple of days, though – that's if I can even track them down after all this time.'

I read him the details from the letterhead and he made a note of them. Then I moved on to a topic I badly wanted to quiz him about: Smith Penney. I told him about my run-in at the hotel bar but he was surprisingly sanguine.

'Ah, don't take any notice of him. He's just throwing his weight about.'

'That's pretty much what Jack said.'

'Who's Jack?'

'Jack Cadison,' I replied. 'The barman at the Transcontinental Hotel.'

Kenny sounded dubious. 'That's another name I don't know. He must be new in town.'

'Kenny, you've been away from Oodnadatta for more than twenty years. There are bound to be one or two new faces in that time.'

He chuckled. 'I suppose so. Anyway, now you've heard it from two sources.'

'That's all very well,' I said doubtfully. 'But my personal experience of Mr Penney doesn't square with the fact that he was the person you asked to go out to George's farm and pack up that crate. Do you trust him?'

'I've known him a long time,' he said simply.

I had to take Kenny's word for it. After all, he'd grown up with Penney and he certainly understood the outback psyche better than I did.

'Have you managed to straighten things out with him?'

'Give us a chance. I only got your wire yesterday. Leave it with me – I'll make sure he knows you're not there to cause trouble.'

We signed off and I decided against telling Sophie that night that the farm might not, after all, be hers. She was carrying enough guilt already without learning that our entire escapade could be a waste of time.

When I went back inside, she was sweeping the floor. Jack Cadison had evidently been wrong about George not owning a broom.

'Bit of a Forth Bridge job, that,' I said.

'What do you mean?'

'Do you know the theory about the Forth Bridge? The idea is that it's so big that as soon as the maintenance crew have finished giving it a coat of paint, they have to start all over again. It's a myth, sadly, but it sounds plausible.'

'So you think my sweeping up is a never-ending job?'

'I think that with all the holes in these walls, there's going to be as much sand in here by tomorrow morning as you've removed this evening.'

As I lay looking up at the stars that night, thinking of Leotta and the warmth of a Devon summer, I heard the unmistakable sounds of amorous coupling from the house.

Those damned walls were just too full of holes.

IV

Kenny's digging into the Sydney legal firm gave us time to fill and nothing to fill it with.

I toyed with the notion of patching up the house a little, using the tools at our disposal and bits of kit we'd brought with us, but in the end there didn't seem much point. Sophie was never likely to live here – nor, come to that, was anyone else. With the mine presumably gutted of its precious stones, there was no reason on God's good earth for anyone to buy a tumbledown ruin in the middle of one of the most barren places on the planet.

George had left her a dud.

It didn't stop Sophie from wanting to tidy the place up and she enlisted Adam in the job as a moderately reticent assistant. I firmly declined and went outside to tinker with the Land Rover.

I didn't even get as far as lifting the bonnet. Idly manhandling the spare tyre, with its jagged hole ripped into it, I came to a decision. It might have been the stupidest decision I ever made but I couldn't sit around here for another few days at a loose end.

Sophie was appalled. 'What are you thinking? You can't make that trip again – and especially not alone.'

I made a calming gesture and invited her to sit down. 'Just think about it, Sophie. It only took us so long because we were skirting Macumba Station on unmapped riverbeds. I've got a much better idea of where I'm going now and, having driven it once, I can negotiate the terrain much quicker so it won't take anything like as long as it did getting here. If I pick up the new tyre I ordered in Oodnadatta I'll be able to take it quicker still on the way back here without the risk we had of a blowout with no spare on board. And I can top up our supplies while I'm in town, maybe do a little digging of my own, see what I can find out about George's relationships with other folk around here. All ways round it makes sense.'

'Not if something happens to you. You'd be stuck out in the middle of the desert with no hope of rescue. Or were you planning on taking the radio with you and leaving us here without any means of communication?'

I hadn't thought of that. It raised the stakes but it was a chance I was willing to take. 'No, of course not. I'll leave the radio here with you so you can contact Kenny at the appointed time each evening. With the increased speed and a spare tyre on the return leg, I should be back here by this time tomorrow in any case. You'll hardly notice I've gone.'

'And what about Smith Penney? I thought you didn't want him knowing we hadn't properly left?'

At least I had an answer for that. 'Kenny's going to talk to him, straighten things out. I'm hoping he won't be a problem for us any more.'

'Why don't we all go back?' Adam asked, not unreasonably.

I shook my head. 'I'm not risking all of us. It's one thing putting my own life in danger but I'm not prepared to do the same to the two of you.'

'Oh, so you do admit you're putting yourself in danger?' said Sophie testily.

'And that's my decision to make. But I'm not taking responsibility for you as well. As long as you keep George's genny topped up with fuel you should have everything you need. It ought to power the radio perfectly satisfactorily too. Now get back to your tidying up and let me get on with restocking the Landy.'

Sophie looked none too happy with the decision but there wasn't much she could do. She stood up angrily, picked up a hammer and started banging nails into the walls.

I was right about the drive back to Oodnadatta: it was much quicker. Without having to take Sophie and Adam's welfare into consideration, I pushed the Land Rover harder than I had on the way out and risked taking on bigger boulders in the flats of the riverbed. She proved well up to the challenge and I picked up the dirt trail where the river intersected with it a couple of miles south of the cattle station. From there the journey was even faster, although I was uncomfortably aware of the dust cloud I was creating and kept a close eye on the rear-view mirror in case someone at the ranch happened to notice. Either they didn't spot me or they were too lazy to check it out and I made it back to Oodnadatta without incident before nightfall.

I caused quite a stir when I walked into the bar of the Transcontinental that evening.

'Well, mate, I didn't expect to see you around these parts again,' said Jack Cadison, a broad grin on his face as he slid a bottle of beer across the counter to me. 'I thought you'd bust a tyre or something and headed back to the White Fellas' Hole.'

'White Fellas' Hole?' I queried.

'Yeah, mate. The aboriginal word for "white fellas' hole" is literally *kupa-piti* so you can probably imagine how that became bastardised to Coober Pedy. But that's only our name for it. In the tribal traditions it's called Umoona.'

'Meaning?'

'Long life, I think – but it's also their name for the mulga tree.'

'Long life,' I mused. I could do with the promise of some of that right now. 'So why isn't it called Umoona on the map?'

Jack sighed. 'Ah, mate, that's a whole can of worms you're opening up there. These guys have lived peacefully on this land for centuries and then some posh white bloke pitches up from England, steals all the goodies from the ground and turns the black-skinned fellas into second-class citizens. You can't blame them for being a bit resentful.'

I certainly couldn't. 'But I think you'll find Mr Stuart was a Scot.'

He laughed scornfully. 'Scottish, English – it's all the same to the locals they robbed.'

I took his point.

Across the room I spotted the town's solitary police officer enjoying a beer at a table with a handful of other men, each as rough as the next. I excused myself from Jack and made my way over. I wanted to test the water. At the very least, I wanted a better response than the one he'd given me last time I tried to report a crime.

'All right, mate,' he said gruffly, nodding to me as I approached their table. 'How's it going?'

I sat down uninvited in an empty chair and put my beer on the table. 'It'd be going much better if some people actually did their jobs like they're paid to.'

He straightened in his seat and frowned. I could tell that he was weighing up whether to take offence or pretend my remark hadn't been directed at him personally. I didn't allow him the time to decide.

'How does one go about reporting a burglary in this town?'

'Burglary? In Oodna?' He seemed amazed that such a prospect could even be contemplated.

'No, not actually in the town.'

The idea of having to do some real work had obviously alarmed him considerably but now he relaxed. 'Oh, well then. Cop shop opens at ten tomorrow.'

I tried to stifle my disdain for his work ethic and stood up. I sensed a mood of tension around the table as the other men waited to see if things would kick off. 'Crime only happens during opening hours, does it?'

I was slightly surprised to see him stand up, too, but instead of towering over me he found himself looking up into my face. I'm not a particularly tall man but my Army training taught me to stand straight and make the most of the height I had. His police training had clearly failed to do the same.

He tried to compensate by sounding tough. 'Crime investigation only happens when I say it does.'

'Must be a joy for the citizens to have you enforcing the law,' I said and turned away before he could think of a retort.

I heard him shout something offensive at my back but I chose to ignore him. I didn't really care whether or not the local constabulary were interested in helping me. Our experience back in Sydney suggested it was unlikely but this clown would have been no use to us anyway. He was one of those types who put on a uniform and believed it lifted them a few levels in the hierarchy. I'd had my fill of those in the military.

It crossed my mind to turn the Land Rover around and head straight back to the farmstead. A night drive might be a good way of avoiding attention, especially now that it was known in Oodnadatta that we were still in the vicinity. I could slip unnoticed past Macumba Station, too, making as much of a dust cloud as I liked: it wouldn't be seen by starlight.

Two things prevented me from doing it. First, I'd arrived

too late in the evening to pick up the new tyre from the garage. That, and the other supplies I wanted to replenish, would have to wait until morning. Second – and much more important as far as I was concerned – I desperately wanted a shower and a clean bed. The thought of another night roughing it was not appealing.

I checked into a room at the Transcontinental Hotel.

It was late when I thought I heard a tentative knock at the door of my room. After checking in, I'd showered, shaved and gone back down to the bar for a bite to eat, then returned to the room and collapsed gratefully into the folds of the soft mattress. I must have been half-asleep because there was a second knock, a little more forceful this time.

I wasn't expecting visitors so I played it ultra-cautious. I tiptoed to the door, grabbing a boot on the way, and stood comically with the toe of the boot in my hand, the heavy heel aloft in anticipation of . . . I don't know what.

'Who is it?' I called stupidly.

The voice on the other side spoke in a hushed tone. 'Let me in, mate. It's Jack.'

That was a surprise. What the hell was Jack Cadison doing creeping around his own hotel, whispering secretively at the doors of guests he barely knew?

I let him in and stepped back from the door. 'What's up?'

He slipped inside, checked the corridor behind him and gently closed the door. 'Sorry about the sneaking about, mate, but I don't think it would be good for either of us if word got out that I was yammering to you.'

He was speaking in riddles. 'What are you talking about, Jack?'

'I'm talking about your continued good health, mate. Those blokes with Constable Doyle earlier on – they're part of Smith Penney's crowd.'

'So what?'

'So you can bet your last cent that he knows you're back in town by now.'

I was beginning to see what he was getting at. 'Damn him. I haven't replaced the last slashed tyre yet. But when we were here the other day you told me he was harmless.'

Jack looked agitated. 'Things have changed. He got a call from Sydney after you left and it's put his back up.'

That must have been Kenny, trying to lean on Penney from his angle. It seemed that idea had backfired badly.

'And now you're back, stirring things up again. If he comes for you a second time, it'll be a lot worse than a slashed tyre, I can promise you that. And if he finds out I've warned you off, he'll be coming for me too. Take my advice, mate, and get out of town – back to the White Fellas' Hole, if I were you.'

'No can do, I'm afraid.' I pointed in the vague direction of the Simpson Desert. 'I've got two rather valuable pieces of cargo out there somewhere that I'm not leaving behind. Thanks for the tip but I'll be out of your hair in the morning. If Penney wants to have a go tonight, let him do his worst. I've seen bigger and uglier thugs than him.'

'But you don't understand, mate.'

There was plenty I didn't understand, but I wasn't sure exactly which bit of it he was getting at. I took hold of both his shoulders and sat him on the bed. From my bag I pulled two bottles of warm beer and cracked them open on the edge of the sideboard. I handed one to Jack and squatted on my haunches in front of him.

'What don't I understand, Jack? Why is Penney all riled up?'

It was then that Jack told me all about Smith Penney. And why he hated George Deakins.

Back in the mists of time, long before Sophie had even been a glint in her father's eye, Penney and Deakins had hung around together, gaining something of a reputation as the bad boys of Oodnadatta. George would drive in from his farmstead every couple of weeks or so, stock up on essentials, and he and Smith would hit the town – such as it was. When the two of them got some beers inside them, no one was safe. It was rumoured that George had tried – and in some cases succeeded in – cuckolding half the men in the area and his propensity for female company had made him *persona non grata* among large swathes of the community, so much so that he was forced to start cutting down on his trips to the metropolis.

Sexual shenanigans weren't the only way the pair made themselves unpopular. While nobody ever quite pinned anything on them, there were suggestions that these bad boys might be responsible for a spate of low-level thefts across an area reaching all the way to Coober Pedy; nothing too major but irritating enough to the populace to make them even less welcome when they were out on a spree.

I could see how the lackadaisical attitude of the local law enforcement might not lend itself to cracking down on a couple of larrikins simply out for a good time. I'd seen Constable Doyle in the company of Penney's crew at the hotel bar and I guessed he'd probably grown up with Penney himself so would be extremely reluctant to put the finger on one of his mates for the sake of a few minor infringements. It truly was the Wild West.

There being no honour among thieves, contrary to the accepted myth, almost inevitably things between George and Smith turned sour. Jack wasn't able to say exactly when, or what had caused the falling-out, but falling-out there was, and it had reached a head in the hotel one hot Saturday night about ten years ago. Penney – by then married and a little less volatile than he had been in his youth – threw a punch at George; George reciprocated in kind and the whole bar kicked off. Jack, who must have barely been out of nappies at the time, recalled hearing Mrs Penney's name mentioned in raised voices and, with hindsight, he suspected George might have had a go at insinuating himself into her favours. That was exactly the kind of thing that Penney would have taken exception to. The fight ended with Penney threatening George openly that if he dared to show himself around Oodnadatta again then Penney would see to it personally that it would be the last time.

'Sounds a bit much,' I said.

'It was. But Deakins obviously took it to heart. For the last decade of his life or more he hardly ever came into town. He was in shortwave contact with a couple of his old mates who'd tip him off whenever Smith was away and George would take the opportunity to sneak in and pick up supplies. I could be wrong but I don't think the two of them ever saw each other again.'

It was a good story but I had questions. 'If they were mortal enemies when George died, why did Penney agree to help when Kenny called from Sydney? Kenny reckons it was simply for the money but there must have been other people around who could have gone out to the farmstead and packed a crate of George's things.'

Jack shrugged. 'Maybe he felt guilty about George being banished for all that time. Maybe it was nostalgia for the years they'd been mates. Maybe he just wanted to make sure George really was gone. Who knows? But George wasn't the only one who'd known Smith since they were young: Kenny grew up here too, don't forget. Smith might simply have been doing Kenny a favour for old times' sake.'

'And when Kenny called again the other day – what upset Penney then?'

'Damned if I know but something did. He was in the bar two nights ago spouting off about ancient feuds and

family rifts. Kept going on about the out-of-towners stirring things up.'

I pricked up my ears. 'What out-of-towners?'

'The blokes who'd been through a few days before you
came along. I told you – he had a run-in with them too.'

This was getting really interesting but even more
confusing. 'Jack, I want you to tell me everything you can
about the out-of-towners and especially how they managed
to annoy Smith Penney so badly.'

'I wish I could help, mate. I didn't hear their convo in
the bar but it ended with another of those brawls that Smith
is so fond of. Well, not really a brawl – more of a scuffle.'

'How many of them were there?'

'Three. All burly blokes. When they first checked in, they
told me they were looking for the Deakins place and Smith
must have overheard them. They were sitting drinking
quietly in the bar later that night when he went over to
them. Like I say, I didn't hear what went on but it wasn't
much of a chat because Smith launched himself at the lead
one within about a minute and a half. The other two had
to haul him off and hold him down.'

'Did Penney tell you about it afterwards?'

'No details. All he said was that the blokes were digging
around in business that wasn't theirs and he wanted to
make damn sure they cleared off out of town.'

'That's exactly what he said to me.'

'Next morning they left and I haven't seen them since.'

I stood up, easing the cramp that was forming in my
legs, and began to pace the room.

'Which way did they leave town?'

'I dunno, mate. They'd gone before I started my shift.'

It was becoming ever more apparent that Smith Penney
could hold vital clues to the mystery of what had happened
to George. He might be able to shed light on the question
of the ownership of the farmstead and mine, too, but right

now I was more concerned with finding three burly out-of-towners who might very well have blood on their hands.

'Could you describe the three men if you had to?' I asked Jack.

'I guess so. Why?'

'Just write down what you can remember of them and keep it somewhere safe. It might be needed.'

I thought I could trust Jack but I didn't want to let anyone in on what I was thinking. It would be safer for him if he didn't know.

'Thanks for the warning about Smith Penney, Jack. And don't worry about me: I'll be gone tomorrow.'

After he left, I lay on the bed staring at the tin roof, trying to put the pieces together. Why did the arrival of three men in Oodnadatta cause Smith Penney such grief? And how did they fit with the story I'd just heard about Penney and George Deakins falling out all those years ago? If they had left town in the direction of Macumba Station, that strongly suggested they were heading for the Deakins farm and were therefore likely candidates for having turned the place over in their search for the metal canister we'd found. But it was a big 'if'. Jack didn't know which direction they'd gone and after our last encounter I didn't feel much like knocking on Smith Penney's door to ask if he had any idea. I badly wanted to get back to the farm but I was still stymied by the lack of provisions. It would have to wait until morning.

The more I thought about it, the more I couldn't escape the notion that the three men were also connected to the hit-and-run that had killed Dolly. That in turn set me thinking about Kenny's latest call to Smith Penney and why that might have triggered another eruption from Penney. What had Penney meant by the 'ancient feuds and family rifts' that Jack had described? I knew Sophie's mother Victoria had fled the farmstead at the earliest opportunity but had there been some kind of disagreement with George which had left a legacy down the years that still hadn't healed? And how did that affect Smith Penney?

It was all too much of a mess and it all seemed to come back to Sophie and her inheritance. What the hell had Uncle George done and why had he dumped it all at Sophie's door?

I grappled with that one well into the small hours but no answers came.

The owner of the town store was surprised to see her first customer waiting outside before she even arrived to unlock the door. In spite of my lack of sleep – or perhaps because of it – I'd been up early and had already paid a visit to the garage, which, fortunately for me, was manned by fellow early risers. I picked up the new spare tyre for the Land Rover and clamped it to the bonnet, and refilled the jerry cans with fuel. At the store, I tried banging on the door from a time that I deemed it reasonable for a shop to be open. I misjudged that by a good hour.

She seemed rather bewildered by my brisk circuit of the store, grabbing the things I wanted and planting them on her counter before thudding a wad of dollars down beside them. 'Someone's in a hurry,' she said as she packed the supplies into two large paper bags, American-style, and rang up the prices on her till. I wasn't in the mood for conversation so I grunted unsociably, picked up the bags and left.

As soon as I stepped off the storefront verandah, I saw him. Smith Penney stood across the street, a few yards from the Land Rover.

He had a rifle tucked under his arm.

My first thought was for the safety of the new tyre. It would be cruel indeed if the same delinquent who had sabotaged our previous spare was going to be responsible for the demolition of the new one.

But Penney didn't seem interested in the car. He fixed

his gaze on me as I strolled across in what I hoped was a nonchalant way.

'I thought I told you to get out,' he said in a low voice.

'Yes, I seem to recall that,' I said, looking up into steely blue eyes. 'But I don't remember you saying anything about not coming back.'

He hadn't expected a riposte and it threw him momentarily. As I walked past him to the Land Rover I said, 'I hope you haven't done anything else to my vehicle. The rental company aren't going to be impressed.'

I heard his footsteps behind me but before I could turn, a huge hand clamped down onto my right shoulder and he span me round like a child's toy. His voice this time was much louder.

'Don't piss me about, you lousy Pom.'

I had already clocked that the rifle wasn't cocked. The bolt was upright and pulled fully back and I could see there wasn't a bullet in the spout. It would only take a moment for him to slam the bolt forwards and load one but I wasn't going to give him a moment. I dropped the bag from my right hand and slammed my clenched fist into his belly.

Without waiting to collect the dropped provisions, I made a dash for the Land Rover. Because it was still early, and because most of its contents had been unloaded back at the farm, I'd left it unlocked so I heaved open the driver's door, threw the second paper bag across onto the passenger seat and jumped in. There had surely been enough time for Penney to recover his breath and his wits and follow me to the car, but as I fired up the engine there was no sign of him beside the vehicle.

I crashed her into gear and floored the accelerator pedal. When I looked in the rear-view mirror I could see why he hadn't bothered running after me. He was standing in the street, the rifle to his shoulder, aiming directly at the Land Rover.

I swerved recklessly to the left, missing an oil drum at the side of the road by a hair's breadth, and wrenched her into second gear. I pulled hard on the wheel and she lurched back to the other side of the street. I had lost sight of Penney in the mirror but I had no doubt he was still there.

My fears were confirmed when a metallic ping ricocheted off the roof of the Land Rover about a foot behind my right ear.

I swore and swerved again, then saw a side street peeling off to the left. I swung the wheel all the way round, hoping to God she wouldn't tip over with the sharpness of the bend, and ploughed round the corner.

Smith Penney really didn't want me around in Oodnadatta.

V

I played down the more thrilling aspects when I recounted my latest exploits to Sophie and Adam at the farmstead later that day. I figured Sophie didn't need any more stress adding to her already agitated state and there was nothing they could do about any of it anyway. Fortunately, neither of them noticed the bullet damage to the roof of the Land Rover: if they had, I'd have been forced to lie to them and I didn't want to add lying to the list of transgressions I'd perpetrated against them on this trip.

They were rather mystified as to why I'd only picked up half the items on the list of supplies but I dodged that one with an enigmatic half-truth: 'It's not like shopping at Fortnum and Mason, you know.'

I quizzed them on the previous night's radio call with Kenny but there was no real news. He'd told them he was still pursuing enquiries about the company, Hamilton and Irvine, but had so far drawn a blank. I hadn't honestly held out much hope for that particular blind alley but we didn't have much else to go on. I didn't tell Sophie but I knew that if Kenny hadn't come up with a fresh lead in the next few days, we'd be sunk. There would be nothing for it but to give up trying to find the truth about George and cut our losses. It might make three burly men very happy but it wouldn't be a satisfactory conclusion for Sophie. Or me.

The two of them had made a pretty decent job of tidying up, all things considered. They'd managed to shore up the house with a few well-placed boards, which would help keep the worst of the sand out, and the broom had clearly been put to good use. If we did end up staying a few days, I thought I might forgo my berth in the open air and risk the indoor creepy-crawlies instead.

After yet another tin-can supper, eaten on rickety chairs on the verandah, I went out to the radio where it was hitched up to the generator behind the house. As I waited for the second hand on my watch to tick round to the allotted call time, I stared out at the open savannah. Over to my left, the sun was sinking towards the horizon, casting an almost unbelievable pink hue over the sand. In the still of the evening, birds and other desert creatures were gearing up for a crepuscular sing-song. If I hadn't had so much on my mind I might almost have relaxed.

Kenny had news.

After some thorough research, for which he'd enlisted the services of Ruth and Carly, he had managed to trace Hamilton and Irvine. The address I'd given him seemed to have vanished from the maps several decades earlier, but the location still existed. Under a new street name, it was situated in a rather luxurious quarter of North Sydney, where the rate of construction of skyscrapers almost matched that of the Central Business District. With the Harbour Bridge connecting the two areas across the big blue divide, both had undergone rapid and aggressive growth in the last few years and both were home to the headquarters of a variety of multinational organisations in their shiny new offices.

I started to get itchy. What did all this have to do with Sophie and her inheritance?

'I'm coming to that, mate,' said Kenny, who was clearly enjoying the tease. 'You remember the document you were telling me about – the exchange of title?'

I told him I did.

'Well, the damnedest thing happened. I was talking to a lovely young lady on the telephone about it and she kindly went away and found Hamilton and Irvine's copy of it in their files. It seems there was a second page that's gone missing from your version.'

That didn't surprise me. The chances were high that George had lost it somewhere in the chaos of his house before he made the decision to hide what remained of it in the canister.

'What was on it?'

'Now you're asking. And I wish I could tell you.'

'Stop playing games, Kenny. What the hell was it?'

'All right, all right – keep your hair on. I can't tell you exactly what was on it because I haven't seen it. What I do know, from what the nice young lady was able to tell me, is that the exchange of title did relate to the farmstead and the mine.'

'And?'

'And they were exchanged for a worthless plot of land here in Sydney.'

I'd read in novels about people scratching their heads in confusion but never believed it happened in real life. Now, however, I scratched my head.

'All right, Kenny, you've got me. What does any of that mean for Sophie?'

'It means, my old friend, that instead of a disused opal mine and a ramshackle farmhouse in the bush, Sophie is now the proud owner of some prime real estate in North Sydney.'

'I thought you said it was worthless.'

'When the exchange of title was made, it was,' said Kenny.

It was starting to fall into place. One of George Deakins's forebears had swapped his opal mine for a meaningless chunk of land on the northern shores of Sydney harbour. When he made the deal, the company must have been rubbing their hands with glee at the prospect of untold riches buried in the red earth near Oodnadatta. But the Deakinses had had the last laugh: the mine had proved next to worthless, while that meaningless chunk of land was now situated bang in the middle of one of the fast-est-growing, wealthiest business districts in the southern hemisphere.

'Hell, mate – Hamilton and Irvine even went and built their own headquarters on it!'

The news was extraordinary and I had to get Kenny to repeat the details to make sure I understood it correctly.

'It was the bridge, Bill. The bridge changed everything. Before 1932, nobody took any notice of North Sydney. You had to travel miles to cross the Parramatta to get to it and the only people who were interested in it were the indigenous tribes who'd lived there for centuries. But after they built the bridge, it opened up a world of possi-bilities – residential and commercial. Well, you know where our house is so you know what a difference the bridge made.'

I thought back to Kenny's drive to work on the southern side of the harbour. It hadn't struck me before but it would have been all but impossible without the bridge.

'Suddenly the land there became a valuable asset and everyone was trying to stake a claim. Hamilton and Irvine happened to have a piece of paper that said one bit of it belonged to them.'

'Who are Hamilton and Irvine?' I asked. 'What do they do?'

'Bit of a mystery, that. They seem to be brokers of some kind but it's hard to pin down what exactly it is that they broker. Plenty of money sloshing about, though. I've driven past the HQ and it's one of the more impressive buildings on the plot.'

'And that piece of paper saying Hamilton and Irvine owned the land . . .'

'. . . was lying. They might have owned it at one point in history, long before the bridge came along, but by 1932 it was unquestionably in the possession of the Deakins family of South Australia.'

My mind boggled. If Kenny was right – and, more to the point, if we could demonstrate that he was right to a burden of proof acceptable by a court – then Sophie was an enormously wealthy Sydney freeholder.

'This is unbelievable,' I said.

'Pretty good, isn't it?'

'But you said a minute ago that you hadn't actually seen the second page of the exchange of title. Why not? Where is it?'

'Ah.' The exuberance vanished from Kenny's voice. 'There's a problem with that, I'm afraid.'

'What problem? You said you were talking to a nice young lady on the telephone.'

'And so I was. She was even willing to accommodate a visit from me to their offices to look it over in person. But when I called back today to arrange a time, I couldn't speak to the same young lady. Instead, I got an extremely frosty reception from an older woman who denied all knowledge of the conversation ever having taken place and refused even to discuss the existence of the exchange of title.'

'What – they shut you out?'

'Looks that way. I can't be sure what happened between the two phone calls but it seems as though someone got to the girl. The problem is—'

'Don't tell me, Kenny. I know all too well what the

problem is. Without that second page, Sophie can't prove anything.'

'What I don't understand is why George stayed out here, in the middle of the desert, when he knew the family no longer owned the mine. He could have gone to Sydney, waved the exchange of title under the noses of Hamilton and Irvine, and retired comfortably on the back rent they owed him for the past hundred years or so.'

Sophie's précis of the situation tallied pretty closely with my own.

'I asked Kenny the same question,' I said. 'He went all nostalgic on me and started reminiscing about growing up in Oodnadatta with George and Victoria. When I tried to get a straight answer, all he would say was that some people are not meant for the city. George, evidently, was one of those people.' I looked at Sophie. 'Fortunately, he didn't make the same presumption on behalf of his heirs.'

Adam didn't seem to be buying it. 'But all that money – who wouldn't want to get their hands on that?'

I thought of Leotta, the one-time lover of an extremely powerful man in the Caribbean. Aside from a cosy pied-à-terre by the sea which he provided, she had never sought the trappings of a wealthy lifestyle, even though they were freely available to her. Kenny was right: some people just preferred the simple life. Hell, my own little cottage on the Dart was hardly the lap of luxury and I was happy. I could have made considerably more money if I'd upped sticks and headed permanently for the smoke of London but that wasn't my style either. I was warming to Uncle George by the day.

'There's more to life than enormous piles of cash,' I said, and Sophie smiled.

'It looks like I'm never going to get the chance to prove that theory one way or the other. Not without that second sheet of paper.'

I drained the beer I was drinking and leaned back in my chair. I'd been trying to figure out a way to get hold of Hamilton and Irvine's copy of the exchange of title. It obviously existed since the young lady Kenny had spoken to first had gone away and found it in the company files. But getting our hands on it – especially with that line of enquiry subsequently being shut down – would be no easy matter. And there was another question I couldn't find the answer to: why, if the document proved they no longer owned the freehold on their site, had they kept it at all? It would have been the work of a minute to burn the papers and then it would only have been the word of a Deakins against the might of their corporation if it ever came to a dispute. All highly duplicitous, of course, but with so many millions of dollars potentially at stake it didn't seem completely implausible. It crossed my mind that there might be a copy of the title in a government land registry somewhere – I wasn't well up enough on the legalities in Australia – but I had a nasty suspicion that any papers as old as the Deakins exchange might have been thrown away long before now. Which just left the Hamilton and Irvine copy.

Another mystery to add to the pile.

'Kenny says he's going to do his best chasing the company but I wouldn't hold your breath. My guess is that the girl he spoke to originally had no idea that the exchange of title was a sensitive document so had no reason not to tell him about it. Someone higher up obviously got involved after that and now it's all under heavy wraps. If Kenny goes poking around asking awkward questions, I guess they might even destroy their copy.'

Sophie looked alarmed. 'But that would be illegal, wouldn't it?'

'Illegal, immoral, unconscionable – pick your adjective,' I said. 'I'm not trying to defend them but put yourself in their shoes. For a century or more they've been sitting on an opal mine that has delivered precious little, from what we can make out. Meanwhile, they've built their headquarters on a patch of land in the big city that must be worth a fortune by today's standards. Now some pesky Pom turns up making waves about an inheritance which, as far as she knows, includes that mine. A well-meaning Sydney lawyer hears of a connection to Hamilton and Irvine and innocently sticks his nose in. Now, nobody involved in the original transaction would still be alive but maybe some sharp-suited high-up at the company realises that they have suddenly become exposed to what could amount to a major liability. If you were in their position, would you be willing to stoop to a little convenient illegality to make the problem go away?'

'But it's not just a little illegality, Bill. If what you're saying is right and somebody at Hamilton and Irvine is out to cover up the whole business, then they've resorted to a lot more than that. They've committed murder.'

It was all getting too confusing. If George had been murdered, then someone knew about the exchange of title before Sophie was even aware she had an uncle. I imagined whoever it was thought they'd dealt with the problem once and for all by eliminating George. They certainly didn't expect his long-lost niece to turn up from England, claiming the Deakins inheritance. But when she did, she needed to be scared off – hence the threatening messages and the attack on Adam. And when it was clear that she wasn't about to be intimidated, then matters escalated horrifically with Dolly's death.

When I explained my thinking to Sophie, she let out a sigh.

'At least that means I wasn't responsible for one death.'

'Nor for the other,' I said, a note of insistence in my voice. 'You've got to stop thinking like that. This thing goes back a hundred years or more; you've only been on the scene for a few weeks. What they did to Dolly was not your fault. What will it take for you to believe that?'

Her head dropped. 'I don't know, Bill. It's all just so horrible. And now we can't even put it right and expose Hamilton and Irvine because we don't have the second page of George's copy of the exchange. Oh, why did he have to be so disorganised?'

Out of nowhere, a momentous thought struck me.

'Hold on, Sophie. Maybe he wasn't disorganised. Maybe he was the exact opposite of disorganised.'

I jumped out of my seat and started rummaging through pockets in the clothes I was wearing, then the jacket I'd discarded over the back of a chair.

'What are you talking about, Bill?'

I found what I was looking for and slammed it down on the table in front of Sophie and Adam.

'Open it up,' I said.

Adam reached forward and unfolded the hand-drawn map of the farmstead.

'Why are you showing us this again?' he asked.

'Think about it. Uncle George did a pretty good job of hiding the first page, didn't he?'

'We had to dismantle a tree to get to it so I'd say yes,' said Adam.

'So can you really see him being so careless that he'd actually lose the second page altogether? I don't think so. I think George knew exactly what he was doing. I think Uncle George deliberately separated the two sheets of paper from each other and hid them in two different locations.'

Something sparkled in Sophie's eyes as the possibility hit her. 'So where is it, Bill? Where's the second page?'

I dropped my finger onto one corner of the map, where George had drawn an arrow and left us another clue in plain sight.

The mine.

*   *   *

The map might have given us a clue to the location of the treasure we were seeking but it left us with precious little to go on in another crucial respect. George's arrow pointed to the north-east but beyond that bare information we had no idea where to find the Deakins opal mine.

I don't think any of us got much sleep that night but whether it was because of the heat or the anticipation I couldn't say. The desert temperatures could drop alarmingly overnight, even at the height of summer, but this was a particularly warm one and the stickiness was disorientating.

We were all awake early so we decided to start our search for the mine before the day got ridiculously hot. We had no idea how long we'd be searching so I stocked the Land Rover for a two-day trip: if we hadn't found it by the end of the first day, we'd turn round and come back to the farmstead to regroup. I loaded up the radio alongside the provisions, although the more remote our expedition, the less I thought we'd be able to reach Kenny.

The remnants of a dirt track ran off to the north-east from the back corner of the house. It wasn't significantly worse than the trail from Macumba Station so we stuck to where it drove a visible route through the brush and hoped for the best. We didn't talk much and Sophie spent a lot of the time staring out at the wilderness from the passenger seat beside me. Adam fiddled with the radio but I suspected it was more for something to do than because it needed any attention. I focused on dodging rocks and maintaining a steady speed.

Kenny had been worried that the mine might be hard to find. His warning had been spot-on about each stage of the journey, from Oodnadatta to Macumba to the Deakins farm, becoming more and more remote. Even he couldn't have foreseen the isolation of this place. I tried to put myself in the shoes of the early Coober Pedy settlers who'd first wandered out here, following seams of opal into the bush.

I found it hard to believe that even the prospect of enormous fields of the stuff could tempt anyone to endure this kind of purdah for years on end but then I was never one to be distracted by shiny objects.

'I know it's tiring but keep your eyes peeled,' I said after an hour on the unchanging trail.

'For what?' asked Sophie.

'I wish I knew. That's part of the problem. Anything that looks different, I suppose.'

Adam grunted in the back. 'Different? Different from never-ending piles of sand and scrub, you mean?'

'That's about it,' I said, and we lapsed back into silence.

Fifteen minutes later, Sophie shouted. 'There, Bill – those stones!'

I stopped the Land Rover and she pointed across to the left, where a pair of dunes created a natural valley that led away to the north. I squinted, trying to see what she had seen, but it took me a moment before I spotted it. At either side of the mouth of the confluence, a neat little array of carefully-spaced pale boulders had been arranged, almost like the lights of an airport runway. George was still guiding us from beyond the grave.

'Christ, that would have been easy to miss. Well spotted, Sophie.'

I turned the car off the track and headed for the valley. The sand was looser here and made heavier going for the tyres but I figured this was what she had been built for and pushed on relentlessly.

A few minutes further on, I was beginning to have my doubts that the boulders had been anything but accidentally positioned.

Adam agreed. 'This can't be it. It's going nowhere.'

Sophie shook her head. 'It was definitely an indicator. The mine is up here, I know it is.'

Five minutes after that, she was proved right. The dunes

came to a meeting point at the base of a rocky outcrop and twenty feet up the slope was a gaping black hole.

We'd found the entrance to George's mine.

What happened next was partly down to Sophie and Adam's inexperience but mostly down to my stupidity. Because we were so keen to see the interior of the mine, we failed to take the kit we were sure to need. As well as being ill-equipped we were hungry and thirsty, having driven without stopping from the farmstead – all contributing factors to our state of not being ready to go underground.

Sophie scrambled up the rock face first and I should have known from the way her boots slipped in the loose sand that we needed better equipment. But I wasn't far behind her and Adam was hard on my heels. When she reached the opening, she stopped and stood still, staring into the abyss like the first explorer discovering a new continent. By the time Adam caught up with us, we must have looked like the Marx Brothers, black silhouettes transfixed comically against a golden sky.

I went in first and ten minutes later we were in deep trouble.

PART THREE: RED

I

The first thing I had to do was rustle up some kind of splint for Adam's busted ankle. At the bottom of a twelve-foot shaft, with a sprained wrist of my own, that was going to be tricky. I forced my foggy brain to function but the problem with that was that it immediately opened up a whole vista of other difficulties: even if I could patch Adam up enough to move him, what then? Sophie was capable at the wheel of the Land Rover but it was down at the bottom of a rock face it couldn't climb and I couldn't see what use it was in any case. We had no ladder, there was no way Sophie could haul us up from the shaft, and neither Adam nor I was in any fit state to start hammering holes into the walls to crawl our way to safety.

I slumped back against the side wall and stared blankly at the red earth opposite me. Adam was still talking to Sophie, high above us in the unstable entrance to the mine, but it was about his injuries rather than how to extricate ourselves from this cul de sac. As I stared, a large black millipede entered the torch's circle of light and slithered lithely down the shaft wall to where the tunnel disappeared into the mine. I shivered and sat up, distancing myself from the wall.

I looked at the tunnel mouth again, uneven and crumbling where presumably George and his ancestors had shuffled through to gain access to the mine itself. Could this really be the main entrance to the site? And if so, how had they managed to extract the opals they dug out of the ground? My heart lurched optimistically and I shone the torch up to the top of the shaft, wondering if I might see a hook driven into the roof as part of some kind of pulley system for winching up buckets of gemstones. As a means of escape, that could offer distinct possibilities.

There was nothing in the roof of the cave but blackness.

The conversation between Sophie and Adam lulled and I took the opportunity to shout up to her.

'Sophie, I need to fix Adam's ankle. Is there anything up there I could use for a splint?'

'I'll find something,' she said, and I heard the shingle crunch underfoot as she left the cavern.

She was back inside five minutes, calling down that the rope was on its way back down to us. I remembered not to look up this time as the cargo came over the edge of the shaft but I felt chunks of gravel and earth fall around me. I pointed the torch upwards and saw a large bundle, neatly packaged in a piece of material, being gently lowered. I stood and reached up to receive it, slackening the rope and shouting to Sophie that she could pull it back up.

Inside the bundle she'd prepared a miniature survival kit. Sticking out at either end of the material was a metal spike that I recognised as part of the Land Rover's grille. I wasn't bothered about the damage to the rented vehicle but two things troubled me about that: first, she'd obviously wrenched it somehow from the car and could have done herself an injury; second, and more worryingly, she'd made the journey down the rock face alone – and back up it again.

'Sophie, you really can't go putting yourself in danger, you know.'

'Oh come on, Bill. I'm a big girl and we've already faced a lot of dangers.'

'That's not what I mean. My motives are purely selfish. I'm not saying you can't handle it but if anything happens to you while we're stuck down here, then we're all dead.'

My bluntness struck home. It was intended to.

Along with the spike, Sophie had included disinfectant, cotton wool and a roll of lint bandage from the first-aid kit to create a makeshift splint for Adam. There was also a flask of water and a walkie-talkie. At least somebody was thinking straight.

I used some of the water to clean what I could of Adam's ankle. The rest we shared between us. Then I lined up the spike with the outside of his leg and bound it as tightly as I could with the bandage. The elasticity of the gauze meant there was no danger of cutting off the blood supply to his foot but equally I wanted it to remain as firm as possible. I had no idea what it might have to go through before we could get him to a medic.

All the while, Adam and Sophie kept up an inane chatter on the walkie-talkie. I tried to zone out of their conversation, laced as it was with lovey-dovey trivialities, and stay focused on the matter in hand. No matter which way I looked at it, I could think of no means of getting either me or Adam to the top of that shaft. That left only one possibility.

I interrupted the walkie-talkie love-in and took the handset from Adam.

'Sophie, there's a tunnel here that leads down further into the mine. I'm going exploring.'

She sounded worried. 'Take care, Bill. You don't know what's down there. Without any maintenance it might have all collapsed. Please don't take any chances.'

'I'll do my best – but I don't see that we have any choice. I'm hoping whatever's down there might give me a clue as to how we can get out again. They must have extracted the opals somehow.'

I thrust the walkie-talkie into a pocket and dropped to my knees, bending further to peer into the tunnel. The torch revealed the same narrow opening as before, widening into a larger space that fell away into darkness. Pushing the torch in front of me, I slid onto my belly and began crawling through the hole, arms stretched ahead. As I'd anticipated, it was tight. I pulled my shoulders inwards, only finding that it made it harder to ease myself along, and I swore as I caught my head more than once on the roof of the tunnel. Fortunately, the narrow bit was only short and my feet were still sticking out in the shaft behind me when my arms cleared the burrow and I could spread them wide for the purchase I needed to haul myself through.

When I stood up, there was a good foot of clearance above me and the light of the torch revealed something much more elaborate than I'd imagined. Although it reminded me of photographs and footage I'd seen of the coal industry back in England, where black-smeared miners toiled underground for hours on end in conditions that made most other hard labour look like a walk in the park, the tunnel stretching out before me was taller, wider and better constructed than I'd have thought possible, given its position in this remote corner of nowhere. Hewn into the earth, which still looked reddish-brown in the light from the torch, it seemed to be carefully engineered and well supported by regular struts and crossbeams of sturdy wood. I patted the wall nearest me to test its solidarity and was pleasantly surprised. My admiration for the opal miners – already at a level approaching wonder – rose another notch or two.

I pressed the button on the walkie-talkie and described to Sophie what I was looking at.

'That's great, Bill, but I don't see how it helps us.'

I didn't either but finally I had a brainwave. Staring hard down the centre of the tunnel, I snapped the torch off and waited. It took a couple of minutes for my eyes to adjust to the total blackness. As I stood hoping that no creatures had made the tunnel their home in the absence of human activity, I nodded triumphantly to myself as I realised that the blackness wasn't as total as I'd first thought.

Way down in the belly of the mine, a sliver of light was becoming visible.

The harder I stared, the more it revealed itself. Without a doubt there was light down there. And unless some renegade troglodyte from the Coober Pedy caves had made a new home out here and was warming himself by a fire, then the light could mean only one thing: somewhere in the network of tunnels stretching out before me there was another shaft.

Sophie was uncertain when I relayed the news over the walkie-talkie. 'Could there be some other source of light down there?' she asked.

'Not a chance,' I replied. 'There's no way any light could get into these tunnels unless there was a hole from ground level. There has to be another opening somewhere up on the roof of the mine. The only question is how to get up there and find it.'

'What do you propose?'

I broke the connection on the walkie-talkie and thought. The logical thing to do would be to send Sophie up onto the top of the hill to scout around and see if she could find another entrance but that option was fraught with danger. From what Kenny had told me, I knew many of these old mines had been abandoned to the elements, with disused shafts covered up by time and dirt, leaving a seemingly innocuous sheet of sand hiding a Swiss cheese of lethal holes. I ruled that out as too risky, for the same reason I didn't want her scampering all over the rock face. I'd have liked to get out on top myself but the Adam predicament – and a twelve-foot sheer drop I couldn't scale – made that impossible. The more I thought about it, heading deeper into the mine seemed the only choice. If I could find the source of the light, then we'd know for sure that there was another way out of this place.

It took Sophie to spot the flaw. She said, 'Even if you find another shaft, how does that help? I still won't know where you are from above.'

I thought some more and came up with a plan: it was a pretty weak one but it was the best we had.

Killing time in a dark, confined space is hardly my idea of an evening's entertainment but there was little else we could do. As we waited for nightfall, I conserved the battery in both the torch and the walkie-talkie. I'd crawled back through the tunnel to Adam and he and I were forced to make small talk, leaving Sophie to her own devices. I tried to warn her to be extra careful around the mouth of the mine and to watch out for any nasties that might be lurking in the vicinity. She gave me another deserved mouthful about being perfectly capable of looking after herself.

I did invoke strict instructions when it came to the Land Rover. I told Sophie to back it up the valley to a point where she was sure she could drive it up onto one of the spurs of sand without any danger then take it as near to the rock face as she could. I was hoping she'd be able to position it on solid ground without having to risk driving it fully onto the roof of the mine but we wouldn't know for sure if that would be possible until we found the new shaft and worked out its position in relation to hers. I didn't want her taking a heavy vehicle into unstable territory unless there really was no other option: I had a hunch the Land Rover would survive if one of those invisible shafts were to give way under a wheel but I'd prefer not to take the chance of it getting irretrievably stuck if it was at all avoidable.

Half an hour before sunset, I started down the tunnel once more. As before, I crawled through the narrow opening, easing my shoulders through and pulling the rest of my dusty body after them. I brushed myself down as I stood up, chuckling ironically at the futility of the action, then peered into the blackness once more. It took a few moments and the glimmer of light was fainter than before but I could definitely make it out down a branch tunnel in front of me.

'We haven't got much time,' I said into the walkie-talkie, wondering if I'd misjudged how quickly the sun would plummet from the Australian summer sky, potentially leaving me in the pitch dark with nowhere to aim for. I fixed my eyes on the glimmer and moved as fast as I could. My boots skittered through loose stones and stumbled over jutting-out rocks but I never dropped my eyes to the floor. As the tunnel twisted and turned through the underground maze, I kept completely focused on the light, trying to decide if it was getting brighter because I was getting nearer, or paler because the daylight outside was disappearing fast. I also made a vague effort to count my steps. I had long since given up hope of trying to tell which direction I was heading – although the fact that I had observed the light in a straight line from the opening was promising. But at least I might be able to give Sophie some idea of how far across the roof of the mine she'd have to travel in search of the shaft.

I kept up a constant dialogue with her over the walkie-talkie. I pictured her somewhere above my head, staring out into the dying light and waiting for a sign from me, and I wondered if she was regretting this whole escapade. I knew I was.

And then, suddenly, I was there. Ten feet in front of me,

like a column of silver dropping from the heavens, the light from the sky outside beamed down in a neat configuration onto the floor of the mine.

'I've found it,' I shouted into the handset, eliciting a pained squeal in response.

'That's great, Bill. Can we celebrate without me losing my hearing, though?'

'Sorry, Sophie.' I was more relieved than I cared to let on but there was still plenty of work to be done. First, I turned back the way I had come and shouted up the tunnel.

'Can you hear me, Adam? I've found the other shaft.'

Adam's voice came drifting through the mine, more distant than I'd have liked: I must have come further than I thought.

'Has Sophie found it up top?'

'Not yet. I wanted to make sure I could still get back to you. Put on your torch, will you?'

I'd left Adam incapacitated on the far side of the narrow entrance to the cavern and I hoped to God that the burrow's dimensions wouldn't prevent the light from his torch being visible from where I stood now. A yellow glow blinked but it wasn't quite where I expected it to be and I realised the tunnel I'd followed had disorientated me. At least I could see it.

'Great. Push it as far into the hole as you can reach and leave it on for me. I'll be back to get you in a bit.'

I put my head into the fading shaft of silver light and looked up. The sky still seemed unbelievably bright outside and I blinked a few times to acclimatise my eyes. I began to wonder if my limited plan was going to work at all: would Sophie be able to see the torch beam when the sun was still so bright? We might have to wait even longer for the night to fall properly. I shuddered at the thought and flicked the switch on the torch.

'I can see you, I can see you!' Sophie yelled, and it was my turn to recoil from the walkie-talkie.

I felt a twisting in my gut but I didn't know if it was relief or apprehension.

'How far away is it from you?' I asked.

'Hard to say – maybe a hundred yards.'

'Damn.'

'What? That's a good thing, isn't it? You could have gone half a mile into that mine and then we'd really be in trouble. At least this is reachable.'

'Not with the Land Rover's winch cable, it's not.' I hadn't actually measured the cable on our hire vehicle but I couldn't imagine it would be longer than a hundred feet and the shaft itself was going to need a decent chunk of that, especially if we were going to fashion some kind of sling.

'Sorry, Sophie, but you're going to have to bring the Land Rover closer to the hole.'

'No problem,' she said chirpily.

She was less chirpy when I explained the dangers.

I told Adam to kill his torch while we waited – there was no point in using up the batteries unnecessarily – and I shut mine down too while Sophie manoeuvred the Land Rover. It was getting noticeably darker and I thought I could make out the headlights of the car flickering across the top of the hole above me. I could hear the engine roaring as she nudged her way nearer and found I was holding my breath when she came back on the walkie-talkie.

'OK, I'm about twenty feet from the hole. I can see it really clearly now.'

'How does the rim look to you?'

'Hold on – I'll have a look.'

'Be careful, for God's sake! Don't go walking about up there. If you need to get closer, shuffle over to it on your belly to spread the load.'

'I'll choose to ignore any implications about my weight,' she said, and I could hear a smile in her voice. Thirty seconds later, her head appeared over the edge of the hole, a good forty feet above me.

'Good evening, Mr Kemp,' she said nonchalantly, as if she'd spent her whole life tramping across deserts and rescuing injured husbands.

I laughed with relief.

The business of getting everything in position took much longer than I'd expected. Sophie unwound the winch to its full extent and dropped the cable down through the hole, letting it play out slowly so as not to damage the rim and bring the whole thing crumbling down on top of me. Only when I had the heavy steel hook safely on the floor, with a few feet of slack to spare, did I tell her to stand down and await further instructions.

The trickiest job was getting Adam from his position at the bottom of the shaft where he'd come a cropper to the spot where we stood at least a chance of getting him out. He was significantly larger than me in all directions and even I had found it difficult to squeeze through the low tunnel into the cavern. I contemplated trying to dig out the passage to make more room but I realised that if that had been a sensible thing to do, then Uncle George or his ancestors would have done it years ago. There must be a reason why they'd left it so tight and I wasn't about to question their mining expertise. Instead, I stayed on the mine side of the passage and dragged him by the arms unceremoniously as he writhed and shouted in pain.

At the mouth of the hole, his splinted foot caught on the side of the passage and he only just managed to haul himself clear before the sand gave way and a wall of dirt crashed down, obliterating the opening.

Even if we'd wanted it, there was no way back.

Adam dusted off the worst of the debris and got to his feet, resting fully on his right foot and leaning on me to keep the weight off his injured left. He threw his arm round my shoulders and together we hobbled towards the torch I'd left at the foot of the new shaft. I could feel him tensing at every step and he let out little grunts each time he edged forwards. I was glad I couldn't see the grimace that I knew would be distorting his face.

When we reached the shaft, I lowered him to the ground as gently as I could and peered up the hole.

'Sophie!' I shouted, and waited for her to appear.

Her voice was anxious. 'Have you got him? Is he all right?'

'See for yourself,' I said, and moved aside so that Adam could lean into the gap and see Sophie.

'Oh, thank God!' she said. 'How's your ankle?'

'Well, being dragged through a disused mine probably hasn't helped but I'll live.'

'All right, that's enough chit-chat,' I said, and resumed my position at the base of the column of light from the Land Rover's headlamps. The sky beyond was a deep shade of indigo and Sophie's face was harshly lit from one side.

'What do you need me to do?' she asked.

'You'll have to go back to the Land Rover to operate the winch – but take care going to and fro. The less you go tramping about up there, the happier I'll be. Give me a few minutes to get Adam shackled up to the hook and when I say, wind it up. If I can make a decent sling somehow, he should have a nice ride to the top.'

'And then?'

'Use the winch to drag him all the way back to the Land Rover. Then you can unwrap him and send the hook back down for me.'

'It'll mean crossing over to the hole again with the hook.'

I wasn't wild about that but it couldn't be helped. 'Just be careful.'

I used a blanket that Sophie dropped down the shaft to
encase Adam as best I could, given my painful wrist. I left
his arms free to stop himself hitting the sides of the shaft.
Then I looped the steel wire twice around the mummified
package and clipped it back onto itself higher up, using the
cable as part of the cradle to bear his weight. It was a real
Heath Robinson affair and I knew it would bite like hell as
the winch tightened but I couldn't help that: the blanket
was not strong enough to support him on its own and if
I'd clipped it onto the hook it would simply have ripped
apart as it went up.

I switched on the walkie-talkie and raised Sophie at the
other end. We'd need them to hear each other above the
noise of the winch.

'All right, let's give it a go. Take it gently to start with
and we'll see what happens.'

I heard the winch fire up and watched as it started to
take up the slack in the cable. When it became taut and
Adam's body began to shift in the dirt, I caught his eye.

'Have a nice trip,' I said.

He smiled grimly and held the cable with both hands
above his head. As the human parcel climbed into the shaft,
he let go with one hand and used it to keep himself away
from the side, with only moderate success. He was about
ten feet up the shaft when he shouted.

'Cut the winch,' I yelled into my walkie-talkie and a
moment later the sound died and Adam lurched to a halt.
'What is it?'

'I – I'm not sure,' he said, his body starting to spin where
he hung. 'If I can just get round to it again—'

I directed my torch straight at him and he shielded his
face with his free hand.

'Don't point that thing at me – shine it on the wall. Over
there.'

I followed where he indicated. There was a dark mark

on the wall of the shaft which I hadn't noticed before. I peered harder but couldn't make it out.

'What is it?'

'Give me a second,' he said, and pushed off from the wall to reach the mark opposite. 'There's something here.'

He put out his hand and I saw it disappear into the wall of the shaft. The mark had been a hole. He rummaged and dug about for a moment, evidently trying to free something from the surrounding earth.

When he drew his hand clear again, a canister gleamed in the torchlight.

'I think I've found it,' he shouted triumphantly. 'It's just the same as the one we pulled from the tree.'

Uncle George was nothing if not thorough, I thought. By sheer chance, we had stumbled on the missing piece of the jigsaw. I didn't understand why he'd chosen to hide it halfway up a shaft in a concealed slot that was almost impossible to find but right now I didn't care. If this was George's buried treasure then we'd found the spot marked X.

We didn't get the chance to celebrate. As I looked up at Adam waving the canister victoriously, loose lumps of dirt and sand began to drop on my head from the hole he'd just enlarged. Even as I watched, a bigger chunk came away from the edge and rained down on me, followed by some pieces from higher up on the other side. It appeared that Adam had destabilised the entire shaft.

'Sophie, take the winch up – now!' I shouted into the walkie-talkie. 'The hole is about to collapse!'

There was no time to consider my position. With the main entrance wiped out, this was the only means of escape and if the shaft came crashing down, I was a dead man under several tons of earth. Adam, dangling from the Land Rover's winch hook ten feet above my head, was my only chance.

I scrabbled to the top of the small pile of sand that marked where earth had fallen from the shaft and launched myself into the air. I knew if I grabbed the wrapped package I was likely simply to tear the blanket apart and we'd both go headlong into the debris below. Somehow, I had to reach the cable itself. I kicked off against the wall of the shaft first with my left foot, then on the opposite side with my right, and suddenly I was high enough to grasp the hook where it was clamped round the wire.

In the heat of the moment, I completely forgot about my injured wrist and the shock of pain that shot up my arm almost made me let go. But my other hand gripped tighter and, as I swung forcibly into Adam's body and he tried to steady me with his freed arms, the hook miraculously held.

Sophie had already snapped the winch into a faster gear and we moved quickly up as the shaft fell apart around us. I buried my head in the material of the blanket, closed my mouth against the suffocating dust, and hoped to God that the opening at the top would hold together until we got there.

And then suddenly we were outside and being dragged across the roof of the mine towards the Land Rover, clinging desperately to one another and gulping in lungfuls of fresh air.

Sophie stopped the winch and immediately began untangling Adam from the cable. I lay inert, contemplating the close call we'd just survived. I stared up at the darkening sky through the beams of the car's headlamps and tried to pull my thoughts into shape. One of them bubbled to the surface.

'Damn – I dropped the walkie-talkie down there.'

Sophie sounded irritated. 'Never mind the walkie-talkie. You could both have been killed.'

I didn't want to think about how close we'd come to that eventuality. I forced myself to focus on the here and now and another alarming thought bubbled up.

'Adam – the canister! Please don't tell me you dropped that.'

I looked over to where he'd rolled himself free of the mummy wrappings, sitting up in the full glare of the head-lamps.

From the folds of the blanket he pulled the canister.

Between us, and despite my injury, Sophie and I managed to get Adam into the back of the Land Rover. Hobbling as he had done underground, he was able to lend his body weight to our endeavours and clambered in awkwardly, both hands still clutching the canister.

'You drive,' I said to Sophie.

'Why?'

I held up my wrist. 'Well there's this, for starters, but you also got the Land Rover up here safely so you're prob-ably best qualified to take it back down again. Whatever you did on the way up, do it again now.'

'I'm not making any promises,' she said guardedly, climbing into the driver's seat. 'Things have changed.'

'What things?'

'We've now got added weight thanks to the two of you, plus who knows what you've done to the surface of the mine's roof with that shaft demolition back there. The whole thing could be completely unstable for all we know.'

'Then you'd better steer clear of where we've just been and get back to where we were as fast as possible,' I said.

She gave me a look which I didn't attempt to interpret and slammed the Land Rover into reverse.

I didn't dare watch as Sophie accelerated towards the edge of the plateau. Instead, I stared straight ahead, seeing the ground where we'd just been parked fall away inexo-rably as the mine caved in. The vibrations of the Land Rover must have been adding to the natural collapse of the shaft and tunnels and I urged Sophie to push the car more to stay ahead of the disintegrating ground.

'I'm going as fast as I can,' she shouted back, then yanked the steering wheel with her left hand. Adam yelled in agony as he was thrown across the back seat and the Land Rover lurched heartstoppingly through 180 degrees, Sophie stamping on the brake at the same time. We were now facing the edge of the raised ground, perilously close to the lip, but Sophie had seen the danger encroaching from behind. She crashed into first gear, opened up the throttle and launched us over the side.

I still have no idea how she kept control of the bucking vehicle as we plummeted down the slope. Incredibly, we avoided any boulders during our descent but we hit the level ground at speed and the front wing of the bodywork took a beating. Sophie held us steady as we flattened out and then eased off the pedal. By the time we regained the trail, we were doing an even fifteen miles an hour and all three of us breathed deeply, any conversation knocked out of us.

As we cleared the entrance to the valley that had initially pointed us to the mine with its array of white rocks, the first gobs of rain splashed onto the windscreen. The drops were huge and loud and sounded more like hail as they bounced off the roof and windows. Beyond the protection of the car, the red sand all around us sent up miniature explosions of dust. Barely two minutes later, we were driving through a giant pond.

'Where the bloody hell has that come from?' asked Adam.

'I don't know,' said Sophie, raising her voice above the noise and peering anxiously through the windscreen where the wipers were having no impact on the torrent of water. 'But I don't like it. I can hardly see the front of the car and it feels like we could slip off the track in a wave of mud at any moment – not to mention the rocks.'

The combination of the teeming rain and the rapidly falling night presented us with a new problem. While I knew that impromptu storms like this were not too unusual, even at the height of a desert summer, I hadn't expected it to happen so fast. Ruby had mentioned the possibility of flash floods but on the other side of the argument was the fact that Australia's colossal interior waterhole, Lake Eyre, had been dry for the best part of a decade. There was nothing to suggest that the drought this year was going to be any different from the last few seasons so we had made only the scantest of preparations for the possibility of rain.

And yet here it was.

Sophie had slowed to a crawl as she negotiated the track ahead but it was growing more invisible by the minute and we were still some distance from the farmstead.

'I think you're going to have to push it a bit more than this,' I said.

'I'm just worried about losing the road and missing the farm.'

I turned round and fished in one of the bags on the back seat, pulling out a compass. 'It shouldn't be too much of a risk. As long as we keep heading south-west, the opposite of the direction we set off in this morning, we should end up back where we started. The bigger risk is not seeing the farm at all through this rain. I'd hate to find ourselves rolling up at Macumba Station unannounced.'

While Sophie maintained a steady speed I did a quick mental calculation. I had a rough idea of the distance from George's place to the mine and, offsetting that against the relative speed of travel of the outward and return journeys, came up with a figure.

'Look, it took us about two-and-a-half hours to get to the mine this morning. Allowing for this weather and our slower speed, if we keep it pretty constant, my guess is that it should take us another three hours or so to reach the farmstead.'

I looked keenly at Sophie. 'Do you think you can maintain this for three more hours?'

'I'm not sure I can,' came a mournful voice from the back. 'My ankle is killing me.'

I considered, then rejected, the idea of using the radio – who was there to call for help, after all? In the event my calculations proved to be pretty accurate and, thanks in large part to Sophie's careful handling of the Land Rover in the pelting rain, we hit the farm almost exactly three hours later. She looked utterly exhausted, her eyes rimmed red with dust and tiredness, but she'd got us back to safety. Adam had fallen into a restless sleep, moaning and turning himself over and over to try and get comfortable – a forlorn hope on the bumpy, slippery track. I had been on lookout duty and my eyes felt as raw and gritty as Sophie's appeared to be.

The storm had not let up for a minute and I wondered what state the house would be in, with its tumbledown walls and gaping holes. My fears were justified: large parts of the floor were soaking wet and the rain was streaming down many of the walls in constant rivulets. In a corner of the living room, a metal bucket stood where Uncle George had presumably rested it during a previous storm, perfectly positioned to catch the drips from a hole in the roof directly above it. It was overflowing.

Parts of the building were dry enough for us to settle in for the night. Sophie bedded Adam down on the settee, which had escaped the damp, while I scraped together a basic meal that would keep us going for now. We were in an emergency so any frills or fanciness were out of the window until we could gather our resources properly in the morning and reassess the situation. I reckoned the house was high enough above ground level not to have to worry about flooding – at least if the rain continued at this rate overnight – but we might have to think again if it was still pouring when daylight came.

I took two plates of cold tinned meat over to where Sophie was sitting on the floor beside Adam but she shook her head as I approached and got to her feet.

'He's asleep,' she whispered, and indicated for me to move away. 'I think we should leave him. I've given him some painkillers so hopefully he'll be able to rest a little and I think that's probably more important for him than food right now.'

I agreed. There was no way of knowing when the next opportunity for rest would come and if Adam was able to find some respite under this hammering rain, then good luck to him. I feared Sophie and I would not be so lucky.

'You look exhausted,' I told her as I handed her one of the plates.

'Thanks. I am. That drive really took it out of me.'

We sat on blankets near the front door and tucked into our unappetising platefuls. It was a few minutes before either of us spoke.

'Bill, I've been wondering about something.'

'Fire away.'

She put her plate down on the floor and turned back to face me. 'What are you doing?'

'What do you mean?'

'I mean, what are you doing out here in the middle of nowhere, taking your life in your hands, with some armed goons probably hot on your tail, to help a couple of newly-weds you barely even know.'

I smiled and put my plate down too. 'I've asked myself the same question once or twice in the last few days.'

'And?'

'And it's not so hard to understand. Besides the fact that I've grown to like you, there's more to this than just your future, you know. Kenny and I go back a long way and I can't just walk away after what happened to Dolly. He'd do the same for me if the situation were reversed. I've got a personal interest in seeing this thing through, and if it makes you a wealthy woman in the process, than that's not such a bad by-product, I'd say.'

Sophie frowned. 'Nothing to do with being an adrenaline junkie, then?'

I studied her face intently. How had she managed to get my number so fast?

'I have been called adventurous in my time,' I admitted. 'And a thrill-seeker. And even headstrong. But I have to say, this little jaunt of yours is really pushing the limits. There were a couple of moments back there in the mine when I found myself wishing I'd stayed at home.'

She threw out a corner of her blanket and lay full-stretch on it, her head resting on one arm. 'I don't believe that for a moment,' she said, and closed her eyes.

I was wrong about our not being able to sleep. Within minutes, Sophie was well away on her blanket and I followed soon afterwards. Not even the vagaries of this capricious climate could keep me from the welcoming arms of Morpheus.

II

I awoke from heavy slumber with the disconcerting sense that someone had been moving around near me; when I looked over at Sophie and Adam, they were both still sound asleep.

I desperately wanted to know what time it was but my smashed watch was giving nothing away. As I stared in vain at it, I realised it was adding to the throbbing from my sprained wrist so I undid the clasp and slipped it carefully off my arm. I thought I could probably get it seen to back in England – it didn't look too badly beaten up – but for now it was useless to me. It had been an anniversary gift from my first wife and there was no way I was going to leave it in the outback so I reached over to my rucksack and stashed it inside a pair of thick socks.

I lay in silence for a few minutes, trying to work out what to do next. It dawned on me that the rain had stopped and there was an oddly refreshing breeze blowing through the house, although it was already hot. I squinted at the holes in the walls, trying to make out where the sun was in the sky, and quickly came to the conclusion that it must already be well into the morning. With no mine left to explore and precious little here at the farmstead to stick around for, I wanted to get moving as soon as we could. But I also wanted to leave Sophie and Adam to rest as long as they were able.

I picked up the canister from the floor by the settee, where Adam had let it fall when he went to sleep. By rights this belonged to Sophie but I didn't think she'd object to me taking a peek at the treasure it might hold – if I could get it open. The last one had proved quite a challenge and I didn't want to start attacking it with a hacksaw while the other two were still asleep. Luckily, this one proved to be much less objectionable and one end screwed off with surprising ease. I wondered how long it had been hidden in that mine shaft.

It didn't matter. What tumbled out of the tube and onto the floor of Uncle George's shack was dynamite. As we had guessed – but I, for one, had hardly dared hope – the canister contained a single sheet of paper embossed with the names Hamilton and Irvine, outlining the other half of an exchange deal that had taken place decades earlier. I didn't need legal training to know that this was the missing link in Sophie's inheritance. This was the vital piece that would allow Kenny to complete the probate jigsaw and establish Sophie as the true owner of that prime real estate in North Sydney. For her, this sheet of paper was the key to untold wealth.

It was also a screaming alarm bell.

If I'd been right about someone high up at Hamilton and Irvine wanting this story buried for good, then this was likely to be the only copy left in existence of the exchange of title. It was what the three thugs had been searching for when they crashed through Oodnadatta, ruffling feathers, before heading out here to turn the place over in their hunt for it. It was looking increasingly likely that it was also the cause of Uncle George's death and quite probably Dolly's too.

It was surely only a matter of time before they came looking for Sophie again.

I shook Sophie and Adam awake, urging them to get up so we could get out fast. Sophie seemed especially groggy but Adam was awake surprisingly quickly, looking at me enquiringly.

'What's happened, Bill?' he asked. 'Why the rush all of a sudden?'

I waved the second page of the document at them and Sophie woke up faster then.

'Is it what we thought it was?' she asked.

I nodded. 'And that means we could be sitting ducks in here. Right now we have the advantage that they don't know we've found it but with Kenny digging around in Sydney they may realise we're still on the hunt. If they think we have any chance at all of finding it, they'll be back. We need to move now and keep out of sight until we can get back to Coober Pedy at least. If we can make it back to Sydney undetected, I'll be even happier. Grab something to eat and pack up your things while I go and get the Land Rover ready.'

As I stepped out of the front door onto the verandah, I could hardly believe what I saw. All around the compound was a sea of mud, washed into an endless red wasteland by last night's lashing storm. Sophie had driven up not too far from the door so we wouldn't get completely soaked as we disembarked but even the fifteen yards to the Landy was like the Battle of the Somme. Our footsteps had been churned out of all recognition by the rain and the car stood forlornly in a thick, greasy puddle of slush.

But the desolation of the landscape was the last thing on my mind when my eyes fell on the Land Rover. Even with its wheels sunk inches-deep in the mud, I could see that all four of its tyres had been slashed.

Shouting at Adam and Sophie to stay where they were and keep down, I turned on my heel and ran back inside. I didn't waste any time trying to scope out whether we were surrounded or if there was anyone around outside waiting to do us harm. Instead, I went straight out of the back door with one thought in my mind: have they nobbled the generator? If someone had put the Land Rover out of action, it would make sense that they would want to do the same to the genny and then we'd really be in trouble.

A moment's appraisal confirmed that that was exactly what had happened. Parts of the generator had been systematically dismantled and removed – it would have been too noisy simply to smash it – leaving the shell of a machine that would be no good without the skills of a mechanic and a stack of spare parts.

I hurried back inside to find Sophie and Adam on the floor of the living room, shielded from the front door by the settee.

'What the hell's going on?' demanded Adam.

'They're back,' I said shortly. 'The people who killed Uncle George and probably Dolly too – I think they've found us.'

Sophie looked horrified. 'But that can't be right, Bill. If they wanted to kill us, why didn't they just do what they did to George? Out here in the middle of nowhere, who would know, and who would care? If they wanted us dead, why haven't they done it?'

'I don't know, Sophie, but I don't really want to stick around to ask them. They've slashed the tyres on the Land Rover and taken the generator apart so we're completely marooned.'

'Maybe that's how they intend to do it,' said Adam quietly. 'Leave us out in the middle of nowhere to die naturally.'

'Of course,' said Sophie, a light bulb going on in her brain.

'What is it?' I asked.

'Listen – George's death could be explained away by suicide.'

'As indeed it was,' I said.

'But they couldn't get away with that for the three of us so they've had to find another way. Stranded in the desert on a wild goose chase – it would be the perfect cover. They don't need to do anything else: they're expecting us to die all by ourselves.'

That part of Sophie's theory made sense. What didn't was the notion that they should want us dead in the first place. Without the vital piece of evidence we'd recovered from the mine, Sophie's inheritance claim was all hot air. I couldn't believe they would resort to triple murder on the off-chance that a court might somehow still find in her favour. No, by rights they should have called off the manhunt and let everything go quiet, knowing there was nothing Sophie could do.

The second page of the exchange of title changed all that. But the mysterious figure pulling the strings at Hamilton and Irvine didn't know that we'd found it.

'What are we going to do, Bill?' Sophie's anxious voice cut across my mental contortions and dumped me right back into the room. 'Do you think they're out there now?'

It was the first thing we had to find out. Regardless of whether the top brass at Hamilton and Irvine were aware of our discovery, we had to address the question of whether or not we were under lethal attack. I took some comfort from the fact that I'd already been outside the house, front and back, and had not apparently attracted any attention from would-be assassins in the vicinity. Likewise, our shouting hadn't prompted any reaction. If there was anyone waiting for us out there, they were keeping damned quiet about it. On the other hand, if their intent was to get us to die of our own accord, out of supplies and out of transport, then they wouldn't need to do anything but wait. As long as we stayed holed up at the farmstead, they'd be quite happy to sit it out and pass the time for as long as it took. Without the Land Rover or the generator, we wouldn't survive long.

There was something else on my mind besides the genny and the car: in the back of the Landy was the radio. We'd left it there as we dashed through the rain to get into the house but I guessed it might still have some charge on it. If it was working, we had a shot at raising Kenny – and the alarm.

'You can't go out to the Land Rover,' said Sophie when I told them of my plan. 'If there is someone out there, it would be suicide.'

'If we sit on our backsides in here doing nothing, that's its own form of suicide too,' I replied, and headed for the door.

I stooped as I opened it and kept my head down as I edged out onto the verandah. The sun was now high over-head and the heat was oppressive. The mud was drying fast and great swathes of the compound were already crusting into dust once more. Where there had been tyre tracks and the semblance of a road leading back towards Macumba, now there was nothing but flat earth, with no delineating features to mark the trail. Even if we could somehow get the Land Rover mobile again, we'd have the devil of a job finding our way back.

I scanned the dunes around the edges of the compound, looking keenly for anything as telltale as a flash of light on a rifle sight or the top of a digger hat – the distinctive headgear with the brim turned up at the side, worn by locals in the bush. I couldn't really believe that any half-de-cent killer would allow himself to be given away by such a feeble clue but it was worth checking anyway.

There was no sign of life this side of the horizon.

Staying low, I crept through the thickening mud towards

the Land Rover. If someone had a rifle, it was unlikely that my speed would make much difference at the kind of range they'd be firing from and I wanted to get a good scout around while I was out in the open. I looked across to the tree where we'd found the first canister and saw nothing different: our tools lay scattered beneath the trunk where we'd left them. The well, too, looked innocuous. In the sea of red earth, the only thing that appeared to have changed since last night was the state of the Land Rover itself.

As I approached it, I did a full circuit, double-checking that my first impression had been accurate. It had. All four tyres sported gaping gashes in their rims. I thought back to the damage Smith Penney had done to the spare in Oodnadatta but this was different. The blade that had caused these tears was smaller, with a serrated edge, not unlike the one I was carrying myself. It made no difference: we were going nowhere. With no indication that I was being spied upon, I abandoned my creeping and walked brashly to the back door of the Land Rover. I immediately saw that it was not properly closed and my heart sank. When I opened it to look inside, I was greeted by the sight of the radio, strewn in a hundred pieces across the back of the vehicle.

'There's good news and there's bad news,' I announced breezily as I threw open the door of the farm and went inside.

'What's the good news?' asked Sophie.

'The good news is that we don't seem to have any company out here in the middle of this scorching desert.'

Adam raised an eyebrow. 'And the bad news?'

'The bad news is we're buggered.'

We ran a perfunctory inventory of our supplies and calculated that we could probably last four or five days on what we had with us, as long as we rationed the food and the water from the well held out. It was precious little time and I knew we had to devise a plan. With Adam's leg putting him virtually out of action – except for some basic domestic chores – it was down to Sophie and me.

I rapidly concluded that someone had to go for help and that someone would have to be me. Adam was in no position to disagree and I brooked no objections from Sophie. My field knowledge left me much better placed to attempt a trek on foot and I reasoned that she would make a much better nurse for her husband than I would. She offered some resistance to the gender stereotype but in the end conceded that I was probably right.

It would be a long and dangerous walk – I estimated it at two full days, taking into account the soaring temperatures and difficult terrain – and we spent the rest of the morning packing and repacking various configurations of rucksacks as we considered a range of eventualities. After lunch we gathered a stockpile of potential weapons in the event of an attack in my absence. Among George's mining paraphernalia we found two rifles and a promising collection of blunt instruments. In addition, in one of the outhouses there was a decent quantity of explosives which might or might not still work. We lugged it all into the house and laid it out in a handy, easy-to-access formation.

I decided I needed to find a safe hiding place for the documents. It struck me that George Deakins had done a damn good job of concealing them himself, with just enough breadcrumbs in his treasure hunt clues to leave a trail that we treasure-hunters could follow. It had taken us to the coolibah tree out there in the compound for the first half of the deed and it had guided us to the mine for the all-important second page. I wouldn't have taken too much exception if his clues had been a little easier to uncover – the canister in the mine shaft could have been missed all too easily – but the fact was that we had found them both and were now in proud possession of a complete document that revealed Sophie Church as the rightful proprietor of a tract of land in North Sydney. I had no idea what it might be worth but it must be considerably more than this dusty red opal mine, abandoned and in ruins, in the cantankerous depths of South Australia.

If I'd intended to stick around any longer, the tree would have attracted me as a hiding place. It had done the job before and proved extremely successful at it. As it was, though, I wanted the documents readily available for easy access. Any one of us could have stowed them about our person somewhere – the more intimate the better, in case of being searched – but I didn't want to put Sophie and Adam in any more danger than I had already. Equally, I suspected that if we found ourselves in circumstances where someone was searching us, I might well be the first candidate, in which case it was no good me carrying them. In the end, I vetoed the idea of any of us taking individual responsibility for them and instead opted for the Land Rover. Out of action as it was, it would be low on the hit list of anyone looking for the documents. It was rugged, fairly close by and well protected. It was also parked in the open in the middle of the compound – an exposed point that appealed to my sense of irony. The treasure would be hiding in plain sight.

I folded the two crucial pages into the undamaged canister and, eyeing the sticky mud where the Land Rover stood, decided to find a sheet of corrugated tin to lie on so I didn't get drenched in the stuff as I crawled underneath it. The slipperiness of the ground acted perfectly in place of the wheels on a mechanic's creeper and I shuffled myself far enough under the Landy to be able to lash the cylinder to part of the chassis. I'd taken the precaution of taping it up inside a blanket and binding the whole parcel with rope.

Finally, I called a halt to the work as the sun sank into

the desert. I had decided to start the journey at night, primarily to avoid the searing heat of the day but also to remain as inconspicuous as possible. They might not be watching the farm but our would-be attackers might well be lying in wait somewhere down the track for anyone attempting an escape. The downside of walking in the dark was that I wouldn't be able to rely on the position of the sun for navigation and my knowledge of the southern hemisphere's constellations was far from adequate. But I had a compass and I reckoned I wouldn't wander too far off course.

Over a cobbled-together meal before I set off, Sophie raised a question that would trouble me deeply over the next few hours trudging across the sand.

'Bill, how well do you know Kenny?'

I was bewildered. What was she getting at?

'I'm sorry, Bill – I know he's your friend but we've got to look at every possibility, haven't we?'

'You think Kenny might have something to do with this? For Christ's sake, Sophie . . .'

I was aghast. Kenny and Dolly had looked after Sophie and Adam like their own children; they'd invited them into their home on the slenderest of acquaintance; Dolly had died in a hit-and-run that might well have been meant for Sophie. Now the girl was entertaining some speculative notion that Kenny might be involved in a murderous conspiracy. I stared at her.

Sophie wouldn't look at me. 'No, I don't really, but we'd be foolish not to consider everything. I'm sorry . . .' she repeated, her voice trailing away.

I considered it. 'No, you know what? You're right. We should look at every possibility. Let's just think about this – pros and cons. Apart from the people at Hamilton and Irvine, Kenny was the only person who knew about the second page of the exchange of title.'

'That's true,' said Sophie. 'But we wouldn't even have known it existed if he hadn't told us about his telephone call to the company.'

'All right. So that's one item in the pro column – unless he told us deliberately to get us searching for it. If we found it, he'd know we had the only other copy. That's a con.'

'Do you really think he'd be willing to see his friend killed for the sake of a piece of paper – not to mention his wife?'

'No, I don't. And that's a definite pro.'

Adam looked up from his plate of rice and tinned vegetables. 'When did we last make contact with Kenny?'

I racked my brains to recall the last time I'd spoken to him. 'Two days ago, I think. We were at the mine yesterday so we didn't put a call in and we haven't been able to today because of the radio.'

'I don't want to put another mark in the con column . . .' began Adam.

'Go on.'

He levelled his gaze at me and said, 'Are we sure he's even in Sydney?'

Sophie looked at him quizzically. 'What do you mean?'

'I mean how do we know he isn't out here in the outback? The radio would work the same wherever he was and he could easily have pretended to be in Sydney when he was actually keeping tabs on us all the time, making sure we never got the chance to tell anyone else about that second page. Think about it: we've only got his word for everything we know about Hamilton and Irvine, from the company history to the supposed phone call.'

'We know they exist – we've seen the letterhead on the exchange of title,' said Sophie.

I interrupted her. 'Yes, but that's all we know. All that we haven't heard directly from Kenny, that is.'

I was beginning to feel a deep sense of unease. I didn't

for a moment believe that Kenny had betrayed us or that he was connected in any way to the shady goings-on that had left us marooned here in the desert. The recollection of his sagging, defeated shoulders under my arm at Dolly's funeral convinced me of that. But there was a growing stack of questions that couldn't be easily explained away and now, with the radio in pieces, we had no way of asking him about them.

Our list of pros and cons was looking decidedly grim.

III

Doubt is an insidious thing and its growth from seed to full triffid can be as rapid and as consuming as any weed. By the time I'd been walking for half an hour in the direction of Macumba Station, my brain was teeming with anxious thoughts.

It wasn't just Kenny that was occupying my mind. I was now seriously concerned that the exchange of title we'd uncovered would be nowhere near as convincing in a court of law as we'd imagined it to be when we found it. Even if we managed to bring it into the light somehow, Hamilton and Irvine would surely be equipped with a veritable army of lawyers and other experts geared up to overturn any claim Sophie might try to exercise. If I were in their shoes, I would impute everything from fraud to murder in order to obfuscate the issue. It would be easy enough to make the document out to be a forgery or, worse, to imply that we might have been the people responsible for George's untimely demise, pointing the finger at Sophie as driven by greed to dispose of her uncle and collect on a supposed fortune. One way or another, we were going to get the legal book thrown at us – and legal books, as any lawyer will tell you, are bloody heavy.

On top of all that, I'd left Sophie and an incapacitated Adam on their own, in a ramshackle shelter, with a nobbled Land Rover, and potentially in the sights of a trio of assassins. The collection of armoury we'd amassed would only go so far, especially in the face of a well-trained, well-equipped foe. I was supposed to be looking after them: instead, I'd abandoned them.

I tried to occupy my mind by focusing on the job in hand. The compass kept me on what I hoped was a consistent course south-west but I only had its magnetic mechanism's word for it. I began to wonder if it might have taken a knock somewhere along the journey, in which case its reliability could be in question. In addition, I had no idea what effect the declination of the earth's magnetic force had in this part of Australia – that is, how far away from true north my compass was actually showing; I knew some places on the planet could be out by a huge number of degrees. After wrestling with the calculations for far too long, I came to the conclusion that none of it mattered anyway. If it was a few degrees out, I'd still be likely to fetch up within a mile or two either side of Oodnadatta. If it was hopelessly wrong, there was nothing I could do about it.

The thought of Oodnadatta was not a comforting one. I'd ruled out knocking on the door at Macumba Station on the grounds that, if there were people hanging around this corner of the Simpson Desert who were out to do us mischief, then Macumba would offer them an excellent base camp. On the evidence of what I believed they'd achieved so far, money would presumably be no object and they would be able to buy the cooperation of the farmhands and ranchers who were stationed there. In any case, the absence of a clear road meant that navigating to the relatively small site at Macumba would be more of a needle in a haystack than locating the much larger settlement of

Oodnadatta. But what would Oodnadatta hold in store? Smith Penney, for one thing, and after our last encounter I didn't relish running into him again. I still had no real idea why he'd taken against our party so violently but I had no inclination to sit down with him and ascertain the reason. My best bet would be to head directly to the Transcontinental Hotel and enlist the help of Jack Cadison. If he could somehow pull together a posse who would be willing to ride out to the Deakins farm, then all might not be lost. We could fight the battle over the land claim later, when we'd returned to the luxury of Sydney.

First, I had to scale the metaphorical mountain of a two-day hike across the bush in extreme conditions. All the warnings Ruby had given me about the natural dangers of the outback haunted my heat-addled brain and by the midpoint of the night I was driving myself crazy with over-whelming and contradictory thoughts and theories.

I'd borrowed Adam's watch, leaving him and Sophie with just hers, and it informed me that it was almost three in the morning. Physically and mentally exhausted, I extracted a tarpaulin and sleeping bag from my pack, crawled inside and fell into a deep, restless sleep.

My intention had been to walk through the night and well into the following morning, delaying rest as long as I dared – or as long as the sun would allow me. Then I would sleep through the hottest part of the day before picking up again as dusk fell, exploiting the lower night-time temperatures to cover more ground. There would be a trade-off as I was likely to be slower in the dark but overall I expected to reach Oodnadatta somewhere on the morning of the second day after leaving.

Instead, I'd given in to complete fatigue hours earlier than anticipated. When I woke, I knew immediately that my plan had gone to hell.

The sun was high in the sky and Adam's watch stood at a few minutes after midday. I'd been asleep for nine hours and my schedule was trashed. Right at the time of the highest heat, when I was supposed to be resting and conserving energy, I was faced with an endurance march in the blistering sun. I contemplated staying put for another few hours but that would push my arrival in Oodnadatta back another day and the supplies in my rucksack – not to mention those back at the farmstead – might not withstand that much of a delay. We were working on a slim margin of error as it was and to lose a full day was unthinkable.

I found some scant protection under a scrubby tree and reassessed my provisions with a view to travelling a little lighter – and therefore faster. I'd packed well, with little excess baggage, so there wasn't much I could leave behind. Finally I settled on a couple of tins of food and a blanket that was meant to protect against the night cold: if I was on the move, I could probably manage without that. I used the fold-up shovel to dig a hole in the sand and buried the tins and blanket in it. I didn't want to start leaving a bread-crumb trail across the barren landscape indicating my whereabouts and direction of travel.

Laid out on the red earth, there looked to be far more than the rucksack could actually accommodate but it had just come out so it must be able to go back in. Weariness and the heat overcame me as I fought with the contents of the rucksack and I sat down heavily in the dirt, finding it was all I could do to reach for the water bottle and drink.

As I tipped my head back to drain the contents, my squinting eyes saw a movement overhead through the scrawny branches of the tree. It was too fast to be a bird and its progress across the sky too straight to be anything other than manmade.

A plane was flying in the direction of the farmstead.

The drone of the engine reached me now and I guessed

it was a four-seater of some kind – maybe the type used by crop-sprayers or the flying doctor. I was grateful that I had taken refuge under the tree; I didn't want to be seen from the air. It was possible that it was a supply plane making for Macumba Station but even as the thought crossed my mind I knew the chances of that were thin. The deadly feeling in the pit of my stomach returned and I seriously considered turning back there and then. Sophie and Adam would be an easy target from the air and they would have no warning that an attack was imminent. I felt sick that I couldn't alert them but the truth was that it would take me a good six hours to reach the farmstead, even if I were able to run – which in this heat was utterly impossible. All I could do was pray that the newlyweds had enough gumption to realise that this was not a friendly visit and enough ammunition to deter anyone from trying to land the plane and launch a ground assault. Whatever the outcome of that particular encounter, I could play no part in it. My only hope was to keep going towards Oodnadatta.

I waited until the plane was a good way past my position before I picked up the rucksack, heaved it onto my shoulders and headed in the opposite direction.

I'd known physical hardship plenty of times before and was acutely familiar with the delightful concept of route marches, in which squaddies are forcibly manoeuvred across miles of unforgiving territory while weighted down with unfeasibly overladen packs. The new factor in my current situation was the unbearable heat. Hydration was a constant concern and I abandoned the strict rationing of my water early on in favour of staying alive. I reckoned there was a good chance I'd happen upon a billabong or riverbed that had been refreshed enough by the recent storm to still have something worth salvaging. If so, I could top up my bottles then. In the meantime, I needed all the water I could lay my hands on.

Sweat was proving another problem. A stream of perspiration flowed down my forehead, dripping into my eyes and making it hard to keep them focused on the compass. Meanwhile, my clothes were wringing wet from the inside out and they clung stickily to my skin. Every step was an effort, every breath a combat with the oppressive air. If I hadn't had the terrifying phantom of Sophie and Adam and their present predicament at my heels, I'd have been sorely tempted to find another tree to crawl under and given up.

I trudged on like this for four hours, pausing every hour to find five minutes' shade and to take on more water. Like the mad Englishman in the Noel Coward song, I braved the highest temperatures the Simpson Desert could offer, in the hottest season of the year, with the lowest chances of success. At least I had the best of reasons for doing so.

It was almost exactly halfway between two of the rest breaks that I heard the sound of the plane's engine returning. Without looking behind me, I dived for the nearest cover, which amounted to little more than a dune slightly taller than the others, and then I rolled onto my back, wriggling out of the rucksack, to see if I could spot the aircraft.

The wind must have been behind me more than I realised because the plane was still some distance away. The noise had carried much further in this direction than it had going the other way and I had time to consider my options. If it was a local farmer or the flying doctor there were plenty of good reasons to flag them down: I could hitch a ride back to Oodnadatta in a fraction of the time it would take me to walk there and I might even get a lift back out to the farmstead with some reinforcements. If, on the other hand, the plane was carrying the thugs whom we knew were on our trail, then they had already been to the farm, done whatever they had done, and were now heading back to civilisation. The very fact that they were in the air right now meant that Sophie and Adam had not been able to put up enough resistance to stop them. I didn't want to contemplate what might have happened to them in that eventuality. Either way, I realised, I had nothing to lose.

I tore off the large white neckerchief that was tied round my neck against the sweat, climbed to the top of the sand dune and began waving like a maniac.

For a full minute I waved, watching the plane pass high overhead and shouting at the top of my voice in case they had somehow missed my on-the-ground antics and would instead hear me over the roar of the engine. A man will do bizarrely irrational things in the face of extreme danger. I'm damn sure it wasn't the yelling so it must have been the neckerchief that did it: as the plane passed the dune where I was leaping crazily about, the wingtip nearest to me dipped and the aircraft began to circle. Describing a wide loop to the south, it came round again, losing altitude all the time, the engine noise swelling and fading as it was picked up and dropped by draughts of wind. It was now making a beeline directly towards me and as it fell from the sky it looked like it was on a collision course with my vantage point.

I stopped waving and scanned the terrain immediately around me. There was no possibility of the plane landing – every conceivably flat surface was not only cratered with mudholes but also liberally bedecked with boulders too large for a light aircraft to negotiate without coming a complete cropper. If I'd stopped to think intelligently about my situation I'd have realised that rescue was a forlorn hope in this patch of desert. However, there was still a chance I might convey a sense of urgency to the occupants of the plane and somehow signal that I needed their help. There wasn't time to work out the exact details right then.

I swiftly changed my mind about the potential for a landing strip when I saw the rifle.

I'd noticed the plane's right-hand window opening as it

descended, with the pilot having to compensate for the resulting yaw. That initial tremble in the aircraft's movement was followed by an elbow and shoulder appearing out of the open window before the stock of a rifle was manoeuvred through the gap and positioned against the shoulder. There was barely enough room for the man to handle the weapon, especially with the gusts that must have been blowing around him, but the barrel fitted neatly between the strut that held the wing and the fuselage itself, and it was pointed unequivocally at me.

At the top of the highest sand dune around, waving a neckerchief to attract the attention of an armed man with clearly hostile intent, I was hardly at my safest in that moment. I tried to dive to my right, towards the little valley between the dunes, but my boots had no purchase in the loose sand and I fell clumsily to my knees in almost exactly the same position I'd been standing. A foot in front of me, the dirt rose up in a fountain of red as a bullet thumped into the ground and I threw myself into a foetal position and rolled down the slope. Without looking back, I scrambled to my feet and ran for cover. Another bullet whizzed past me as I sprinted towards the largest boulder I could see and I executed a feet-first slide into its shade, hearing a third bullet ricochet off the stone above my head.

Only now did I turn to look at the aircraft and I realised the gunman must either have had excellent luck or be something of a marksman. To have got three shots away in the space of those few seconds, and to come so close to hitting his target, was a pretty impressive – and alarming – feat.

I had a little respite while the plane circled round for another pass so I considered my position. I was now on the wrong side of the boulder, exposed again to an approach from the aircraft. I knew I'd have to move. I wondered if I could simply switch round to the other side of the rock, then keep going back and forth for subsequent passes until their fuel ran out; but I realised they could circumvent that tactic by the simple expedient of realigning the plane and coming at me from the side. I needed somewhere more protected where I could get myself properly hidden and hope that they would lose interest and go away if they couldn't find me.

About fifty yards to the north, beyond where my ruck-sack was dumped in the brush, a large boulder lay up against the wall of a sand dune. It stood about six feet tall and, where it touched the dune, created a crevice on its underside that I estimated was just about the right size to hold a man. If I could get there unseen and crawl into the nook, I had a chance of shaking off the plane – and its occupants. I thought about grabbing the rucksack as I went past but there didn't seem much point and it would only slow me down. There was also the strong possibility that it wouldn't fit in the crevice and might end up giving away my position.

The plane was banking at the far end of its run and if I'd tried to move to the boulder then I'd have been spotted for certain. With the aircraft still at a considerable distance, I took the opportunity to switch to the opposite side of the rock I was using. I could make the dash for the big boulder after they had gone by this time: it would be difficult for them to see me from behind as they repositioned for another pass and I'd have a good few seconds to make the sprint. I hoped it would be enough.

As I rounded the rock I heard a voice shouting in an unmistakable Australian accent.

'There he is!'

I flung my arms around my ears and dived for safety. A bullet punched into the dirt near my feet but I was now out of the direct sightline of the plane. This was my moment.

Glancing up at the aircraft, its nose rising again as the

pilot prepared to bank, I dug my boots into the ground for traction and launched myself towards the boulder like a sprinter out of the blocks. Fifty yards was going to take me a good ten seconds, I figured, and that might give the pilot enough time to circle far enough round for the rifleman to spot me running. If he did, I was back to square one: moderately protected by the habitat but still an identifiable target. I'd cross that bridge if I came to it. My first priority was to reach the crevice.

I kept low and moved as fast as I could, dodging the rocks and scrub that filled the valley between me and the boulder. All the time I kept my eyes fixed on the crevice. The plane could wait until I got there. As I neared my hiding place, I saw that it actually opened up into a larger hole than I'd imagined and I thanked whatever higher power organised things in the universe that this, at least, was a lucky break. I took the baseball batter's technique once more and slid inelegantly into the gap, my feet ploughing into the softer dune at the back of the crevice and my backside taking the full force of the much firmer boulder. Rolling onto my stomach, I edged myself deeper into the crack until my head was level with the opening. Only then did I squint upwards against the blazing sun and try to spot the enemy.

With the sun high and the plane low, I thought I stood a decent chance of seeing it. Now, though, the dune ran straight out in front of me to my left, obscuring half the sky, and I could see no sign of the aircraft. I strained my ears for a clue and after thirty seconds or so the engine crept into earshot. I tried to work out how far away it was but the gusting winds were sure to be deceptive and I couldn't hazard a guess. All I knew was that it was getting louder.

In another ten seconds, the plane burst into view, very low and very fast, almost directly overhead. It swooped over the top edge of the dune right in my eye line and was gone behind me almost before I'd realised. I buried my head in my hands, clamping my digger hat onto my skull in an attempt at camouflage, and stayed put. The plane was clearly executing a low pass over the valley and I took that as a good sign. It meant they had lost sight of me and were forced to try this low-level, close-up search. I was pretty confident I couldn't be seen from the air in my current position so all I had to do was wait. It was only a matter of time before they'd give up.

The plane made two more passes over the same stretch of the valley and I heard more random gunfire before the engine whined and the aircraft climbed rapidly away to the west. I thought the shooting must have been an exercise in pure hubris as I was sure they couldn't see me and none of the bullets came anywhere near my hiding place. But I didn't want to take any chances so I stayed motionless with my head buried under my hat for a full five minutes more. I listened hard as the wind blew through the brush but there was no sound of the plane returning. My heart was still pounding from the sprint – or the gunshots – but the danger seemed to be over.

When I finally looked up and peered out from my hole, I realised it had barely begun. I was staring into the glossy black eyes of a taipan snake.

IV

The inland taipan of central Australia is, by some distance, the world's deadliest snake. It may not have the highest casualty rate – the infrequency of its encounters with humans is due mainly to its remote habitat – but its victims are the least likely to survive. Aboriginal Australians, who gave it the misleadingly pleasing name *dandarabilla*, have lived with it for thousands of years but it's only recently that it was properly classified and catalogued, a hundred years after it was first described by the early European explorers. Some believe that sea snakes are the most toxic of all, but the inland taipan outvenoms them by around four times. Little wonder it has earned the nickname 'the fierce snake'. Its extreme toxicity can hardly be overstated: one bite can carry enough venom to kill a hundred men. And it's both fast and accurate, with its repeated strikes almost invariably delivering a lethal dose – every time.

All this I had learned from my research and from Ruby McKenzie. And it meant that, of all the dangerous critters I could have faced on this trek, the taipan was the one I had feared most.

'Oh, don't worry about it,' Ruby had said. 'You won't see one, and if you do you just need to make sure you stay away from it. It'll be more frightened of you than you are of it and you'd really have to be going some for it to want to bite you. They'll only do it in self-defence – they're a pretty placid sort on the whole.'

I was far from convinced that this particular specimen had been given the same lecture in herpetological behaviour as I had. Its head raised several inches from the ground and its dark, stubby snout poised for action, it looked decidedly angry from where I was lying. As for steering clear, that was an option that simply wasn't available to me. I was backed into my hole with no way out other than past this vicious-looking killer.

There was something mesmerising about the silky skin and the glistening head that returned my stare. In its coppery summer colours, with the first six inches of its six-foot body darkening almost to black, it was a truly impressive sight, if you're in the mood for lethal reptiles. The beady little eyes were fixed on me and I sensed it was preparing to strike.

I tightened the grip on my hat with my left hand, bringing it over my face to shield everything below my eyes. With my right hand, I reached down and grabbed a handful of the soft, red dirt that I'd scuffed up as I dived into the crevice. I took a deep breath and, in as swift and smooth a movement as I could manage, I hurled the sand at the snake and leaped to my feet simultaneously.

The taipan was a blur as it launched itself in my direction. I tried to swat away the lunge with my hat and felt a sharp scratch on the knuckle of the middle finger of my left hand as I went flying past it, heading for open terrain. I ran for twenty seconds, past the rucksack, past my previous hiding place and up on to the dunes once more. I didn't care if the plane was still in the vicinity – I needed to get away from the snake.

At the peak of the ridge, I finally stopped and looked

back. From this distance, I could see the snake near the entrance to the crevice, resembling a broken twig as much as anything, and it seemed to have calmed down, with its head now back at ground level. As I watched, it slid along the bottom edge of the dune and vanished into a crack in the sand.

I noted the exact point where it had disappeared then sat down in the scorching earth. I hardly dared to look but I knew I had to force myself to inspect my finger, which was now throbbing gently. If I had taken a full bite from the snake's fangs, the chances were I was done for. While I was carrying anti-venom in the rucksack, the toxicity of the lethal liquid was highly likely to outdo any restorative qualities that the medicine could offer. I turned my hand over and looked at the knuckle. The fleshy skin over the joint had what appeared to be a scratch but there was no blood visible on the surface. From the look of it, I'd have said I'd got away without the skin being broken – and therefore without receiving a shot of the taipan's venom. The throbbing in my hand told a different story.

The fact that there had been no recorded cases of deaths from a taipan strike in nearly twenty years was small consolation. I didn't want to become the first.

I had to move fast.

I ripped off a strip of material from the bottom of my shirt and subdivided that to make two bandages, one larger than the other. The smaller one I wrapped tight round my wrist, using my teeth and my right hand to increase the tension until I could feel the blood pumping under the pressure. I tied it as best I could then repeated the procedure with the larger bandage, which I wound round my upper arm. I was hoping that the combination of the pair of tourniquets might prove more efficacious than a single effort.

After that, I went looking for my knife.

Keeping a close eye on the fissure where the snake had vanished, I headed quickly for the rucksack. As I neared it, I saw that the gunfire I'd heard during the last two passes of the plane had not been random at all. The rifleman had been taking potshots at my kit – and he'd been bloody accurate about it too. The rucksack lay in the middle of a slightly damp patch of earth that was drying rapidly in the heat, marking the demise of the water flask that had been stowed inside the bag. I upended the sack unceremoniously and kicked through the contents with one boot. For now, I wasn't bothered about the damage to my kit – what I needed was the knife.

I fell on it eagerly and pulled it from its leather sheath, grabbing a cigarette lighter with the other hand. I flicked the lighter into life and held the flame under the tip of the knife for a few seconds to sterilise it as far as I could in these most unsterile of conditions. Then I put the sheath in my mouth and chomped down on it with my teeth: this was going to hurt. As I dug into my knuckle with the blade, I tried to divert my brain from the searing pain by wondering just how much flesh I would need to remove. Like Beethoven's deafness, it was another of those damned unanswerable questions so I erred on the side of caution and went deep.

I peeled back the skin and screamed into the desert.

The mopping up exercise didn't take me long. After I'd bound the wound with the cleanest bit of material I could locate – which was hardly clean at all – I fished around for the anti-venom, which had fortunately survived the aerial attack. It had never been our intention to call on it but it made up a reassuring part of the first-aid kit and I was grateful for it now. In an ideal world, the drug would have been administered intravenously by a medical professional for the fastest, most productive result but there was no chance of any such luxuries here. Instead, I bared my belly and jabbed the syringe into the subcutaneous layer, pumping the liquid in evenly but quickly. I had no idea if that was the most effective site – or method, come to that – but I wanted the anti-venom in me and that seemed as good a way as any.

Now I could begin to worry about the damage to my kit – and there was plenty to worry about. Aside from the water flask, the compass had taken a direct hit, rendering it useless. The needle was gone and the dial shredded by the impact of a bullet. With no direction finder or, more importantly, means of hydration to achieve the minimum basic requirement of staying alive, I was more or less finished. Disorientated by the attack from the skies, I was already unsure which direction I had come from and in which direction lay Oodnadatta. I hazarded a guess from the position of the sun and the layout of the valley, working out that the large boulder where I'd met the taipan was roughly to the north of the dune from which I'd waved at the plane. But roughly wouldn't cut it now: if I was to make it out of this, I would need to point myself precisely towards the town and get there fast. There was no other chance of survival.

I abandoned most of the remaining kit, as well as the rucksack itself. Without water, everything else was academic. I dropped a few of the smaller, lighter items – including my damaged wristwatch – into the pockets of my shirt and trousers, took a final calculation of the likeliest direction, and set off into the wilderness once more.

An hour later, I knew I was hopelessly lost.

It had occurred to me to try heading due south in an attempt to stumble across the road between Oodnadatta and Macumba Station but I'd ruled it out for a couple of reasons. Firstly, there was no guarantee it would even be visible after the rainstorm – the track to George's farmstead

had completely disappeared, after all. And secondly, if I was
to make it back to Oodnadatta, then going south followed
by west in order to go south-west was two sides of a
right-angled triangle. I needed the hypotenuse.

I was regretting that decision now. With only the sun for
guidance, and with no idea where it was meant to be at this
time of day and in this season of the year, I was out of my
depth and rapidly running out of time. The heat was leaving
me parched and I could almost feel the moisture draining
from the core of my body as the sweat poured out of me.
The surrounding desert was a barren wasteland of red, dotted
with greeny-brown scrub and carapaced with the relentless
blue of the sky. At least it would be a colourful way to go.

I didn't know whether I should be conserving my energy
in the heat of the afternoon or ploughing on while I could
still walk. I feared that if I stopped and rested, or took
shelter from the sun, my lack of hydration would make it
all but impossible to get up and get going again as evening
fell. Meanwhile, I suspected that the venom could be
working its way through my system and I could only guess
how long it would be before it began affecting my vital
organs. While I deliberated, I stumbled on through the
sub-Martian landscape. As long as my feet kept moving, I
reckoned, I had a chance.

And then I saw something that my eyes couldn't explain.

Gazing into the distance, where the blue and red collided
in a dazzling horizon, I noticed the strip of land nearest the
sky starting to divide itself up into segments. It was a fine
division into roughly equal parts and it was indisputable
now, even to my heat-addled brain. Thirty yards nearer to
the phenomenon, I understood. The straight lines dividing
the horizon were tall, vertical structures that my mind
finally recognised as wooden poles. As I neared, I could
make out that they were linked by thin cables from apex
to apex.

I had happened upon the old telegraph line that had traversed the country from north to south for a century.

The sight of a manmade assembly gave me an unexpected thrill. It was a symbol of the civilisation that I had almost forgotten existed, even after such a short time, and the scale of it was a sobering reminder of what humans are capable of as a species.

More to the point, this telegraph line might be my salvation. For if the telegraph was here, then the Ghan rail track couldn't be far away.

I'd just reached the nearest wooden pole when I stopped dead in my tracks. For all its engineering brilliance and ability to connect one side of the continent with another, the Ghan was going to be absolutely no use to me. The frequency of the service currently stood at twice a week and there were plans in place to drop it to just once. The chances of my arrival happening to coincide with a passing train were slim at best, even if the hapless driver was willing to stop for a nutcase flagging him down in the middle of the desert – which seemed highly unlikely to me. I could follow the tracks, of course, but even that was a fifty-fifty longshot. I had no idea where on the line I had intersected it and Oodnadatta could be many hours' trek . . . in either direction. If I got it wrong, there was zero chance that I would reach the next stop.

I leaned my back against the telegraph pole – one of thirty thousand from coast to coast, I recalled uselessly – and let my legs buckle so that I slid down to the ground. Resting my forearms on my knees, I slumped my head forwards and stared at the ground between my legs. Now that I had stopped, I registered just how fierce the sun was and I picked my hat off my head and adjusted it further back, trying to cover the nape of my neck. I rubbed the top of my shoulder and found it tender to the touch. The skin was turning decidedly leathery and I knew I was burning badly. Somewhere down the line I was going to need some soothing ointments.

It was then that the realisation hit me: the prospect of my ever needing soothing ointments again was melting as rapidly as I was in the sweltering heat. All of Kenny and Ruby's warnings had been in vain. This crazy Englishman had broken just about every rule of bushcraft in the manual and now here I was, roasting quietly in the oven of the Simpson Desert, with taipan venom probably coursing through my veins, never to be found and facing the very likely eventuality of my carcass being picked clean by whatever carrion birds populated the skies in these parts.

It was the not being found that bothered me most, for some reason. At least if there's a body, then friends and family have something physical to focus on, something they can gather round and share reminiscences about. A funeral might be predominantly a sad occasion, but I can't say I've ever been to one that was completely devoid of humour. Somebody always has a ribald story to tell about the deceased or some anecdote to reveal how witty they were and how much they'll be missed. But a funeral without a corpse is just another kind of séance – remembering the departed in spirit rather than in body – and I was never one for that kind of mawkish stuff. Better to be forgotten than to be permanently missing in action, with its futile sense of desperate hope.

Something in my back pocket was digging into my buttock and I shuffled to reach it. I pulled out the lighter that I'd shoved in there without thinking and stared at it. There was a dent in the fluid casing where I'd been sitting on it and I idly wondered if I'd broken it – not that it mattered now, one way or the other. I flicked it open and snatched at the wheel, sending sparks across the valve and igniting the butane jet at the first attempt. In the blinding sunlight the flame burned evenly and beautifully, as calm and efficient as always, and I marvelled as I saw its constancy.

Then I marvelled as I saw its potential.

I snapped the lighter shut and jumped to my feet. From the scrub nearby I yanked and broke off as much dry brush as I could carry, returning to the telegraph pole and shaping the branches into a pyre around it. For fifteen minutes I gathered and built, crafting a bonfire that was as tall as I was and spread ten feet across at its base. I was surprised at how energetic I felt and I wondered if I was suffering from an incipient madness caused by the snake bite that might prefigure some kind of rabid descent into oblivion. There was no point worrying about that so I kept working. By the time I'd finished, the stack of combustible material towered over me and the telegraph pole looked like some kind of skirted stick man if he'd been painted by Hieronymus Bosch.

I didn't care about how it looked. I cared about whether it would burn. I'd torn off another strip of my shirt and laid it from the heart of the bonfire to the outer edge to act as a kind of wick. Now I fished out the lighter once more and put its end to the flame.

My expectation had been that the bonfire would go up pretty quickly but the speed at which the wood ignited still took me aback. I moved away a few paces from the pyre and by the time I turned round the flames were already licking the pole itself. A wall of orange blew up in front of me from the tinder-dry brush and a new wave of heat pounded my face. I hadn't thought it could get any hotter out here but I was wrong. My biggest concern had been that the dry branches would burn themselves out before the pole had a chance to catch light but I was wrong about that too. Decades of exposure to the desert climate must have left it totally bereft of any moisture and it blackened in minutes and carried the flame high into the sky. The thought crossed my mind that it might have been eaten away inside by termites or some other minuscule creatures, leaving it additionally susceptible to the fire. It didn't matter to me: what I was after was the complete and utter destruction of this telegraph pole. I had nothing in particular against it – it seemed a perfectly adequate telegraph pole to me – but it was the sole target of my temporary pyromania. As the wood crackled and broke apart, it did exactly what I had hoped it would do. Less than five minutes after I'd applied the lighter, the top of the pole disintegrated and it came crashing to the ground, smashing into the remaining flames and sending out an explosion of sparks that erupted frighteningly close to me. With the top of the pole came the telegraph wires and, as they fell, they snapped.

Somebody somewhere would be experiencing disrupted communications.

At least, that was my sincere hope. The whole point of bringing down the telegraph wire was to bring it to somebody's attention. With luck, there might be a bunch of people whose connection to the outside world had been rudely interrupted by my actions and they would feel the need to send out a representative to investigate. I didn't know how long that investigation might take but with so many dependent on the line for communication I hoped it wouldn't be too long. In the meantime, there was nothing I could do but wait. I didn't dare move away from this spot until somebody came looking for the problem.

Exhausted, overheated and still terrified about the toxin lurking around the edges of my system, I surveyed my surroundings. Within about fifty yards of the smouldering fire were four coolibah trees of varying size and health. I picked out the one with the bushiest, leafiest branches and walked over to it, throwing myself into the shade. I positioned myself so I could see the smoking wreck of the telegraph pole and would be able to attract the attention of anyone who came investigating. My only aim now was to stay awake. It would have been the cruellest of ironies for a rescuer to have flown over and me to have missed it because I was off in the Land of Nod.

Staying in the shade and trying to move as little as possible to conserve my energy, I resorted to mental arithmetic and memory games to keep myself conscious. I plumbed the depths of my childhood recollections for the kind of game my parents played on long car journeys; working my way through the alphabet for the initial letters of countries, animals, authors – anything that would stop me sinking into a heat-induced torpor. I tried to remember as many elements in the periodic table as I could, running out of steam long before I got to the noble gases. I ran through every list I could think of, from the names of the seven dwarves to the fifty states of the USA. When I realised the list-making itself was sending me to sleep, I changed tack. Now I began rehearsing familiar processes in my mind, from stripping a Lee-Enfield rifle to imagining the journey from my home in Devon up to London – a journey I'd made more times than I cared to recall thanks to the regular employment I was offered by the Western and Continental Insurance Co Ltd before it all went sour in the Caribbean. As thoughts are inclined to do, mine wandered off into stray territory, wondering what the hell I would do for work if I ever made it back to Blighty. There's not much around for unloved insurance agents, especially if one of the biggest companies in the business has put a black mark against your name. The money I'd been given at the end of that little escapade would keep me going for a while but I couldn't retire on it.

I chuckled aloud at the thought of retirement. Nothing seemed less likely to me at that precise moment.

When I felt my eyelids dropping again I decided I had to move and damn the energy conservation. My whole arm was sore and I held it close to my body as I crawled to my feet. The sun had moved further round beyond the burned-out telegraph pole but the heat was still fierce. I shielded my eyes with my good hand and scanned the sky, starting in the direction that I imagined Oodnadatta might be. From there, I searched to the west, then the north. When I reached the final cardinal point, in the direction of where I'd come from, my jaw dropped open.

Smudging the far horizon was a plume of black smoke.

PART FOUR: BLACK

I

I don't know if it was the heat, the venom or the over-whelming sense of responsibility but I threw up under the coolibah tree.

The pall of smoke could mean only one thing: Uncle George's farmstead was on fire. There was nothing natural in the desert that would create such a huge cloud if it was set alight and I doubted that the ranch hands at Macumba Station would have allowed their buildings to go up in flames like that. It could only be the Deakins property.

A rush of possibilities flew through my mind. I wondered if Sophie and Adam had performed the same trick I'd executed with the telegraph pole, setting the farm ablaze to attract attention and raise assistance. But I could think of no circumstances that would force them to take that kind of risk: the likeliest arrivals on such a scene would be people who were only too happy to wish harm upon the young couple and a fire would offer them ideal cover if they decided to approach matters with lethal intent. Besides, Sophie and Adam still had supplies to keep them going for a few more days so why would they resort to signalling in such a terminal fashion?

Much more likely was that a delegation from Macumba

had paid the farm a visit and the blaze was the result. How it could have occurred did not bear thinking about but the welfare of my two companions – for whom I had developed something of an avuncular accountability during our time in Australia – weighed heavily on me.

And now I had a dilemma. My instinct was to be guided by the smoke and head back to the Deakins farmstead as quickly as I could. It would take hours and there was no guarantee I'd make it – I was still without water and, although the temperature would begin to drop as the day shaded into night, it was still lethally hot. My chances of survival were remote, to put the best possible spin on it. And even if I made it to the farm, what was I going to be able to do? If the place was ablaze now, it would be totally gutted by the time I reached it and I'd be of no use to anyone who might still be alive around there. In fact, I'd be much more of a hindrance, needing medical attention and probably rapid hospitalisation. If Sophie and Adam weren't dead already, I might be directly responsible for killing them by putting them in an impossible quandary.

The alternative was barely more palatable. I could stay here, under the coolibah tree, and hope that somebody turned up. I couldn't be sure who that might be – my best shot was that it was someone from Oodnadatta sent out to investigate the break in the telegraph line – but if I was really lucky, I might be able to get myself seen to and also despatch some urgent assistance to Sophie and Adam at the farm. However, I couldn't escape the thought that none of the options I had turned over in my head had the slimmest chance of working out. By far the likeliest eventuality was that I would die here under this tree.

The stench of my own vomit, by now a lure to a quite extraordinary number of flies, provoked me to action. I got up from my seat at the base of the tree and evaluated the others nearby. None of them had quite the protection that this one provided but equally they would not offer the constant, unsavoury reminder of my stomach contents. I stepped out into the full glare of the sun, surprised at what a difference the tree's shade had made to the temperature, and shuffled across to one of its neighbours. My view of the telegraph pole was slightly more obscured here but I was confident I would still be able to advertise my presence to anyone happening along the route of the wire – as long as I was still alive.

For some reason, I had imagined that help would come from the skies – that it would be a plane that came to investigate the telegraph line. I was wrong: I saw the trail of dust through the heat haze long before I heard the engine and I knew a vehicle was heading up the line in my direction. It was coming from the south and I guessed I must have wandered quite a way north-west during my desert perambulation. There was a long time when the car didn't seem to be getting any nearer and I half-wondered if I was indulging myself in one of those mirages you see in films set in the desert. Then, all of a sudden, it appeared really close and I could identify it as blue and probably a Toyota Hilux or Datsun Sunny truck – the Japanese had been making serious inroads into the ute market for years, although I still favoured the good old reliable Landy. At that moment, however, I didn't care whether the car was Asian, British or manufactured on Mars.

Although time was of the essence, I wanted to see what would happen when the occupants of the vehicle found the destroyed telegraph pole so I stayed under the tree to wait and watch. The car – I could see now that it was indeed a Datsun – was still half a mile away and motoring pretty swiftly, throwing up its trail of dust for a good few hundred yards behind it. Its route was taking it some distance from the telegraph line, although seemingly parallel to it, and I realised that it must be following the rail tracks

of the Ghan. There must have been a solid surface free of
rocks beside the track that served as a road for ease of
maintenance. As the vehicle approached the point where
I'd burned down the telegraph pole, it slowed and I could
see there were two men inside. The passenger was a dark
blur on the far side of the car and I couldn't make him out
but the driver, with his window wound down, was in full
view, and I saw that it was Jack Cadison.

I couldn't have been more relieved if it had been George
Deakins himself.

Still nursing my weakened arm, I moved out of the shade
of the coolibah tree and began hurrying towards the vehicle.
But I stopped dead when I saw it lurch into life again and
pick up speed, heading north and moving fast away from
me. As it went, I caught a glimpse of the passenger, waving
an arm out of the window as if signalling to the driver,
pointing further up the track.

Jack Cadison's companion was Smith Penney.

At first, I couldn't figure out what the hell was going on.
Why were Jack and Penney sharing a ride in the ute? They
had clearly come looking for the damage to the telegraph
line. So why had they subsequently raced off, away from
Oodnadatta, in a direction that Penney had evidently deter-
mined for Jack? I couldn't tell if they'd seen me scurrying
towards them from the coolibah tree. If they had seen me,
were they deliberately leaving me to die in the desert? From
my short acquaintance with Jack, I found that hard to
believe. But maybe he was acting under duress from Smith
Penney. Was it possible that they hadn't seen me at all,
with their focus drawn by the charred stump of the telegraph pole? Maybe I'd been camouflaged by the tree or
had faded into a khaki background. But that still didn't
explain why they'd taken off to the north.

I watched forlornly as the dust trail drifted away. As I

stared after it, my heart leaped hopefully: the cloud had reappeared a little way over to the right, on my side of the telegraph line, and began moving back in my direction.

As I watched, the explanation revealed itself to me. Unable to cross the rail tracks, even in a ute, Jack had driven on to where the tracks crossed a dry riverbed on one of those rickety steel bridges that populated the line every so often. He must have manoeuvred down into the riverbed, crossing underneath the bridge supports and emerging on the opposite side of the railway.

Level crossings were an infrequent luxury on the Ghan.

The ute's speed had dropped on this side of the tracks and I took the opportunity to make my way back to the relative sanctuary of the coolibah tree. If it had been anyone other than Smith Penney in that passenger seat, I'd have been throwing myself in front of the car, desperate to attract their attention. As things stood, I needed to know whether he and Jack Cadison were friend or foe.

Jack pulled the car up near the telegraph pole and both men got out. I was alarmed to see Penney take a rifle out and shuck it onto his shoulder as they moved towards the pole, looking around them warily as they went. I glanced at the pole itself and could see why they were nervous: this was clearly no accidental damage.

Jack kicked around in the black ashes of the fire for a while, bending down once or twice to check something out, while Penney had his eyes glued to the ground, searching the loose red sand. He looked up, studying the coolibah trees, and called to Jack.

'Over here.'

'What is it, mate?

'Our culprit,' said Penney with more than a hint of menace in his voice. 'These footprints are recent. Whoever made them is still around here.'

Jack took off his hat and scratched his head before

flapping away flies from his face and putting the hat back on.

'Why would they do this?' he asked, gesturing at the telegraph pole – although I didn't get the impression his question was directed at Penney.

'I don't know, mate, but I reckon our chances of finding out must be pretty good. If they're still around, then we're sure as hell going to find them.'

Penney got to his feet and started striding purposefully in the direction of the first tree I'd hidden under. As he walked, he took the rifle from his shoulder, pumped a round into the breech and held the stock as if ready to fire. I didn't like the look of that and I knew the other coolibah wouldn't detain him for long so I began to scout around for options. Aside from the fact that essentially there were none, I thought I might be able to make a half-hearted run for it if I headed in the exact opposite direction, using my current coolibah as cover. If Penney spotted me when I was in the open I knew I'd have no chance but if I could get far enough away that I could cross the rail track, forcing them to take the ute back up to the riverbed before they could come looking for me again, there was just a possibility that I could evade capture. God knows what I thought I'd do then. At that moment I couldn't think further than one minute to the next.

Behind me I heard Penney shouting to Jack.

'Someone's heaved up here. We're looking for a wounded animal. He can't get far.'

I didn't look round. I was now close enough to the rail line to be able to see the tracks and I fixed my eyes dead ahead and ran as fast as I could. If I could just make it to the sleepers I might be able to bury myself far enough into the dirt that I wouldn't be visible from the ute.

'Hey – you there!'

I thought it was Jack's voice but I wasn't about to turn round to check.

I hit the track, danced across the sleepers and dived for the deck. As I did so, a gunshot rang out.

There was more indistinct shouting between the two men, then the sound of the car engine firing up. As I had suspected, they were going to try and flush me out. Going back up to the riverbed to cross the tracks again would give me at least a minute and I thought about switching back to the opposite side. But the only cover there was the coolibah trees and I knew they would offer little protection against Penney's rifle. Besides, I was no kind of opposition for two fit men with a weapon and a vehicle: in the heat of the chase, I'd forgotten the damage to my arm – both the wrist sprain and the snake bite – and squalls of pain were shooting up to my shoulder. I let out a cry as much in frustration as in agony.

Cornered and immobilised, I could do nothing but wait.

II

'What the hell did you think we were going to do to you?'

Jack shot me a sideways glance as he steered the ute across the rough terrain towards Macumba Station. The three of us were packed tightly across the bench seat in the cab of the Datsun.

I didn't really have a sensible excuse so I gave him the truth.

'I'm sorry, Jack – I didn't know if you were on my side or not.'

Smith Penney, sandwiching me on the other side, gave a grunt.

'Don't mind him,' said Jack. 'He's got a grudge against everyone until you tell him different.'

I looked sidelong at Penney, who stared impassively out of the window at the fading sunlight. 'Does that still include me?'

I recalled the last time our paths had crossed, when he'd sent a bullet pinging off the roof of my Land Rover. Mind you, I'd also managed to land him a punch to the gut so maybe we weren't that far from even.

Penney sat in silence for a good ten seconds before

replying. 'Jack set me straight on a few things,' he said eventually.

My comment to Jack was heartfelt: 'That was very good of you, Jack. Much appreciated.'

'No worries, mate,' he said. 'Seems like a few wires might have been crossed all round.'

'What do you mean?'

Jack began to regale me with the full story. Two days before Sophie, Adam and I had swung breezily into Oodnadatta, three other strangers had turned up in town. This much I already knew – Jack had described them as burly thugs. What Jack hadn't been able to tell me when he paid a late-night visit to my room at the Transcontinental was how exactly they had succeeded in upsetting Penney. Apparently they had pretended they were old friends of George Deakins and were hoping to look him up as they traversed the continent on some kind of field trip. The history between Uncle George and his erstwhile pal had been unknown to them and they had inadvertently stumbled upon the one person they would antagonise by mentioning his name.

'You can see why Smith here took exception to their hanging around in Oodna,' said Jack.

I couldn't really but this wasn't the moment.

'Trouble is, Smith can't resist a bit of a bust-up and he got one the next night.'

I remembered what Jack had told me about the thugs outnumbering Penney and leaving him the worse for wear. 'Three to one isn't exactly fair odds,' I said.

'I can take a punch,' he said. 'As you're well aware. Besides, I got my own back.'

'What did you do?'

He shrugged. 'About the same as I did to you. Stuffed up their spare tyre and invited them to bugger off back to Coober Pedy.'

'The White Fellas' Hole,' I said, more to myself than anyone else. I still had questions over Jack's attempt to warn me about Penney but I wasn't about to drop him in the deep end by revealing he'd come to my room specially to do it. If the two of them had found a way of joining forces that allowed them to work together on this little jaunt into the wilderness, I was hardly going to rock the boat.

'You might have had good reason to run them out of town but what did you have against me and my travelling companions?'

'I thought you were more of the same,' said Penney. 'I'd just about had enough of people poking their noses around in our business. We should be allowed to get on with our own lives without some snooping Sydney bastards messing things up.'

Jack interrupted. 'I think I might have stirred things up a little there, too. I happened to mention to Smith that Sophie was related to George.'

That would have set Penney off for sure, I thought. If he was operating on such a hair-trigger that even the mention of George's name could have him reaching for his rifle, then the prospect of an actual living relative rolling into town must have properly driven him over the edge.

'You really didn't like him, did you?' I said.

We fell into a hot, tetchy silence. Jack's handling of the ute was much more accomplished than my own wrestle with the Land Rover and he also had the advantage of knowing the terrain. He swerved and dodged the rocks ahead of us and seemed to sense instinctively which ones he needed to avoid and which he could simply plough over. As a result, we were moving much faster than my previous trip across the desert plain and I estimated we'd be at Uncle George's place in less than a couple of hours. It would not be a comfortable ride but I don't imagine any of us cared much about that.

As we drove I pondered the last half-hour, in which I'd lurched between black despair – fully expecting to be executed and have my body dumped somewhere anonymous for the scavenging birds to pick clean – and utter euphoria when Jack and Smith had leaned down and helped me up from my sitting position by the rail tracks. Penney had sported the stony poker face I'd always seen but Jack had been all smiles.

'Why did you run, mate?'

'You were shooting at me,' I retorted. 'What was I supposed to do?'

Penney grunted. 'I was just trying to get you to stay put.'

'Well that's a bloody funny way of doing it. You seem to forget that you've already had a damn good go at putting a bullet in me.'

He gave me a long, hard stare. 'Mate, if I'd wanted to put a bullet in you, you'd be leaking like a colander. Back in Oodnadatta, that was only meant to frighten you off. And just now, I was shooting into the air, trying to make you stand still so we could come and get you. But no – you had to go and be a bloody hero, didn't you?'

I hadn't felt much like a hero but I was damned if I was going to admit that to him.

'You did give us the runaround, mate,' said Jack.

'Good.'

Between them, they'd tried to fuss over my injuries. Penney was less than sympathetic about my wrist sprain – he called me a 'bloody idiot, traipsing around those mines' – but seemed genuinely concerned about the taipan bite.

'Show me the anti-venom you used,' he demanded.

'I can't. I left it back there with the snake.'

Penney tutted. 'Where did you inject it?'

I showed him the pinprick mark on my belly.

'How deep?'

'Deep enough,' I said, hoping I was right.

'Well there's nothing else we can do about it now.' He turned to Jack. 'We'll have to get him straight to the doc when we get back to town.'

'Town?' I said, looking between them anxiously.

Jack nodded. 'Time is always the biggest factor with snake bites. Even if you've got the anitvenom in you, you still need urgent medical attention. It was a bloody clever idea of yours to burn down the telegraph pole. If we hadn't found you when we did, you'd be a goner for certain.'

I put as much steel into my voice as I could muster. 'There's only one place we're going and that's the Deakins property.'

Jack went from nodding his head to shaking it. 'Not a chance, mate. If we don't get you back to town, I can't answer for what might happen to you. Snake bites are nasty little buggers at the best of times and the taipan is the worst. We've got to get you to a doctor.'

I sat down in the sand where I was standing. I didn't care how childish it looked; I wasn't going to be moved on this topic.

'It's the Deakins place or you can leave me here.'

Jack and Smith Penney looked at each other. I tried to work out who was in charge. Then Penney shrugged and walked off towards the ute.

Jack looked back at me. 'Just don't come running to me when you're dying of convulsions and organ failure.'

'Scout's honour,' I said, making the boy scout salute.

Now we were making rapid progress towards the plume of black smoke that still lingered on the eastern horizon and I was praying to a god I didn't believe in that Sophie and Adam had somehow made it out of there alive. I conjured up all kinds of horrific images in my mind and spent the next half-hour trying to dislodge them again. Had the three thugs made it to the farmstead? And then there was the plane that had buzzed me and pushed me into sharing a crevice with a killer snake. Had that reached the Deakins farm, and if so, what had followed? The aircraft had been unable to land in the valley where I'd seen it but the farm stood in slightly more open country and I found it hard to believe that an experienced pilot wouldn't have been able to find somewhere to put his bird down before they launched an assault on the house.

My biggest worry was the smoke. It was obvious to me that the main farm building had gone up in flames but how had it happened? Was it a scorched earth plan by Sophie and Adam to put their pursuers off the scent? After all, if the assassins believed they were already dead, maybe they'd have called off their manhunt. Sophie certainly had the wherewithal to set the place ablaze using the mine explosives so it wasn't a completely vain hope. And it was much better to contemplate than the alternative, which was that the thugs had penned them in at the farmhouse and resorted to arson. If Sophie and Adam stayed inside, they'd die from the effects of smoke inhalation, assuming the fire itself didn't get them; if they made a run for it, the killers would be shooting fish in a barrel.

Despite the heat, I shivered.

Jack broke into my thoughts. 'Oh yeah, mate, I nearly forgot. There was a phone call for you last night.'

'A phone call?'

'Kenny Hines. Said he hadn't heard from you for a couple of days. Sounded worried.'

'I'll bet he did. We were supposed to be in contact every evening but I haven't spoken to him since the day before yesterday. What did he say?'

Jack smiled. 'That was the interesting bit. He wanted to speak to Smith here.'

I looked at Penney, who was still giving nothing away. 'And . . . ?'

I turned back to Jack, who shrugged. 'Don't look at me, mate. He hasn't told me anything. But when the news came in at the hotel that the telegraph wire was down, Smith came right over to me and pretty much ordered me to come out here with him. Didn't you, mate? I've been trying to put two and two together ever since.'

'It pains me to say it,' said Penney at last, 'but you were the only one I could really trust.'

'Oh, thanks, mate. I'm touched.'

I couldn't tell if Jack was being sarcastic but there was a definite glint in his eye.

The tension was unbearable and I raised my voice towards Penney. 'What the hell did Kenny say?'

Finally, Smith Penney broke into a broad smile.

'How much longer?' I asked Jack.

'Twenty minutes; maybe more. Have you got a plan?'

With a shock, I realised that I hadn't. I could have spent the last hour devising some fiendish scheme for what we'd do when we reached the Deakins farm. Instead, I'd wasted it turning over what Penney had told me about Kenny's phone call – and all to no avail.

Actually, that wasn't quite true. I knew a hell of a lot more about what was behind the murder and mayhem than I had known an hour earlier but the outcome was the same: it didn't make Sophie and Adam any safer.

I had never seriously doubted Kenny's loyalty but it was good to have my faith in him confirmed. He'd come up trumps with background information about Hamilton and Irvine but his inability to reach us on the shortwave radio had left him both concerned and in a quandary. Not only did he need to track us down but he also needed to make sure the new information reached us safely. His long history with Smith Penney meant that Penney was the only person to whom Kenny was prepared to entrust the details.

And the details were explosive.

After Kenny had first contacted the firm and was met with such a helpful response from the unwitting receptionist he'd spoken to, things had turned tricky pretty quickly. He'd already told me that his second call to Hamilton and Irvine had been a good deal frostier than the first and he feared for the corporate future of the poor receptionist he'd originally chatted to. From that, I had devised the notion that someone high up in the company had been trying to close Kenny's enquiries down and possibly close us down too – and now Kenny had confirmed it. The chairman of Hamilton and Irvine was someone named Charlie Dacre.

'What did Kenny find out about him?' I had asked Penney.

'Not him – her.'

According to Kenny, Charlie Dacre was not a nice lady. It had taken Kenny and his two reliable sidekicks, Ruth and Carly, several days to trace her footprints through the sands of Sydney commerce and what they had found evidently left an unpleasant odour. At first they had struggled to find any information or anyone willing to talk about her but they had finally managed to track down a former staffer who spoke to Kenny on condition of complete anonymity. While the grumblings of a disgruntled ex-employee should probably be taken with a pinch of salt, the gist was clear: Charlie Dacre was not above all kinds of underhand ploys and plots to get her way, even skirting the fringes of corporate law to maximise her profits and her position. She'd been widowed at a young age, with a child to look after, and while some people buckle under that kind of adversity, she had fought her way through by developing a hide like a rhinoceros and a first-class business brain, which she combined with a dubious morality to devastating effect.

She had assumed her current role just a few months back
by wresting control of the business away from members of
both the Hamilton and Irvine families, using every seedy
tactic from bribery to blackmail. It appeared she left a trail
of destruction in her wake, alongside a baying pack of
delighted shareholders.

So far, so shark-like. But where Charlie Dacre seemed
to differ from many of her ruthless counterparts in business
was that she had a reputation in certain circles for not
stopping at the fringes of the law: she was willing to trample
all over the boundary and go swanning about in the fragrant
meadows of criminality. Nothing had ever been proved –
she was too smart an operator for that – but rumours
abounded. Investigations by tax officials and fraud detectives
had been unable to pin anything more concrete on her
than a parking fine or two but the mole clearly suggested
that she was prepared to stop at nothing to achieve her
ends. While the word 'murder' had not actually been used
during the interrogation of the witness, Kenny was apparently willing to believe anything of Charlie Dacre.

So I had a name but precious little else. The evidence
may have looked strong from where I was sitting but, to
use Kenny's legal terminology, it was decidedly circumstantial. We had nothing to link her directly to anything that
had happened out here in the outback over the past week
and only Kenny's hunch to put her in – or, for that matter,
anywhere near – the frame. I was willing to trust Kenny's
hunch above pretty much anything else but it wouldn't
stand up in a court of law.

Meanwhile, we had the little matter of three homicidal
thugs in a scorching desert to deal with. They had already
shown Smith Penney they were happy to use violence if
they needed to and the attack on me from the air had left
little doubt that they would do whatever it took. Dolly's
death, of course, had already demonstrated that but that

was just another thing to chalk up in the 'circumstantial' column.

For now.

'So what are we going to do?' Penney sounded energised.

'I haven't decided yet. I'm beginning to think we should have gone back to Oodnadatta.'

'I told you that,' said Jack. 'We need to get your arm seen to and—'

'Not for me – for reinforcements. Why the hell didn't you bring a radio with you?'

Penney grunted. It seemed to be one of his primary means of communication.

'All right, mate,' said Jack. 'No need to go on about it. We were only supposed to be hopping up the train track to see what had happened to the telegraph line. We weren't expecting to be quartermastering another Gallipoli.'

'It's hardly the Great War,' I said morosely. 'And I'm not exactly asking for an Anzac army. But a radio would have been nice.'

Penney let out a short, barking laugh and Jack fell silent for a few minutes.

'Well we can't just roll up and walk in the front door,' he said eventually. 'Those bastards will be watching the farm for sure. Whatever's happened to Sophie and Adam, they'll know that they've still got to take you out of the game.'

That gave me an idea.

'You're right, they know about me. But they don't know about the two of you – at least, not that you know the background to all this. As far as they're concerned, you could simply be heading out to the Deakins farmstead because you've spotted the smoke on the horizon and are worried that someone might be in need of assistance. I'd be surprised if they were willing to take you out unless they knew for sure that you were in the know. That would be too much collateral damage and there's already more than enough of that. No, my bet is that they'll play the waiting game and see what happens when you get there. If you don't look like you're going to cause trouble for them, they might just leave you alone. Of course, if Sophie and Adam are still around to blab everything to you, then it'll be a very different story.'

Jack said, 'So what are you proposing?'

'Drop me off a quarter of a mile or so from Uncle George's. You've brought more than one rifle, I hope?'

Penney laughed. 'What do you take me for? There's a bloody arsenal back there.' He jerked a thumb over his shoulder towards the flatbed of the Datsun, which was shrouded with a large, grubby tarpaulin. I gave silent thanks for the naturally suspicious instincts of the outback larrikin in his native environment. Or maybe Penney just liked guns.

'I thought this wasn't Gallipoli?' I quipped. Before he could respond, I said, 'I'll take a rifle and stay well back. When you drive in, the innocent white knights coming to the rescue, I'll keep an eye out for any movement around the fringes of the compound. Even if they don't believe you're as innocent as you're going to appear, they won't be expecting a pincer movement from fore and aft.'

'And if they decide they don't like the look of us?' Jack sounded worried.

'Don't panic. I'll try not let them take any potshots at you. If you take reasonable precautions – like not wandering about in the open or inspecting the perimeter too closely – then with a bit of luck we might get away without a confrontation. And if it does come to a shootout, then at least we've got even numbers and a . . . What did you call it, Penney?'

'A bloody arsenal.'

'Right. A bloody arsenal.'

So they dropped me off as we approached a bend in the track that concealed the Deakins farm. The smoke had thinned during our journey but the plume was still sickeningly visible as it rose above the dune where we stopped. I indicated that I would skirt round to the left, coming in towards the farmstead from the west. I wanted to get well away from the track and I reasoned that if the three thugs were hanging around, they would have split up and spread out. My guess was that they were most likely to be watching from the west and south, partly to avoid staring into a setting sun but also to keep their escape options as open as possible. The track fed into the compound at the south-west corner and that's where I thought their attention might be focused. If I could set up a position overlooking the fence, with the sun behind me and a clear view of the house, I should be able to spot anyone keeping watch nearer the buildings without being seen myself. It was a long time since I'd used my weapons training in anger and I'd never been in the field as a sniper but I'd have to do the best I could. I just hoped Smith Penney kept his rifles in good working order, and that my enfeebled arm would stand up to firing one if it came to it. I grabbed one from under the tarp – complete with telescopic sights – and slung it over my shoulder, marvelling at Smith Penney's sophisticated collection of weapons. Maybe he needed them for hunting or something.

I kept low as I ran for the base of the dune. I was wary of the muzzle being visible over the top of the slope. The glint of gunmetal catching the light of the dying sun would be a dead giveaway to a trained eye.

Behind me, Jack stuck the Datsun into gear and took off towards the farmstead. I cursed him for not waiting longer: I would have perhaps half a minute before he pulled up outside the house and I would need every second.

I kept to the base of the dune as I moved fast to my left.

In my head I counted off fifteen of those Army instructor seconds, then cut sharply to my right, scrabbling up the dune and throwing myself down into the sand just below the peak. I glanced behind me to check the location of the sun and saw that it would blind anyone who looked over in my direction from the compound. This position would have to do.

I was totally unprepared for the sight I encountered when I put my head over the lip of the dune.

The building at the heart of the farmstead – George's home – was a blackened husk. It had no roof, half its walls had collapsed and any remaining timber clinging to the stonework was roasted to charcoal. The holes I'd complained about just a few nights earlier were now open gashes in the structure and the contents of the house had been melted into black sludge, with most individual pieces of furniture and personal effects indistinguishable from the rest. I felt the nausea rise in my throat again: if Sophie and Adam had been inside this conflagration when it went up, they would have faced a horrifying end.

I didn't have time to contemplate that possibility as the Datsun appeared at the gate of the compound over to my right. Immediately, I started scanning the dunes beyond the perimeter for any sign of activity. I saw nothing.

Jack swung the ute in a wide arc round the well, coming to a halt near the front door of the house, not far from the Land Rover, which was still parked where Sophie had left it, its tyres in shreds. I wondered if the cylinder lashed to its chassis had succumbed to the firestorm but from where I was, the Land Rover's bodywork looked as if it had escaped the flames and I was hopeful the cylinder had too.

I smiled as I watched Jack trying to make his entrance look totally innocent and unimpeachable. Smartly, he left the tail end of the car closest to the building, allowing for swift and easy access to the armoury under the tarpaulin.

Smith Penney opened the passenger door, nearest to me, and climbed out, leaving the rifle out of sight in the cab. That was smart too – it would be reachable if required but it would have put any watchers on immediate alert if he'd emerged with it.

I peeled my eyes as Jack and Penney walked slowly up to the building and I heard them call out through the burned-out door, making out they were a rescue party looking for survivors. That wasn't so far from the truth but it was important that they played the role for any onlookers' benefit.

Jack took a step onto the verandah then checked himself, looking at the soot he'd just picked up on the sole of his boot. He steadied himself against the doorpost to do it and realised he'd just done the same thing with his hand. He brushed the ash off on his shirt and stepped back again. He and Penney stood for a moment, looking uncertainly around the compound, then raised their sights higher. I worried that they might be looking for me and ducked down under the lip of the dune. If they spotted me and tried to attract my attention, they'd immediately give away my position to anyone in the vicinity and we'd be done for.

I waited thirty seconds before peeping back over the crest, my rifle still cradled against my shoulder in readiness. The two men had split up and gone in different directions, Penney to the rear of the house and Jack towards the well. While Penney stayed close to the building, making use of its shelter, Jack was moving into uncomfortably open ground and I took another look around the perimeter, hoping to pinpoint the enemy. I could see nothing and I was starting to wonder if I'd been wrong and maybe the farmstead wasn't under surveillance at all. I couldn't figure out any reason why they would abandon their manhunt, leaving me alive. After all, shutting down any legal enquiries into the ownership of the mine involved much more than removing Sophie and Adam: Kenny and I would both be dangerous to them. But in the absence of any evidence of their whereabouts, I had nothing to work with.

Then, as Jack approached the well, Sophie ran yelling out of the nearby outhouse and all hell broke loose.

III

My avuncular instinct kicked in and I almost shouted out to Sophie to take cover again. I managed to resist and Jack did the job for me but not until the action in the compound flushed out a shooter.

From over to my right, on the far side of the entrance to the farmstead, a gunshot rang out. I caught the flash of the muzzle in my peripheral vision and thought I'd be able to identify its location through my rifle sight. First, I checked down in the compound and saw Jack cradling Sophie under an arm and steering her swiftly towards the well, where they crouched together out of the view of the gunman.

I turned my attention back to the fence and lifted the rifle sight to my eye, resting the stock gingerly in my injured hand. I flicked back and forth a couple of times across the area I'd identified then saw the leaves of a eucalyptus rustle suspiciously. Our man had ducked back into the under-growth but from my vantage point above him I could make out his black shape and the straight, dark line that marked out the barrel of his weapon. At this distance, I'd have no problem picking him off but that was not my plan. No matter how strong my anger towards him at putting Sophie and Adam at risk, I couldn't justify taking him out in cold blood. And I'd be putting myself in danger if I tried. I still didn't know where his two pals were and I didn't fancy giving away my position to a pair of thugs who, I had to assume, would be heavily armed and on a lethal mission.

There was another factor affecting my thinking: if I could somehow get down to the gunman's location and surprise him from behind, he might be more useful to us alive than dead. It would be a high-risk manoeuvre but one with significant pay-offs if it could be achieved. Besides, my staying put would help no one and I might as well keep moving to reduce the chances of being found.

It was important that Jack and Sophie were not about to go dashing around the compound; when I looked back at them, I was optimistic about that. Sophie was curled up in a foetal position and Jack was crouching over her, shielding her from any possible attack. They didn't look as if they were going anywhere any time soon.

I shimmied down from the crest of the dune and landed on firmer ground at the bottom. Keeping my head down and sharing the weight of the rifle between my hands as best I could, I scurried inelegantly round to the right, stopping when I reached the point where the track cut through the slope on its way into the compound. I knew this would be one of the most dangerous parts of the operation, leaving me potentially exposed to anyone watching from inside, but there was no other way. I estimated the distance to the dune on the other side of the track at fifteen yards and reckoned I could cover the ground in two or three seconds, flat out. While I was not in peak physical condition – snake bites can have that kind of effect – I thought I could manage that short a sprint.

There was no point trying to hide or stay low. I was out in the open and would be clearly visible to anyone looking towards the farm entrance. I was confident that the gunman I was hunting would not be able to see me from his position but there was always the chance that he'd already moved somewhere else. And there were his two mates to be taken into consideration, too.

I fixed my focus on the base of the dune opposite and ran.

Out of all the crazy decisions I'd made in the past few days, this had to be one of the craziest. Miraculously, I got away with it.

I sprawled headfirst in the dirt and winced as the momentum rolled me over onto my damaged arm. Although I'd heard no shots fired in my direction or shouting to indicate I'd been seen, I didn't want to stick around so I scrambled to my feet and kept moving around the base of the dune. Behind me, the desert stretched out in a carpet of red earth dotted with green and brown bushes, but in front I had plenty of protection from the mounds of sand that provided the natural oasis for the farmstead. I'd calculated that the fence itself was perhaps twenty feet inside the dune I was currently skirting, which meant I'd have to scale it, descend the other side and creep up to my target, all without being noticed. As I said, a high-risk manoeuvre.

When I reached a point roughly equivalent to where I thought the gunman was, I stopped and caught my breath. Looking up to the crest of the slope, I saw the taller branches of the eucalyptus tree where he'd dug himself in and knew I'd got it about right. The earth in the mound was firmer here but I thought I could get enough of a foothold to climb it without making too much of a racket. The biggest problem was the rifle, which I considered trying to use as a kind of walking stick but which seemed more of a hindrance than a help at this point. When I got to the other side, I'd be at too close range for it to be much use anyway so I took another bold decision and left it at the base of the dune. Instead, I took out the knife that was strapped to my belt. Guerrilla tactics were going to be the order of the day.

As I climbed, I listened for any further activity in the compound. I could hear no voices and I hoped Sophie and Jack were keeping their heads down and staying where they were. Penney, I couldn't second-guess. His intemperate nature might lead him to try something stupid but, like me, he was operating on the working hypothesis that there were three armed men around the place somewhere and I suspected that might curtail his recklessness somewhat. It didn't honestly make too much difference to me whether he tried something or not: what mattered was that the attention of my quarry was firmly on the farmstead and its occupants, rather than on the potential for an ambush from behind. I thought it was safe to assume that they wouldn't be expecting Jack and Penney to have teamed up with me so there would be no reason for them to wonder where I was at that particular moment. They would probably imagine that I'd died out in the desert. Meanwhile, with Sophie still charging about the place, offering herself up as a target, all they had to do was sit with their rifles poised and wait for an opportunity to strike.

I wondered how long they would wait. Night would fall fast when it came and it wasn't too far off now. If I were in their shoes, I'd want to get the whole thing done and dusted in daylight, which meant they might be preparing to rush the farm at any time. On the other hand, I'd seen no sign of anyone other than my single shooter and he didn't seem to be communicating with anyone else. Was it possible that he was a lone watchman on the lookout for my return to the farm? Perhaps he had simply been detailed to keep Sophie and Adam – if Adam was still alive – penned in until starvation or heatstroke got them. I began to feel slightly more optimistic about our chances.

At the top of the ridge, I poked my head over and saw him immediately.

Favouring my right side to avoid the possibility of crying

out in pain if I landed on my weak arm, I slid noiselessly down the far side of the slope and vaulted the fence. As I planted my boots on solid ground, the shooter moved his head and for a moment I thought I'd been rumbled. But he wagged his head more violently a second time and I realised he was trying to shake off the ubiquitous flies that would be obscuring his vision. If he turned round now, I'd be a sitting duck. The only option was to move forward – and fast.

I covered the ground between us in seconds. Abandoning any effort at concealment, I dived the last few feet and landed heavily on him just as he heard my movement and tried to spin round. His shift in position meant that my outstretched arm – intended to wrap around his neck and shoulders – instead made full contact with his left cheek and the knife I was brandishing sliced into the skin near his ear. He let out a piercing scream and writhed underneath me but I was pinning his arms against his chest, where they clutched his rifle, and I slammed my free hand down over his mouth. Pain shot through my bandaged wrist and forearm but I held firm and forced his head backwards, lifting his chin and making it difficult for him to breathe. Sensibly, he stopped wriggling and concentrated instead on taking in heavy breaths through the part of his nose that I'd left unhindered. I stared menacingly into his face, willing him to understand that I would not be impressed if he made any further sound. He seemed to get the message.

Without taking my eyes off him, I listened for reactions elsewhere in the compound. I'd expected to hear shouts, gunshots, running feet – anything to indicate that my victim's pals were coming to his aid.

I heard nothing.

'Are you alone?' I hissed into the face of my hostage. I could see fear and pain in his eyes and I thought I could exploit that. I brought the knife in tight to his throat and

let him feel the hard, bitter edge of the steel blade. I repeated
the question.

He nodded nervously, the flesh of his chin making uneasy
contact with the blade, but it meant nothing. He could be
telling the truth or he could just as easily be lying.

Keeping my injured arm clamped across his shoulder
and my hand over his mouth, I put the knife blade between
my teeth and took hold of his rifle, which he was still
grasping uselessly against his body. He released it without
a struggle and I tossed it away with as much force as I
could muster from my prone position. It didn't go far but
I was happy that it was too far for him to be able to reach.
In disarming him, I'd allowed him to free one hand but I
had the blade back against his throat before he could capi-
talise on that and he lay still, the blood from his cheek
dripping into his hair and onto the ground beside his head.

'You'd better be right about that,' I said. 'Otherwise it'll
be more than your ear that's sliced open.' I pushed the
blade against his skin one more time to emphasise the point
and he nodded again. 'Now don't move.'

I eased myself off him and to my knees, the knife never
more than two inches from his face, and maintained eye
contact as I patted him down for other weapons. It was a
bodge job of a search but it was all I could manage under
the circumstances. Finding nothing, I backed off from him
and got to my feet. Without looking away, I went over to
the rifle and picked it up, pointing it immediately at him.
The knife I slipped back into its sheath on my belt. My left
hand was almost too weak to support the forestock but I
didn't let him see that, balancing the stock under my right
shoulder and taking the bulk of its weight on the trigger
guard.

'Get up.'

He leaped into life but I didn't want that so I waved the
muzzle at him menacingly.

'Slower.'

He checked his pace and got to his feet, holding his hands high in the time-honoured tradition of prisoners the world over. I indicated for him to turn round and head for the compound.

The distance from the perimeter fence to the well couldn't have been more than sixty yards but the time it took for me to run across the open space felt like a lifetime.

I'd told my hostage to keep walking towards the well and called across to Jack that he was on his way.

'I don't think he's armed but you'd better frisk him when he gets there,' I shouted.

'Leave him to me,' said Jack, and I hoped that wasn't a note of mild glee in his voice.

I kept my rifle trained on our prisoner all the way across, as I'd told him I would, but I was also looking out for movement around the edges of the compound. His colleagues – if they were there somewhere – might just think it expedient not to allow him to be captured and to take him out as he walked to the well. But he wasn't moving as if he was expecting to be cut down at any moment and I took heart from that.

It was a very different matter when it came to my stepping out into the open, however. The hostage had reached the well without incident and I caught glimpses of Jack's head popping up and down as he ran a much more thorough search than I had. Then he span the man around and pushed him to his knees against the low wall of the well. I couldn't see Sophie at all, and I assumed Penney was somewhere in the house itself. I still didn't know what had happened to Adam.

It occurred to me that I could get Jack to bring the ute over and pick me up but that would have involved too many risks: Sophie would have been left minding the prisoner and

Jack himself would have had to emerge from his shielded position, get to the car, drive it over and then get us both back to safety, all under the potential eye of two more killers. I wasn't prepared to risk that just so he could rescue me.

Instead, I ran for it.

I'd decided I would head for the Land Rover first, take a brief pause there to collect myself, then go on to the well. In the heat of the moment, however, and in the absence of any gunfire from around the compound, I didn't stop. I reached the well and threw myself to the ground beside Jack, who was pointing a pistol at our hostage. Behind him sat Sophie, whose face lit up when she saw me, then darkened again as she spotted the bandages on my arm.

'Bill – are you OK?' she began, but I cut her short.

'We don't have time to talk about my health right now. We need some answers.'

I turned to the prisoner and stared hard at him.

'Seems like you were telling the truth. Where are the others?'

His expression didn't change. There was a steely contempt in his face. 'What others?' The accent was unquestionably Australian.

Jack made as if to thump him but I held out a restraining hand.

'There are lots of ways we can do this,' I said. 'We can all be nice and you can tell us what the hell is going on. Or it can get nasty.'

Out of the corner of my eye I saw Sophie grimace but I ignored that. The man didn't look like he was going to change his mind, even with my not-so-veiled threats, so I brought in the cavalry.

'Penney!' I shouted towards the house.

'Everything all right?' he answered.

'I need you to do a little job for me.'

From inside the house, Smith Penney stepped onto the verandah and, for the first time, our prisoner's defiant look faltered. As he watched Penney stroll over from the house, a rifle resting casually on his shoulder, his expression changed to one of alarm, then sheer terror. Perhaps he was remembering – and regretting – the beating he and his chums had given Penney back in Oodnadatta. Comeuppance can be a powerful motivator.

Jack and Penney grabbed an arm each and hoisted the hostage to his feet. As they dragged him back towards the house I switched my attention to Sophie, who looked almost as terrified as the man they'd taken away.

'What will they do to him?' she asked.

I shrugged. 'Whatever it takes, I guess. This is now officially a war zone. But let's not think about that. What happened to Adam?'

Instantly, Sophie became focused again.

'He's over in that outhouse,' she said, pointing in the direction of the corrugated iron shack near the coolibah tree where we'd found Uncle George's first treasure. 'We split up when we saw the men arrive and hid in different places. He's fine.'

'Not fine enough to look after you.'

'That's hardly fair, Bill. He's injured.'

'He's not the only one,' I said acidly.

An anguished cry came from the house and I knew Jack and Penney were at work getting information from their prisoner. I needed to distract Sophie so I took her by the arm and began marching her towards the outhouse. After my own sprint across the compound and Penney's much more laid-back saunter to pick up the hostage, I was confident there were no snipers lurking in the trees around our little oasis.

We reached the shack and I yanked open the door. There, hunched among an array of rotting tools and a rusting bicycle, sat Adam. I offered him an outstretched arm, which he took and hauled himself to his feet.

'Bloody hell, Bill – I'm glad to see you.'

At that moment the feeling wasn't particularly mutual. I'd have felt much better disposed towards this sallow Englishman if he'd shown more of a protective instinct towards his wife.

'Let's sit under the coolibah tree,' I said, and led the way across to the shade. What I really wanted was to get Sophie out of earshot of what was going on inside the house but even the tree wasn't far enough. I mentally blocked out the sound of the prisoner being interrogated and faced Sophie and Adam.

'Now, tell me everything that's happened since I last saw you.'

Sophie insisted on rebandaging my arm and checking me over for signs of deterioration from the snake bite before she would tell me anything. I was feeling surprisingly chipper, given what I'd been through, and I was optimistic that the anti-venom had done its work successfully. Or maybe the dose of taipan juice I'd received had been less than I feared. I would still need to see the medics when I got back to civilisation but I wasn't about to keel over.

To the backdrop of the occasional grunt and cry from the house, I heard the story of how the three thugs had rolled up at Uncle George's in their big black Range Rover, armed to the teeth and out for blood. The plane, it seemed, never made it as far as the farmstead. My fear that its occupants were set on an aerial assault of the house had proved unfounded and I guessed it must instead have been taking supplies – possibly including weapons – to the troops at Macumba Station, where I knew a makeshift airstrip was carved into the sand. That would also explain the delay between my being buzzed and the cloud of smoke appearing above the Deakins property: the private army had been waiting for fresh provisions before launching its latest attack on the ground.

Fortunately, Sophie had been on lookout when the Range Rover arrived and she'd watched it wheel through the entrance and come to a dusty halt near the well. The men were clearly well-drilled and waited some time before emerging from the vehicle. When they did, they did it in formation, skirting out in either direction to cover the front of the house. By then, Sophie had picked up Adam from the settee where he was resting, thrown his arm round her shoulders for support and sneaked out of the back door. As they passed the generator, she had the presence of mind to grab its metal frame and pull it over, blocking the door to hinder the progress of anyone who might come after them. Then they'd made off as quickly as they could to the nearest section of the fence, where they'd hunkered down in the bushes as the thugs searched the house.

Finding the place empty, the three men had begun to comb the compound, starting at the well and taking in the two outhouses. Sophie and Adam had used the opportunity to change position, moving around the fence towards the entrance in the hope of an escape. When the men came up with nothing in the outbuildings, they regrouped on the verandah and rested for a cigarette.

'Sounds like they were thorough,' I said.

Sophie nodded. 'And they didn't stop there. After they'd finished their smoke, they started on the fence. One went to the main entrance, not far from where we were hiding, another went out the back and the third headed over the other side.'

She pointed to a spot near where I'd ambushed the hostage.

From their starting points, the trio had worked anticlockwise around the perimeter, poking rifles into bushes and peering up the trees that encircled the compound. For one brief moment, Sophie explained, two of the men were completely out of sight, while the third – the one who'd started at the entrance – had his back to Sophie and Adam.

'I knew we would be caught if we stayed where we were, and Adam didn't fancy heading out into the bush with his leg the way it is, so we made a beeline for the outhouses,' she said.

'Which they'd already searched,' I said, nodding appreciatively. 'Smart girl.'

Sophie smiled. 'It worked, didn't it?'

'It worked. What happened then?'

'I'm not too sure. I could only see through cracks in the corrugated iron so I didn't get a proper view but when they finished their search they went back to the house. The next thing I knew it was a raging inferno. Two of them – that one who's inside now and one of the others – came dashing out and they just stood and watched it for about ten minutes. I'm not sure but I think the third one might have got caught up in the fire.'

I shuddered. 'What did the other two do?'

'They talked for a bit – it looked like they were trying to work out what to do – then one got in the car and drove away. The other one went and hid in the bushes, where you found him.'

'I hope to God you're right about the third one,' I said callously. 'If not, he might still be around here somewhere.'

A noise from the house that sounded like a heavy piece of furniture falling over cut into our conversation. Moments later, Jack and Penney emerged onto the verandah, carrying the hostage between them, trussed up like a turkey. They dumped him unceremoniously into the dirt outside the front door and came over to where we were sitting under the tree. From where we were I could see that he was still conscious and I wondered what Penney in particular had done to him: there had been a score there waiting to be settled.

'Well?' I asked as they neared the shade.

Jack grinned. 'He's quite talkative when you get to know him.'

'Anything useful?'

'His name's Ron, if that's any help?'

'I said "useful".'

'Ah, right, mate. You mean like the fact that there'll be reinforcements on their way?'

I looked at him sharply. 'He told you that?'

Jack waved his hands at me in a placatory manner. 'Don't worry, mate – he doesn't think they're coming back tonight.'

'Doesn't think? Is that the best you've come up with? They could be back at any moment.'

'No, mate – it'll be night soon and I don't think they'd risk it in the dark.'

I wasn't so sure. We were likely to be heavily outnumbered, whatever time of day or night they arrived.

'Where did they go for these reinforcements?'

'Macumba Station. Seems like there's a few more of them camped out there.'

'A few? Do you know how many?'

'Three or four, he thought. Ron hadn't seen them himself as they were still on their way from Coober Pedy when he and his buddies left Macumba to come here.'

'Talking of his buddies, what happened to the third one who was here?'

Jack pulled a face and looked at Sophie. 'Did you see it?' he asked her.

Sophie shook her head. 'We were hiding in the outhouses. What happened?'

He drew in a slow breath, considering his words. 'Apparently they all went out onto the back porch for a ciggie after they'd searched the place. Somebody had knocked over the generator and left a load of fuel lying about and . . .'

'And cigarettes and diesel don't mix,' I said.

'Something like that.'

Penney spoke for the first time since coming out of the burned-out house. 'Must have gone up like a bomb.'

'It did,' said Sophie forlornly. She had turned a shade of sickly green and I knew why: she had been the one who knocked over the generator. According to her scoring method, this would be the latest death for which she was holding herself responsible.

I stood up and took control of the group. 'We don't have time for a forensic dissection of the fire and we can't bank on the reinforcements not arriving tonight.'

'What do you suggest?' said Jack.

'I suggest we get ready to repel all boarders.'

Four faces stared at me incredulously. It was Sophie who spoke.

'You want us to stay and fight?'

'I don't really see what other options we have.'

'We could make a run for it,' said Jack. 'I know the Landy's out of action but three of us could fit in the cab of the ute, and Smith can look after Adam on the flatbed.'

'Why me?' said Penney.

'Because you're used to it,' Jack replied. 'These Pommie bastards wouldn't last five minutes in the back over this ground.'

I stamped on Jack's idea pretty sharpish. 'We're not making a run for it. We're effectively in a bottleneck here and the only way out is past Macumba Station. I don't feel like walking into the mouth of the lions' den right now, do you?'

'We went cross-country before—' Jack began.

'And we're not making the same mistake again. Especially not with a car full of people. With five of us on board we couldn't carry enough supplies and if we drove overnight there's a high chance we'd end up lost – even with your local knowledge. No – our best bet is to batten down the hatches and build ourselves a bunker in whatever time we've got before they arrive.'

Penney looked animated. 'Like the Alamo?' he said.

'You can be Davy Crockett if you like,' I said, 'but I'd read up on your American history before you take that analogy too far.'

He looked confused but I didn't pursue it. We had work to do.

For the next few hours I pushed everyone as hard as I could. Jack and Penney were the fittest and I put them to the hard labour of constructing walls around the blackened shell of the farmhouse using whatever materials they could find. Penney wanted to tear down the two outhouses for iron cladding but I stopped him: I wanted to put Sophie in one of them, as far out of harm's way as I could manage, and the injured Adam in the other. At least they would have a chance if the main building fell to the attackers.

Adam himself was dragooned into filling empty sacks with sand from a nearby dune. He'd been keener than anyone to stay put and positively leaped at the prospect of hiding in one of the outhouses. My estimation of him hadn't risen in the weeks I'd known him and his overt lack of care for Sophie was high on my list of reasons why. I've never been able to understand spouses who don't realise what a jewel they have at their side and instead take them for granted. I just hoped that, if Sophie was going to see through his pusillanimity, she would do it sooner rather than later. From where I was standing, she deserved better.

Sophie and I worked on the interior of the farmhouse, rearranging the charred remains of the furniture into buttresses and bulwarks against intruders. By the time we'd finished ripping fixtures from the walls and piling up everything from the bathtub to the settee, our barricade wouldn't have looked out of place on the streets of Paris in the June Rebellion. I didn't think any of our efforts would offer much protection against the kind of weaponry our enemy was likely to be packing but we had to do something.

Ron spent the evening bound to a charred wooden chair, gagged and largely ignored despite his muffled pleadings. If and when any action came, he'd have to take his chances.

By nine o'clock, the sky was black. We could have gone on working by the light of the ute's headlamps but I was worried about the possibility of providing an easily identifiable beacon to anyone approaching. We were enough of a sitting target without giving away our exact location. We ate frugally and I told the others to try to bed down for the night. Sophie insisted on being included in the two-hour watch shift that I drew up, which would see us through to the first wisps of dawn, but I took the first watch.

It gave me no pleasure to realise that I had been right and Jack had been wrong. A few minutes before midnight, when I was due to hand over the watch to Penney, I heard a car approaching.

I left it longer than I should have done, trying to confirm that what I was hearing on the wind was, in fact, an engine. When I saw a glimmer of light silhouetting the dunes either side of the farmstead entrance, I waited no longer. I roused the others quickly and they all moved to their allotted places. Sophie helped Adam to his outhouse then crossed the compound to the other, which I could see from my vantage point near the front door. I was stationed behind the bath, which had been wedged on its end, with a couple of armchairs holding it upright. If I crouched, I could actually climb inside it but I had no idea if the metal cocoon would offer any protection against a bullet. I'd already hammered out the plughole, leaving a neat, round perforation that I could use for observation or for sniping. Jack knelt behind an upturned wardrobe to my left while on my right Penney lay outstretched on the ground, the muzzle of his rifle poking out through a low gap in the timbers. Around him was a makeshift foxhole of chairs, boxes and cushions that would offer about as much cover as my tin bath.

On the plus side, I reckoned we might enjoy the benefit of surprise. The approaching forces couldn't know how many of us there were lying in wait for them. But I realised with a nauseating feeling in my throat that we were just as much in the dark as they were: we had no idea how many of them there would be and I could only hope that Ron's guess had been an overestimate. We could probably see off two or three reinforcements – any more than that and we'd be in serious trouble.

The lights rounded the corner of the dune and my heart sank. Two Range Rovers entered the compound at speed and had to pull up fast to avoid colliding with the immobilised Land Rover. Out of the doors piled . . . how many? Four? Five? And every one of them looked armed to the teeth. When I spotted the gunman from the plane illuminated in the beam of the headlights, I stopped counting and let fly with my rifle. Jack and Penney followed suit and the men scattered like ants from vinegar. One or two jumped straight back into the cars, which swung round and headed for the gate. The rest split up towards the trees.

Then Penney fired again and the sky lit up orange.

It took me a moment to work out what had happened. The leading Range Rover had been blasted into the air and was only now coming down, a ball of flame that crashed to the earth on its roof. The car behind swerved recklessly to avoid it and the passenger door flew open, throwing its occupant directly into the burning wreckage. As the screams rent the night sky, I looked over at Penney, who was looking back at me stony-faced.

'What the hell?' I mouthed.

With his free hand, he picked up a neatly-tied bundle of red sticks and waved them at me.

'Dynamite,' he said simply. 'I buried some out there earlier.'

He was obviously more of a marksman than I'd given him credit for.

Jack, meanwhile, was popping off at anyone he could see outside. With the compound lit up by the fireball, there were few places to hide. The second Range Rover had swung side-on and stopped, and the driver had climbed out of the far door, from where he was now setting up a shooting position. If he got the chance to square up to us things might get sticky, so I launched a couple of bullets in his direction and he abandoned that plan, running off towards the gate.

I heard another shot from Jack and saw a man spin away and fall to the ground over to my left. Return fire started from behind the coolibah tree and I heard a bullet ping off the outhouse where Sophie was hiding. I hoped she was keeping her head down. Penney and Jack both pointed their rifles in the direction of the tree and let off a volley of shots in quick succession. A cry went up and the return fire stopped.

I tried to figure out how many might still be at large out there in the blackness. I thought I'd seen six emerging from the cars and with the two drivers that would make at least eight. One driver was never going to get behind the wheel of a car again – Penney had made sure of that – and the coolibah tree man sounded like he might be out of action too, along with the one Jack had floored and the poor bastard who'd fallen into the conflagration. That still left four by my reckoning and I couldn't see where they were.

'Hold your fire,' I shouted to Jack and Penney, and the night fell silent.

'Did you see where they went?' I whispered.

Penney shook his head. I turned to look at Jack, who said, 'There are two in the trees over to the left and the driver of the second Range Rover ran off out of the gate. I don't think we'll be seeing him again.'

'That still leaves one unaccounted for,' I said, and Penney immediately started moving.

'I'll flush them out,' he said, heading for the back door of the house.

'Wait,' I ordered, but he'd already gone.

Enough light from the compound reached the back door to reveal Penney's silhouette breaking to the left as he stepped outside. It seemed to me like a suicide mission but then Penney had been a constant source of surprise to me and I didn't want to underestimate him now.

'Let's give him some cover,' I said to Jack, and we both began peppering the fence line over to our left.

Two minutes later I heard a gunshot from the direction of the coolibah tree and I signalled to Jack to stop. There had been no return fire from the trees that Jack and I had been targeting and without a visible enemy we were just wasting ammunition. I wondered what Penney had been up to over by the coolibah and I didn't have to wait long to find out. Less than ninety seconds later he was back at his post in the house.

'Another one down,' he said, and I chose not to ask any more questions.

The minutes ticked by and I started to get nervous. There were two men unaccounted for and if they moved stealthily they could be anywhere by now. The flames from the Range Rover were dying down and it was darkening across the compound. I was most wary of an attack from the rear so I turned round in the bathtub and sat with my back to its floor, training my rifle on the door where Penney had been silhouetted only minutes earlier.

As I watched, I became aware that the chair where Ron had been strapped had vanished. For much of the gun battle, he'd been bouncing up and down, his futile shrieks muffled by the gag in his mouth. It had vaguely registered with me when Penney went out to the coolibah tree that the chair was no longer standing upright but I thought Ron had probably tipped it over to keep a lower profile as the bullets went whizzing through the ruins of the house. Now I wasn't so sure. I crept over to where the chair had stood and put my hand straight into a warm, wet pool that spread across the floorboards. I lifted the hand to my face and, even in the darkness, knew it was blood. I reached out to feel for Ron and discovered him soon enough. It was the work of a few seconds to find a wrist tied behind his back and establish that there was no pulse.

The revving of the Range Rover engine brought me spinning back to face the front again. I ducked into the bath and peered out through the plughole. One of the remaining men was scrambling to get into the car. The door was still open as the other man, evidently in the driving seat, took off, ploughing straight through the middle of the still-burning wreckage of the first vehicle on his way to the gate. Bits of smouldering material attached themselves to the underside of the Range Rover and I heard Penney bark a short, humourless laugh.

If Jack was right – that the eighth man had long since fled – then we were alone once more. Thirty seconds later, out in the desert beyond the dunes, the other Range Rover exploded.

I stared at Penney, who calmly showed me his two empty hands. He had no more dynamite.

IV

It looked like a hell of a mess to me but the clean-up operation was remarkably smooth.

One of the few benefits of this part of the country being relatively lawless was that nobody cared much about a bunch of missing mercenaries. The battlefield was unlikely to be stumbled across and even if it was it would be next to impossible to uncover the story of what happened there that night. The charred remains of the Deakins house and a pair of gutted Range Rovers would not reveal the secrets of the half-dozen or so bodies that would, in any case, be unidentifiable soon enough. The abandoned rented Land Rover might raise a few questions but if a semi-retired insurance investigator couldn't deal with that, then I'd lost my touch.

'We can't just leave them here like this,' said Sophie, trembling, when Penney first mooted getting out of there fast. She'd emerged from her outhouse to a hellscape of fire and brimstone and, although not a medical expert, I feared she might be suffering from shock.

'Got any better ideas?' he asked her baldly.

She hadn't.

While the others prepared to leave in the Datsun, I spent some time alone with her, taking her out of sight of the carnage and calming her down. As gently as I could, I explained that we could spend hours digging graves but that wouldn't prevent the dingoes and other wild creatures getting to them and we'd only be putting ourselves at greater risk of discovery. Besides, I reasoned, their demise had been the direct result of their own violent intent; we'd merely acted in self-defence. If the matter were ever to go before a court, we'd be cleared by any jury of malfeasance in a trice in regard to their deaths. I don't think she was convinced but she could see that arguing about it was going to get her nowhere.

Adam seemed equally appalled and from his reaction I suspected he'd never seen a dead body before. He climbed onto the flatbed of the ute and sat there, staring silently at the devastation around the compound. He'd be no use to us so I took Sophie to him and left them comforting each other while I helped Jack and Penney get our things together. The last item I packed was the cylinder containing the all-important title exchange documents. I retrieved it from the underside of the Land Rover, stowed it in a rucksack and handed it to Sophie without a word. She nodded without looking at me and slung it immediately on her back.

We were ready to go in less than twenty minutes and I was glad of it because I didn't want to stay there a moment longer than was absolutely necessary. I knew we'd have to pass the second Range Rover on our way out, which would be another source of anguish for Sophie, and I had severe doubts about Smith Penney's plan to head for Macumba Station. He assured me it would be safe and we could get the urgent medical attention we needed but it was one place I'd avoided throughout our entire time at Uncle George's on the basis that it might be harbouring our pursuers. For all I knew, that could still be the case.

Penney was adamant. 'We've got them all,' he said. 'And the guys at Macumba are mates of mine – and George's. If there is anyone else still lurking about there, the ranch hands will side with us rather than them.'

'Even if they've been paid?' I asked.

Penney seemed genuinely affronted. 'What do you take us for – a bunch of hicks? Money means nothing around here. Hell, it comes out of the ground in great big lumps and does anyone care? Everyone is here because they want to be. Yes, of course we're all hoping to hit a bloody great opal seam but it's not the financial rewards we're after; it's the thrill of the chase. Some people play roulette, some go crocodile hunting, but we're all after the same thing. That's what you city people just don't get. It's not about the money. Money's just a means to an end. What we're looking for is something much more valuable than dollars. We're looking for something that makes us feel alive.'

Smith Penney had surprised me again.

I took him at his word and we headed for Macumba Station. Penney travelled in the flatbed with Adam. Sophie was sandwiched between me and Jack, who watched the road ahead grimly as he drove.

Fortunately there was enough room on the track to pass the remains of the Range Rover about half a mile out of the compound. I turned Sophie's head towards me as we approached, cupping her face with both hands and staring deep into her eyes, and Jack took the ute round the left-hand side of the wreckage so she could avoid having to look at the mangled jumble of steel where two of the gang had met their grisly end. I could see her eyes were damp but she held my gaze and I couldn't help feeling a surge of tenderness towards this sensitive but indomitable woman whose feckless husband lay inches away behind us.

It turned out Penney was right: anyone at Macumba who had seen or heard anything from the direction of Uncle George's farmstead certainly wasn't saying anything. The ranch was operated by a skilled team of hands who covered the vast area it occupied on horseback. The five who were currently stationed there all got out of their beds to welcome us, even though it was the depths of the night, and hot coffee was quickly served. Sophie nursed hers gratefully but I opted for something a little stronger – someone dug out a bottle of Japanese malt, crafted in the Scottish style, and between us we made major inroads into it. I didn't even know the Japanese distilled the stuff but one of our hosts apprised me of its century-old history and how rare imports could be bagged from the right supplier for a price, even in these remote parts. It was a very different kind of malt from my favoured Glenlivet but in my present frame of mind it was unadulterated ambrosia.

I tried to talk to the manager – a rough-hewn, round man in his forties by the name of Jordan – about what his men might find if they were to venture in the direction of the Deakins mine.

He cut me short. 'Don't know, don't want to know. That land isn't owned by the company that runs Macumba Station so we've got no call to go turning over any stones. I don't think anyone's been out there for years apart from old George himself.'

'But you've been quartering a dragoon of armed men who were on their way there,' I said stupidly.

Jordan fixed me with a stony look and Jack – who'd been listening from a nearby armchair – got up and came over.

'I don't think you've got that right, mate,' he said, staring me squarely in the face. 'If Mr Jordan says nobody's been out there in years, then nobody's been out there in years, all right?'

I smiled and raised my glass to the pair of them. 'My mistake.'

When the reunion with Kenny came, it was emotional. Sophie ran crying across the airport tarmac and threw her arms around him as if he were her long-lost father. In a way, I suppose he was. He'd certainly been able to deliver an inheritance that would mean she never had to work again. But that didn't count for much in Sophie's estimation, I could tell. To that extent, she shared the view of Smith Penney: that money was next to meaningless in the grand scheme of things and what really mattered was what you did with your life.

I held out a hand for wagging but Kenny ignored it and gave me a big bear hug instead.

'My God, am I glad to see you,' he said, his voice swamped by my shoulder and his tears.

I think some of Sophie's feelings stemmed from the fact that she'd openly doubted Kenny back in the desert. Now she recognised he was as solid as I knew him to be and she was overwhelmed by it. He had sacrificed so much to further her inheritance claim – up to and including the love of his life – and she would never be able to repay him.

The journey back to Sydney had been an odd one, for various reasons. Jack and Smith Penney had first driven us back to Oodnadatta, where we'd received the necessary medical attention for snake bites, snapped ankles and shock respectively, and we stayed a couple of nights in the Transcontinental Hotel to recuperate. I knew it might take weeks for me to eradicate the venom fully from my system and I would have to take things gently, but I felt well enough to indulge in reasonably normal daily activity. There being little else for us to do, much of that naturally revolved around the hotel bar and on our second night of relaxation I even coaxed an apology out of Smith Penney for the damage he'd caused to the Land Rover's spare tyre and roof.

Word soon got round that the three crazy Englanders had come to some grief in the outback – although the details were hazy – and we became minor celebrities during our brief stopover. We even enjoyed a cursory visit from our friendly neighbourhood police officer but he was just as useful as he had been the last time I spoke to him and we were not troubled by the law again. By the time we left, wild stories were developing about what we'd been up to but I figured nothing was quite as wild as the truth and let the gossipers get on with it.

Jack Cadison drove us to Coober Pedy, whence we were to hitch a plane ride to Adelaide. We could have caught the Ghan train but I, for one, was in dire need of something a little less gruelling and the luxuriance of Sydney demanded that we get there as soon as possible. The flight from Adelaide would be a matter of hours and Kenny had promised to pick us up from the airport and take us back to his place for hot baths and soft beds. He had news, too, he said, but that could wait until he saw us in the flesh.

All through the journey, Sophie and Adam were awkward with each other. I couldn't make out whether she was angry with him or he with her but there was a distinct frostiness between them that left me uncomfortable. They had known each other such a short time and, thrust into the nightmare we'd shared over the past few weeks, things looked set to go one way or the other. Either they'd be forged with an unbreakable bond or they would fall apart under the intensity of the pressure. It wasn't my place to go sticking my oar into their relationship but I couldn't help feeling that the latter was far more likely.

When Kenny greeted us all on the tarmac, Adam held back. He was hobbling about using a stick he'd acquired in Coober Pedy and it didn't make for an easy hug. I wondered if he was using it as an excuse not to get up close with Kenny but concluded he was just being his usual maudlin self. Sophie hooked her arm into Kenny's and left Adam to fend for himself, which I took as a bad sign.

As we drove back across the Harbour Bridge I tried to get Kenny to tell us his news but he insisted there would be time for that over dinner. After some badgering, to which Kenny paid no attention whatsoever, I relented and sat back to admire the ever-impressive view over the shimmering bay. It struck me that it had only been a matter of days since I'd seen it but the desert made me appreciate the water all the more.

When we finally heard what Kenny had to say, over a sombre meal that we all knew wasn't up to Dolly's standards, it was more than a little depressing.

'Even with Uncle George's copy of the exchange of title, the chances of getting anywhere legally with Hamilton and Irvine are pretty slim,' he told Sophie. 'I've been doing some pushing at this end and they're not going to budge.'

Sophie shrugged. 'You know what? I'm not sure if I care any more. Let them have it.'

I was surprised at her nonchalance about the whole business and I told her so when we were alone on the balcony later that evening.

'Has something happened?' I asked tentatively.

'What do you mean?'

'It's just that we've been through so much – Kenny's been through so much – it seems a bit odd to throw it all away with a casual remark. Don't you think he deserves more than that? Don't you think Dolly does?'

As soon as I said it I thought that might be a bit much and indeed Sophie started weeping silently. I put an arm round her shoulders and she leaned into me, resting a hand on my chest.

'I don't know what to do for the best, Bill. The fighter in me wants to see this thing through to the bitter end, to make sure there's some justice for Dolly and to honour George's wishes. But Adam says I should just let it drop – that I've suffered enough already and there's such a low probability of coming out of this with anything anyway. I'm really torn.'

I put a hand on top of hers and she lifted her face to look at me. 'Never mind anyone else – what do you think?'

She looked impossibly tired but I was sure there was a spark in her eyes.

'I think it could be worth one last shot,' she said.

I smiled. 'I think so too.'

Kenny pulled out all the stops over the next few days, sounding out his lawyer chums and wading through acres of business regulations and the niceties of ancient torts. At the same time, he made overtures towards the legal department of Hamilton and Irvine, trying to discover whether they would even be willing to discuss the ownership of the respective parcels of land here in Sydney and out there in the desert. Somehow he managed to set up a meeting with the firm's top lawyer for two days hence.

'Bill, I'd like you to come with me,' he said that evening.

'Why? I've got no legal training – I'll be no help to you at all.'

'Not so, old friend. You may not have the cerebral qualities required for this fight but your physical presence might be just what we need. And it'll give me a bit of moral support.'

I couldn't argue with that, so I agreed. The next morning Sophie took me suit-shopping in downtown Sydney and I came back with a beautiful, off-the-shelf, lightweight tan number from a Chinese tailor in the back streets of Paddington. My tie I selected from the extravagant range on offer, opting for a pattern of Anderson tartan: I thought it might remind the senior executives at Hamilton and Irvine of the Auld Country. The gesture was as much to amuse myself as anything else but if I was going to head into the lion's den with Kenny, then I wanted to look the part, even if I was a total fraud.

Adam had demurred on the shopping expedition on the grounds that his ankle was still giving him gyp but from what I could see it was firmly on the mend. He'd even abandoned the stick and seemed to be moving fairly comfortably around the house. Maybe – like many men in my experience – he just wasn't the shopping type.

When the time came for the meeting, Kenny drove us to the company's headquarters in North Sydney and I immediately saw what he'd meant about it being worth a fortune. Fifteen floors of glass and concrete rose above us, towering over the neighbouring skyline and dominating the landscape for several blocks in each direction. It couldn't compare with the whoppers going up across the bridge in the Central Business District but it was still a pretty nifty piece of real estate. I could understand why the money men behind Hamilton and Irvine might be reluctant simply to hand it over to a nonentity from England.

We mounted the summit in a lift whose back wall was made of reinforced glass, offering sumptuous views south over the harbour. The higher we climbed, the more impressive this extraordinary city looked and by the fifteenth floor my jaw was wide open. A nudge from Kenny brought me back to reality as the lift doors offered a tuneful 'ping' and slid easily apart.

A barrage of suits faced us on the other side. Six or seven men of varying greyness were apparently queuing up to meet this upstart lawyer and his English associate. One – taller and more expensively dressed than the rest – stepped forward and offered a hand for shaking.

'Miles Moreton,' he said, his mouth breaking into a grin that revealed some equally expensive dentistry. 'Head of the legal department at Hamilton and Irvine.'

Kenny observed the niceties, taking the proffered limb and giving his name before turning to introduce me.

'This is my colleague, Bill Kemp.'

'Mr Kemp.' I'd expected his palm to be damp from the humidity of the city, like everyone else's I'd met, but the air conditioning was better than that. His handshake was bone-dry and rock-solid.

Our party adjourned to a nearby conference room, where Kenny and I were offered chairs with our backs to the view, which I thought a little mean-spirited. Five of the suits sat opposite while the other two took up positions at one end of the room, parked against the wall, where they immediately took out notebooks and settled in for the duration. On the table in front of us stood carafes of water and upturned glasses together with little bowls of mint imperials.

'Please, help yourselves,' said Moreton, gesturing at the refreshments.

We both declined and Kenny opened the heavy leather compendium he'd been carrying, shuffling some papers officiously. I had no idea what he'd got up his sleeve but that wasn't what I was there for. My job on this occasion was muscle.

'You're aware that my client has recently acquired a document with rather significant implications for your company,' said Kenny, sliding a sheet of paper across the table to Moreton. 'That's not the original, by the way.'

Moreton didn't touch it but eyed it suspiciously from his seat.

'Would you mind waiting a moment?' he asked.

I saw Kenny bridle slightly. 'What for?'

His question was answered by the opening of the sturdy oak door. A woman of thin, weaselly bearing stepped over the threshold and, without looking at anyone else in the room, took a seat at the head of the table, nearest the door. She adjusted her position fastidiously before casting her gaze around the table, settling finally on Kenny and me.

'Mr Hines and Mr Kemp, I assume?'

We nodded. I felt nonplussed by this interloper but Kenny seemed to be taking it all in his stride.

'Delighted to meet you. I'm Charlie Dacre. It's my company you're attempting to defraud.'

The woman certainly had some front about her, and I was about to launch into an angry tirade when Kenny surreptitiously placed a calming hand on my leg. I lapsed into silent fuming.

'Miss Dacre, how nice of you to join us.'

'Actually, it's Mrs Dacre. And I wouldn't have missed this for the world,' she said, her mouth creasing into an oily smirk. 'It's not every day you meet your nemesis, is it?'

Kenny inclined his head slightly and pulled a face. 'Interesting choice of word but I'll take it. I've got broad shoulders.'

'That's what you are, isn't it?' said Mrs Dacre. 'Retribution? Revenge?'

I couldn't help myself. 'Revenge for what exactly?'

'For whatever wrong you believe has been done to your client, of course. Although I'm not quite sure what that's supposed to be. Perhaps you can enlighten me?'

'With pleasure,' said Kenny. He rifled through some more of his papers and drew out another sheet, which he slid in Mrs Dacre's direction. One of the minions reached forward and completed its journey to his boss.

'What's this?'

'That,' announced Kenny, putting all the sobriety of his legal training into his voice, 'is a writ requesting your presence before a federal judge to resolve the disputed ownership of the building in which we are currently sitting. There's also the ownership of the Deakins mine in South Australia to be resolved but I imagine this one will be of more concern to you.'

I watched Mrs Dacre closely as she assimilated this news.

I thought I saw a tiny twitch in her left eye but she covered it well and turned to Moreton.

'Miles?'

Moreton reached over and took the writ, perused it for a few seconds then pointedly slid it back towards Kenny with a single extended finger.

'Oh no,' said Kenny. 'You can keep that copy. And there's a few more documents here for you to look at.' He pushed a sheaf of papers across the table, his eyes never leaving Moreton's.

'We'll need to consider the matter,' he said smoothly. 'But I wouldn't hold your breath. These things take time.'

'Fourteen days to register a counter-claim,' said Kenny, utterly unruffled by the proceedings. I knew he was good under fire but this was something else. They'd managed to rile me but Kenny was calmness personified.

To my surprise, Mrs Dacre sprang up, quickly and without notice, like a jack-in-the-box leaping into life.

'You don't seem to understand, Mr Hines,' she said, leaning forward on both hands, her spindly fingers splayed out on the table in front of her. 'What Mr Moreton is saying is that we don't recognise your claim. It has no validity in law, and we will not waste precious time negotiating with a back-street hack and his Pommie sidekick.'

Kenny didn't move. 'I'm not interested in negotiating, Mrs Dacre. I'm interested in proving once and for all that my client owns the land this building stands on and is therefore entitled to the best part of half a century's lease-hold payments. Now I'm prepared to admit that the first few years might not have yielded much of a return but for the past – what shall we say? – decade or so, this has been some of Sydney's most prestigious real estate and that counts for something. I'm guessing we might be looking at upwards of three million but we're happy for the courts to decide the exact sum. How about you?'

It was Mrs Dacre's turn to bristle, and she almost growled at Kenny as her face turned a burning red.

'You haven't a goddamn chance,' she spat. 'I don't care what you think you found out there in the outback but I can tell you this much: it won't stand up under scrutiny for a second.'

'Well, I respectfully disagree,' said Kenny, folding his compendium closed and getting up. He smiled amiably at Mrs Dacre. 'I think we've got rather a strong case. Don't you, Bill?'

The question was rhetorical, I knew, so I simply rose to my feet beside him and we headed for the door, sidestepping Mrs Dacre as we left.

'That was a hell of a show,' I said as Kenny cracked open the whisky and poured out two decent tumblers on the desk. 'I thought she was going to explode.'

'So did I. And did you see the office juniors? They've obviously never heard anyone speak to the boss like that. I couldn't tell if they were terrified or delighted.'

We clinked glasses and I sat in one of the chairs opposite Kenny's throne.

'Was it all a bluff?'

'Not all of it,' he said. 'The exchange of title is real enough, as you know, but just how much weight that'll carry in a federal court is anyone's guess. It's the only copy and we've got a pretty unbelievable story to tell about how it came into our possession – that's if the judge will even accept a fifty-year-old deed as evidence. Other than that, it's all a bit "he-said-she-said".'

'More "she-said-she-said".'

Kenny chuckled. 'True. And don't forget, Mrs Dacre does have home advantage over Sophie.'

'That shouldn't matter, though, should it?'

'Shouldn't, mate, but you never know. These judges can be funny buggers.'

'When you lay it out like that, it sounds as if Sophie's got a pretty thin case.'

'Hard to say. Might depend on how the judge is feeling on the day. If we're lucky, it'll be one of those anti-corporate blokes with a fondness for an underdog and a pretty face and Sophie will walk away with the lot. But it could just as easily go the other way.'

'And then what?'

'Then she goes home with nothing. Or at least no worse off than she was when she arrived.'

I swirled the amber liquid in my tumbler and sipped it, relishing the heat that it carried round my mouth and down my throat.

'So it's one big roll of the dice,' I said.

'You could put it like that.' Kenny put down his glass and leaned on his elbows. 'But there's one difference between Sophie Church and Charlie Dacre.'

I thought there was clearly more than one but I bit. 'What's that, then?'

'Sophie's got nothing to lose.'

'While Mrs Dacre . . .'

He picked up my thought. 'Mrs Dacre has got a fortune at stake. My guess is she found out about the exchange of title soon after taking over the company – possibly quite by accident – and has been trying to shut down the implications ever since. Starting with George himself.'

'So why didn't she destroy Hamilton and Irvine's copy of the exchange of title?'

Kenny shrugged. 'Who knows? Arrogance on that scale can make people do strange things. Maybe she kept it as a reminder of what she had achieved – and what she stood to lose.'

I smiled. 'And then you went and drew attention to it by sweet-talking her receptionist, which meant she had to get rid of it.'

'It would have been the first time she knew for sure that we were on to the document. I don't think she expected us to find out about it.'

'Then why the threatening letters? They warned that the mine didn't belong to Sophie – and it turned out they were telling the truth.'

'I think she was just trying to throw Sophie off pursuing the claim by any means necessary. As long as there was a chance that George's copy could still be found, she didn't want anybody going anywhere near the Deakins farm. And let's face it, most normal people would have given up and gone home after threats like that, wouldn't they? Especially after what happened to Adam. And Dolly.'

His voice broke, and I reached for the whisky bottle to top up his glass.

'And there's no chance we can pin Dolly's death on Mrs Dacre?'

Kenny shook his head and drank deep. 'There's no evidence to connect her to the hit-and-run. We'll be lucky if we can make Sophie's claim to the land stand up.'

'Seems so wrong,' I said. 'Mind you, after that performance back there, I bet she wishes she'd got you on her side of the table. Especially if she's looking at the wrong end of three million dollars.'

Kenny sat back in his chair. 'To pay that kind of settlement would probably ruin the company. As a bare minimum she'd have to hand over the building and all its contents. If it were to go really badly for her, Hamilton and Irvine could be bankrupt – except for the mine, of course. But then I can't really see Mrs Dacre scrabbling about on her hands and knees in that red desert looking for what's left of the opals, can you?'

I had to admit that I couldn't.

We spent the next couple of hours poring over the documents in Kenny's folder but whether it was down to my lack of legal knowledge or the fumes of the alcohol, I didn't seem able to take in the fine detail of his arguments. He made it clear that Sophie's case was a real fifty-fifty chance but it made total sense that she should at least give it that one last shot we'd talked about. With the vital piece of paper from Uncle George's mine, it was just possible she might come out on top.

'Let's call it a night, shall we?' said Kenny as the clock above his head ticked towards five. 'I think we can say we've done a good day's work.'

'You're the boss,' I said, and began to tidy up the drinks while he locked the documents in a wall safe that I hadn't noticed before. He'd just spun the dial on the door to seal them safely away when we heard shouts from downstairs. Carly and Ruth were both raising their voices but it was impossible to tell why. Then one of them screamed and heavy footfall hit the stairs leading up to Kenny's office. I shot a warning look at Kenny and started to move swiftly towards the door, hoping to get behind it before the foot-steps reached it. But I was too slow and the door crashed open.

Staring angrily at us, sweat across his face and a gun in his hand, stood Adam Church.

V

For a long moment, it seemed Adam had no idea what he intended to do when he reached Kenny's office and the stand-off felt interminable. It crossed my mind to take advantage of his hesitation by jumping him, but I never like the idea of charging an armed man when I've got nothing to defend myself with, so I vetoed that in favour of talking.

'What the hell's going on, Adam?'

'Shut up, Kemp,' he said through gritted teeth, his eyes fixed on Kenny, a dozen feet behind me on the other side of his desk. As he spoke, he brought the gun up to eye level and I saw that it was a Smith and Wesson Model 36 – a stubby-nosed power pack of a handgun that has been in production for more than two decades and remains the favoured revolver of police departments from Malta to Malaysia. I watched him steady it with both hands, in the style of the military. I liked that even less but I was too far away from him to reach the gun before he had a chance to pull the trigger and it wasn't my body in the firing line so I didn't feel justified in making that call.

'All right, all right,' said Kenny, a tremble discernible in his voice. 'Let's not get overheated, shall we?'

'Too late for that,' said Adam. 'I've suffered more heat than I want in a lifetime thanks to your fun and games.'

I was bewildered. This was not the Adam I knew, the pasty, craven lump of a boy who'd somehow persuaded Sophie Carrington to marry him and settle for a life of stockbroker-belt mediocrity as the wife of an accountant. Even his voice was different, now tinged with the Australian drawl I'd become so used to hearing. He had a look on his face that I hadn't seen before, and the look was determination. I couldn't figure out how it all fitted together and I could only think of one way to find out.

'What are you playing at, Adam? Why have you got a gun?'

Now his gaze broke off from Kenny and fixed on me. 'I thought I told you to shut up.' He switched back to Kenny and spoke in a low, threatening voice. 'You just wouldn't be told, would you?'

'Told what?'

'Told to keep your nose out of business that didn't concern you.'

Kenny raised an eyebrow. 'You mean Sophie's inheritance?'

'That's horseshit and you know it. She isn't entitled to that land any more than you are.'

'So who is entitled to it, Adam? You?'

He smiled mirthlessly. 'That's exactly who, Kenny.'

This was getting more confusing by the minute. I wondered if Kenny had any better idea of what he was talking about than I did but from the look on his face I doubted it.

'What are you talking about, Adam?' I asked.

His fury took me by surprise. 'That's my inheritance, not hers, and I don't care what bit of paper you've got that says otherwise!'

'What do you mean, your inheritance?'

'What do you think I mean? I mean it belongs to me. And that exchange of title is the only remaining document that can challenge that, so if you don't mind, I'd like you to hand it over.'

Kenny didn't move and Adam wiggled the gun in the direction of the wall safe.

'I haven't got all day.'

I badly wanted to keep him talking. I was edging imperceptibly closer to him, and if I could squeeze another foot or so in his direction without his noticing, I might stand a chance of grabbing him.

'I'm probably being a bit stupid here, Adam, but what on earth makes you think it's your inheritance? I mean, I know you're married to Sophie but Uncle George left his estate to her, not you. From what I've seen of her, I'm sure she'd be willing to share it with you, as her husband, but the law says it's rightfully hers.'

'Damn the law,' he said. 'Without that bit of paper, it's mine.'

I moved half a step closer and he snarled in a way that suddenly rang a familiar bell. Pieces of the jigsaw fell into place.

'Good God,' I said feelingly. 'It's you – you're the child. Mrs Dacre is your mother.'

His tone was sarcastic. 'Finally the penny drops. And I thought you were supposed to be the clever investigator.'

The barb struck deep. That was exactly what I was supposed to be. And yet somehow I had missed all the clues under my nose, all the evidence that now seemed so clear and obvious: Sophie and Adam's whirlwind romance, his eagerness to track down the vital document, his reluctance to get involved in the fire-fight with the thugs at George's farmstead. The whole time he'd been working the other side of the street, just waiting for his chance to step in and clean up the only obstacle that stood between him and what he believed was his birthright. It was a hell of a length to go to but if it hadn't been for Sophie's tenacity and a slippery sheet of shale, he might have got away with it.

'You've put Sophie through all this just to get your hands on that land?' I asked incredulously.

He shrugged. 'Like Kenny said, it's got to be worth millions.'

'And George Deakins – were you responsible for his murder?'

His face turned ugly. 'I don't like that word, Kemp. I prefer to think of it as collateral damage.'

Kenny interrupted him. He sounded pained. 'What about Dolly – was she collateral damage too?'

Adam at least had the good grace to look guilty at that. 'She wasn't meant to die. The accident was supposed to warn you off pursuing Sophie's claim.'

'Let me get this right,' I said. 'You knew there was only one piece of paper that could stop you inheriting—'

'Actually there were two. Hamilton and Irvine had their own copy buried deep in the files. My mother discovered it soon after she took over the company. That one is long gone now, of course. Which just left George's copy. I must say it's been quite a treasure hunt.'

Kenny said, 'How did you know about Sophie?'

Adam smiled. 'Most people will tell you anything in the face of imminent death. I wasn't there myself, of course, but I'm told George was very forthcoming about his will – and his beneficiary.'

I thought of Uncle George, his lifetime of opal-hunting reduced to a lonely, terrifying showdown in the red desolation of the Simpson Desert.

'He didn't spill the beans about everything, though, did he?'

The smile fell away as quickly as it had appeared. 'The

idiots killed him before they got the exchange of title. We had to find another way of tracking that down.'

'By finding Sophie.'

'Exactly.' He looked at Kenny. 'You need to get some new associates in London. They seemed to make very heavy weather of locating her. I didn't really have any trouble at all. It was getting hold of the title deeds that proved the problem.'

I snorted. 'And I was the convenient hired help that led you straight to them.'

'Hardly straight,' he said. 'I think you might say it was a little more round-the-houses than that. I even endured a black eye in the process.'

'Deliberately to throw us off the scent?'

'Of course. Verisimilitude is important in these matters, don't you think? Mind you, I didn't expect to be dropped down a mine shaft.'

'Couldn't have happened to a nicer person,' I said acidly.

My mind raced as I relived the experience we'd endured in the outback. I didn't care about Adam but he'd placed Sophie in extremes of danger that couldn't be justified, no matter what the prize. I wasn't too impressed by what he'd put me through, come to that. And all that time he'd been using us both – not to mention Kenny, Jack Cadison and Smith Penney.

Kenny said, 'What if Sophie hadn't agreed to marry you? It's not the most reliable of plans, is it?'

Adam shrugged. 'It seemed like the most direct route. Sophie Carrington, the lonely orphan adrift in London, manages to turn things around and make a name for herself with her catering business. All that's missing from her perfect life is the man of her dreams. And who should walk in . . .'

'Tugs at the heartstrings,' I said. Another thought struck

me that sent a chill down my spine. 'Wait a minute. The tyres and the radio in the Land Rover – that was you, wasn't it?'

Adam smiled superciliously. 'I had no need of them. I knew I was being rescued.'

'And you needed to make sure that Sophie and I couldn't be.'

His grin was ugly.

'But your leg was smashed up. How did you manage to sabotage the Land Rover like that?'

'You fell for that one, too. It was never as bad as I made out. Once you'd splinted it in the mine, it improved pretty quickly. I just thought it might be useful cover for me if you believed I was out of action. Turned out I was right.' He smirked again. 'It was very good of you to leave your knife available for the tyres, by the way.'

That smarted but I ignored it. I had another, simpler question for him. 'You were married to Sophie. Why didn't you just ask her to give you the deed?'

He snorted contemptuously. 'Don't be stupid, Kemp. People don't just hand over a fortune worth millions of dollars.'

I knew he was wrong but I also knew he wouldn't believe me.

'So you were willing to remove George, fly half way round the world and marry someone, then come back and wage some kind of miniature war in the outback to get your hands on it. How many people have died, Adam? Is it really worth all this?'

I thought I might be close enough now to have a go at ambushing him but talk of the multitude of deaths he had caused seemed to jolt Adam back into the present. He took two steps back and realigned his weapon on Kenny. My opportunity had gone.

'Enough talking,' he said. 'Give me the document.'

'And then what?' I asked. 'You think you can just destroy it and walk away as if nothing has happened? Or are you planning to kill us both – and Sophie?'

Kenny's voice had calmed down and the tremble had left it. 'You're not going to fire that gun, Adam. You haven't got it in you.'

'Is that right?' he shouted, and he twitched the trigger. A flash exploded from the muzzle and I heard the window behind Kenny shatter.

Before Adam had even adjusted to the recoil, I was on him. I went for his arms, hoping to sweep them away from his target and, at the same time, unbalance him and bring him to the floor, but I misjudged his athleticism. He kept his feet as I went hurtling past. I managed to get enough contact to avert his aim but I knew I'd become his immediate target now. Without looking back, I headed for the window. A shot rang out from behind and the glass cascaded away. I followed the myriad shards out, hoping that I had remembered the building correctly and there was a porch over the entrance to break my fall. Otherwise I'd be hitting the ground from the height of the first floor with some momentum behind me.

It was still one hell of a shock as my body thumped into the stonework above the door. Catching my breath, I heaved myself over the lip and dropped to the ground as another shot rang out from the window above. I didn't dare think about Kenny – or the women downstairs, who I hoped had made a swift exit. I guessed that the sight of Adam's gun had prompted the scream I'd heard and that they'd probably made a run for it. I wondered if they'd had time to phone the police.

For the moment I was protected by the porch, but I wouldn't be able to stay there long. Adam might lurk by the window but, more likely if he realised he hadn't hit me, he'd be on his way to hunt me down. I hoped my dramatic exit had convinced him I was carrying the title deed and that would draw him away from Kenny. But I had a sickening feeling the last shot I'd heard had not been fired in my direction.

I counted to five, then started running.

I'd barely hit my stride when I heard a voice screaming my name. I checked my sprint and looked around. Dolly's little blue hatchback was parked on the far side of the road, pointing towards the city in the direction I was running.

At the wheel sat Sophie, a look of terror on her face.

Instantly I changed my trajectory, dashing into the path of the traffic to get to Sophie and shouting to her at the same time.

'Drive!' I roared as I rounded the bonnet of the car. Grabbing the handle, I swung open the door and leaped into the passenger seat as Sophie took off at speed. I span round to look behind us and saw Adam emerge from Kenny's building. He ran directly into the road, where a car screeched to a halt to avoid him, and levelled the gun in our direction.

He obviously thought better of loosing off a bullet or two in a busy Sydney street. Instead, he turned the gun on the driver of the car and signalled to him to get out. Then he took up the driving position himself and the car lurched into motion.

The hunt was on.

Sophie was in a high state of distress and it was all she could do to hold the car on the road.

'Was that . . . Adam?' she stammered as we negotiated the afternoon rush hour through the Central Business District, a potential killer on our tail.

'I'm afraid so,' I said, grateful for the practice she'd had avoiding rocks in the desert. 'It turns out your husband isn't all he seemed to be.'

'Was he shooting at you?' She sounded incredulous.

'And at Kenny.'

'Did he get you?'

I was amazed that her first thought was not for herself or her marriage, but for me and Kenny.

'Not me,' I replied. 'But I think he might have hit Kenny.'

She gave an involuntary cry and put a hand over her mouth. Tears welled in her eyes.

'Don't start thinking about that now,' I said. 'We can't do anything to help Kenny unless we can get away from Adam. Right now, he's following us in a black Mercedes.'

I saw her eyes flick to the rear-view mirror and she gasped. 'I see it.'

I turned to look back again and saw that he was gaining on us. I didn't fancy the chances of Dolly's little runaround against the horsepower of the Merc, especially with traffic to dodge, but I had a plan.

'Take the slip road to the left,' I told Sophie. 'But leave it to the last possible moment.'

The Mercedes was close and steering up the right-hand side of us. The manoeuvre was designed to throw Adam, who I was hoping would not be expecting us to head in that direction. Sophie did exactly as I asked, swerving violently and very late across the solid lines that marked the exit onto the distributor road that led to the Sydney Harbour Bridge.

'Perfect,' I said as the Merc went sailing by and on up the street.

We joined the steady stream of traffic feeding onto the bridge approach and I told Sophie to ease off the gas. The last thing we needed was to make ourselves conspicuous in any way.

I changed my mind about that damn fast when I looked back and saw the Mercedes join the same line a hundred yards behind us. Somehow Adam had managed to circle back in the one-way traffic and pick up the scent once more.

'New plan,' I said, and Sophie hit the floor.

As we raced up the outside lane towards the pylons that marked the start of the bridge proper, I checked my wing mirror. Sure enough, Adam was picking up speed behind us. Sophie, her face now set in a look of grim rage, began swerving out into the opposite lane to overtake the vehicles in front. As she dodged in and out of the oncoming cars, they blared their horns, their drivers gesticulating furiously. It was reckless, brave and insane and there could only be one outcome.

Sophie wrenched the wheel to the left to avoid colliding head-on with a shiny yellow Ford Falcon but it clipped our rear wing and threw us into a spin. By some miracle, we didn't hit anything on our side of the carriageway as we turned a full 360 degrees before lurching back onto the opposite side. We ploughed across the lanes, narrowly missing two other cars as we went, and smashed into the vast stone pillar that formed the trunk of the south-eastern pylon.

All around us the traffic screamed to a stop, and it gave us the crucial seconds we needed. I pointed at the pedestrian nooks in the pylon and ordered Sophie to take cover there, then I leaped out of the car and ran in the opposite direction, onto the bridge itself. Looking back, I could see that the Mercedes had become gridlocked but Adam had got out and was following on foot. I hoped Sophie had got to safety and tried to make myself as visible as possible to Adam, jumping up and down as if to catch sight of him. When I was sure that he had seen me, I headed for the nearest steel girder and flung myself behind it.

I reckoned he would reach me within thirty seconds so I had to think fast. He still had his gun with him – I had no doubt of that – but what I didn't know was whether he was prepared to use it on a crowded highway. It seemed that he'd thrown all caution to the wind in his crazed obsession with the inheritance so I didn't want to take the chance. I had to draw him away, both from Sophie and from the throng that was now building up as drivers emerged from their cars to see what the hell was happening.

Above me on the stanchion of the bridge, a maintenance ladder was bolted to the framework. I looked higher and saw that it fed directly through a hole onto the top of the steel arch that spanned the bay. I estimated the arch itself at less than ten feet wide but at least it would take this armed maniac away from innocent bystanders. I started up the ladder and poked my head through the hole just as Adam rounded the stanchion below me.

He let off a bullet that flew wildly past the steelwork but by then I was out onto the arch. A set of steps led up the centre of the girder, with two or three feet either side of them, and I started to run. The grey arc of steel carved through the air in front of me and I kept my head down, focusing closely on the steps. Fortunately, they were evenly spaced and I quickly got into a routine but at one point I dared to avert my gaze to the water far below me and immediately my head swam. The vertiginous height and the limited width of the girder hit my brain like a sledge-hammer and I had to stop. I fell to my knees and flattened myself onto my belly, attempting to make myself as small as possible a target for the man I knew was climbing the bridge behind me. I couldn't wait for more than a few seconds and as soon as I felt my balance system readjusting I jumped to my feet and recommenced the ascent. A gusty wind was blowing in from the ocean and I had a feeling it might be preventing Adam from popping off any more shots: he would need to get significantly closer to me to make it worthwhile trying.

I stopped again. To my left, a web of giant Meccano struts formed enormous X shapes connecting the two sides at a distance of 150 feet or so. I considered stepping out onto them – the centre of the web seemed more secure somehow than the narrow arch – but a statistic surfaced from the back of my mind and forced me to reconsider. Sixteen men had died in the construction of this bridge, and I was not willing to offer myself up to it as the seventeenth.

And then something happened that made me rethink everything.

I looked down the steps and saw Adam, thirty feet below and hesitating as he stared back at me. Despite the adrenaline coursing through our systems, I think the realisation of our current situation hit us both at the same moment and he wavered, then squatted. Bracing one knee against the steps, he took aim with the revolver and fired.

I smiled down at him.

'That's five,' I shouted into the wind. 'You're out of bullets.'

I watched him calculate that I was right and then he stood and began walking slowly and steadily up the steps towards me, his jacket billowing like an untrimmed sail.

'It's over, Adam. You had a damned good go at pulling it off but you have to accept it – you've failed.'

He was twenty steps away now, hefting the gun in his hand and pacing cautiously, putting his feet sideways on the treads for maximum contact.

'What are you going to do, Adam? Push me off?'

Fifteen steps. Ten. Five.

When he finally stopped, he was close enough for me to see the veins standing out in his neck and the manic look in his eyes, which never left me for a second.

Then, with a sudden jerk of his arm, he shied the revolver at me.

My reactions were swift and I ducked out of its way. I heard the weapon clang against the metal behind me and glanced round to see it arcing away towards the water. I didn't wait for the splash four hundred feet below: I was ready for Adam's next move.

In one seamless motion, he tore the jacket from his shoulders and hurled it in my direction. At the same moment, he propelled himself at me, but as his body shifted position he gave me a clear view of the arch beyond. Two steps behind him, an arm outstretched towards his flailing legs, Sophie was clinging to the bridge.

She must have made only the slightest contact with him but it was enough. Adam's course through the air was sufficiently diverted and he hit the steel beside me. The momentum took him on another two feet and as he rolled over the edge I flung out a hand to try and grasp his shirt.

My hand came away empty, and Sophie screamed.

VI

The blue Sydney sky I had come to know and love was clouded over on the day we packed our bags to leave.

'All set?' I asked Sophie as we locked up Kenny's front door for the last time.

She nodded and heaved her rucksack onto her shoulders.

I studied her profile from the back seat of the taxi as she made polite conversation with the driver in the front. The bubbly young woman I'd met a few weeks before was gone. Sophie seemed older and sombre, a weathered traveller who had experienced more in this one short trip than most people do in a lifetime. She would be able to face anything life could throw at her and I wondered what that might be. Like Mrs Dacre, she was now widowed young and would carry that shadow with her on her journey. I knew she would also carry the ghosts of Uncle George and Dolly Hines, however unjustly, and I hoped it wouldn't embitter her.

The taxi pulled up at the rank outside the hospital and we got out. We knew the route to Kenny's room well by now but it was with mixed feelings that I realised this would be the last time we walked it.

He was in decent spirits for a man who had taken a

bullet to the gut and we were under strict instructions not to get sentimental.

'How was she?' he asked brightly as soon as we went in.

'Give us a chance,' I said, pulling a second chair round to the bedside to sit next to Sophie, who was already holding Kenny's hand in hers.

She leaned in and spoke softly. 'She's a broken woman – but then who wouldn't be if your son plunged to his death off the Sydney Harbour Bridge?'

Kenny nodded grimly. 'Depressing places, prisons. To be honest, I was amazed that she agreed to see you.'

'Well, it turns out that she was my mother-in-law all along,' said Sophie. 'It would have been rude of her not to, don't you think?'

'And did you say what you wanted to say?' asked Kenny, gripping Sophie's hand a little tighter.

She nodded and dropped her eyes. 'Nothing particularly earth-shattering.'

'You don't have to tell us,' I said.

'No, it's fine. I just wanted to know why, really. Why she thought it was all right to turn me into a victim of her scheming. Why she felt people's lives could be thrown away for the sake of some extra dollars in the bank. Why she'd driven Adam to the point of self-sacrifice in order to please her. Why . . . just why.'

'What did she say?'

'What could she say? Like your precious Beethoven analogy, there are no answers, are there? But I wanted to look her in the face as she admitted that.'

'Well I don't imagine you'll be enjoying much in the way of family reunions, even if you wanted to,' I said. 'The cops say she's looking at twenty years – at least.'

Sophie fell silent as she contemplated that. Mrs Dacre would be an old woman by the time she was freed from prison but I reckoned Adam's death would turn out to be the greater punishment.

'There's another "why" that's been troubling me,' said Sophie, looking up at Kenny again. 'I still haven't been able to work out why the exchange of title happened in the first place and why Uncle George went on living at the farm.'

Kenny leaned back into his pillow and smiled. 'Now there I can help you a little. I haven't just been lying here doing nothing all week, you know. And I've had to keep Ruth and Carly busy while I've been away.' He turned to me. 'I've decided to keep the practice going, by the way. I couldn't put those lovely girls out on the street.'

I was glad for him and said so. He waved it away and went back to his narrative.

'Anyway, they tracked down an old-timer in Coober Pedy who knew Valentine Deakins – do you remember, it was his name on the deed? Valentine was George's great-grandfather but he died before George was born. And before I was, come to that. Now I can't tell you why Valentine did the swap in the first place or what Hamilton and Irvine thought might be in it for them, but it was the early days of mining in the area and folks in the outback were a law unto themselves.'

'Not much has changed,' I said.

Kenny ignored that. 'So for reasons that are now lost in the mists of time, the exchange took place, but it seems that Valentine never exercised his rights over the Sydney plot. In return, the company allowed him and his family to stay put and pull whatever gemstones they could find out of the ground. Maybe they struck some deal that he would mine it on their behalf and they would split the proceeds. Who knows? The point is that the Deakins family remained on the property and after old Valentine shuffled off this mortal coil, his son just carried on. By the time it got to George, he'd never known anything different from that way of life so he obviously decided to stick with what he knew. I shouldn't think anybody at Hamilton and Irvine remembered or even knew about the deal from decades before but George certainly did – hence his careful secretion of the exchange of title. Do you remember the wording of his will, Sophie?'

She thought for a moment. 'He wanted everything to stay in the family.'

Kenny nodded. 'And with your mother gone, that meant you. I think he trusted me with his will because he knew I wouldn't let it lie until I'd found his nearest relative. We could be as stubborn as each other in the old days.'

I said, 'Why didn't he just send the exchange of title to you for safekeeping?'

Kenny shrugged. 'I can't answer that one. My guess is that he wanted to keep it in his own custody for as long as he was alive and the farm was as safe a place as any. But the hand-drawn map suggests that he wanted us to have enough clues to be able to find it in the event of something happening to him.'

'Do you think he suspected someone was onto him?' I asked.

'No idea. But whether he concealed the canisters recently or they've been hidden away for years, the fact was that he wanted them to be found so that members of his own family could decide what to do next.' He leaned forward again and studied Sophie closely. 'So what are you going to do next, Sophie?'

Her answer was unequivocal. 'I'm going home and I won't be rushing back. I think I've had enough of Australia for a while.'

'That's a shame,' said Kenny. 'I was hoping we might see a bit more of you now that you're a fabulously wealthy property owner in Sydney.'

Sophie shook her head. 'I don't want to deal with all that. In fact, I'd like you to sort it out for me.'

'Sort it out how?'

'Sell it. Get rid of it all. I don't want it and I don't want to have to think about it.'

Kenny looked at me and I looked back and shrugged.

'Whatever the girl wants,' I said.

We sat in silence for a minute or two, appreciating the stillness after the madness of the last few weeks. Kenny's beeping heart monitor was the only thing that interrupted the tranquillity and even that was gently hypnotic.

'What will you do with the money?' he asked eventually.

'Give it to a koala sanctuary or something.'

I couldn't help laughing and Sophie shot me a stern look. 'I'm serious. Let the money do some good, at least.'

'All right; but if you're serious about giving it away, what about an aboriginal charity? I'm sure Ruby McKenzie could recommend a good cause.'

Kenny leaped on the notion. 'That's a brilliant idea, Bill. Give something back after everything the white fellas have taken from them.'

Sophie nodded eagerly, a light creeping back into her eyes. 'We're agreed, then. The money goes to charity – but only after we've done something in memory of Dolly. I know we can't bring her back, and Mrs Dacre being in prison is a flimsy kind of justice for her death, but I'd like to honour Dolly's life with some kind of gesture. What did she love, Kenny?'

He thought for a moment, then said, 'She loved you.'

Sophie's head dropped and she dabbed the corner of one eye. It was clear that, even in the short time she'd known Dolly, she felt the same way – and still did about Kenny.

'I thought we weren't getting sentimental,' I said.

'Oh, bugger off, Bill,' said Kenny.

I tried to keep the atmosphere cheery as we boarded the Qantas flight for the first leg of our journey home on the

Kangaroo Route via Singapore. I'd stocked up on airport blockbusters and newspapers and as we settled into our seats I said, 'I'm not expecting much from the company over the next day or so.'

'That's all right, Bill,' said Sophie. 'Neither am I.'

The lightness in her voice told me she was joking but I suspected there was a darker undertone. Just the previous evening we had shared a long, intense conversation about . . . well, about society and its problems, really, but the problems did seem to keep coming back to men. Men, she averred, were responsible for much of the planet's ills and by Sophie's reckoning the world would be a much nicer place if it were run by women – Mrs Dacre excepted, of course. I found it hard to disagree and I told her so.

'But don't write us all off in one stroke,' I said. 'There are a few of us around who aren't as wicked as all the rest.'

She'd smiled at that and leaned over to plant a kiss on my cheek.

'You're not too bad, I suppose.'

I blushed then added, 'And Kenny, of course.'

'And Kenny.'

Now, as the Boeing 747 taxied to its runway for our departure from Sydney, I suddenly wanted the flight to last as long as possible. Sophie Carrington evidently had a gloomy opinion of men; I had around twenty-five hours to change her mind.